Praise for *Sur*

"The vivid descriptions create a mental movie of one family's life during the 1920s and 1930s. Prepare for a raw emotional experience. *Surviving Southwood Avenue* stuns the senses with its pure honesty. The story's intimacy amplifies themes of love, betrayal, weakness, and survival. The believable dialogue enriches the reality of each character's experience and allows the reader to become invested in their welfare. This is a fast-paced, can't-put-it-down book. Melissa Simonye's labor of love is a fantastic tribute to her grandmother, Stella. Fans of memoirs, historical fiction, and drama will not want to miss *Surviving Southwood Avenue*."

—Five-Star Review by P. Rosenthal, *Readers' Favorite*

"*Surviving Southwood Avenue* by Melissa Simonye is an amazing book ... This partly fictional memoir is beautifully written as the characters leap off the page, especially Stella, and we share every hardship she suffers. While this is a harrowing read, it reminds or informs us of a time when children were seen and not heard, and also how a young child believes how helpless they are. It also shows the strength of the human spirit. Today, we live in a much kinder world, and this book is a lesson that reminds us of it. Inspirational."

—Five-Star Review by Lucinda E. Clarke, *Readers' Favorite*

"Author Melissa Simonye shares the heartfelt tale of her grandmother in this riveting true story based in Columbus, Ohio ... The author pulls on the heartstrings of every reader and keeps them glued from start to finish ... Even with the subtle instances of torture and abuse, I would gladly recommend *Surviving Southwood Avenue* to young adult readers as well. This is a story of hope and love in the face of cruelty, and how one person can truly become the matriarch of a family and inspire the world."

—Five-Star Review by Ronél Steyn, *Readers' Favorite*

"Fleshing out a family story with imagination and admiration for its heroine, *Surviving Southwood Avenue* is an inspiring historical novel ... Indeed, this story is about persistence and grit ... A plucky survivor finds happiness after a childhood of trauma."

—*Foreword Reviews*

"Simonye dramatizes her grandmother's harrowing childhood in this debut historical novel. At its best, the author's observant prose contains brilliant, psychologically revealing details ... An admirable if upsetting account of childhood abuse and resilience."

—*Kirkus Reviews*

"*Surviving Southwood Avenue* by Melissa Simonye takes one on a roller coaster of emotions as one sees the consequences of broken families, especially on children. Melissa ensured all the events were captured vividly, which made one invested in the storyline. The characters were well-developed, and the steady narration also added to the overall beauty of this amazing work. This was a great read, and I look forward to more by this wonderful author."

—Five-Star Review by Frank Mutuma, *Readers' Favorite*

"*Surviving Southwood Avenue* is an inspiring story of strength, perseverance, and courage as author Melissa Simonye bases her novel on her grandmother, who endured an emotionally and physically abusive childhood. The author skillfully presents a theme of family dysfunction ... Simonye's novel is intended as a tribute to the indomitable spirit of a remarkable woman."

—*BlueInk Review*

"*Surviving Southwood Avenue: A Story of Family Secrets and Resilience* is a historical coming-of-age novel set during the Depression years. It opens with Stella Irene's birth in 1916, following the family's experiences and contrasting Stella's life with that of her mother Clara. *Surviving Southwood Avenue* is ... a powerful story of adaptation and change that allows readers to better understand the decision-making process and perceptions of a mother and daughter whose disparate backgrounds change their views of life and their place in it ... Libraries seeking discussion points about family secrets, survival, and how these decisions ripple across generations of values and ideals will find much to recommend and appreciate in how Melissa Simonye spins *Surviving Southwood Avenue,* which explores losing trust and gaining wisdom with equally strong acuity."

—D. Donovan, Senior Reviewer, *Midwest Book Review*

"Inspired by true events, *Surviving Southwood Avenue* counsels parents and caretakers to pay attention to the unsaid words of their children ... In Stella's voice, the narration provides a view into the innocent world of a child. This adds another level to understanding the unbelievable impact of such atrocities on a child's mind and heart ... The well-written plot forced me to keep flipping the pages until the very end. Although Stella's story is quite dark and gut-wrenching, it is also a testament to the strength and perseverance of human character. *Surviving Southwood Avenue* by Melissa Simonye urges society to do better for those who can't protect themselves. At the same time, she inspires the survivors to rewrite their story."

—Five-Star Review by Ankita Shukla, *Readers' Favorite*

SURVIVING

Southwood Avenue

A Story of Family Secrets and Resilience

MELISSA SIMONYE

Surviving Southwood Avenue
Published by Snowy Mountain Press LLC.
Denver, CO

ISBN: 979-8-9905341-0-0
FICTION / Biographical
FICTION / Historical / 20th Century / General

Cover and interior design by Victoria Wolf, wolfdesignandmarketing.com, copyright owned by Melissa Simonye

SNOWY MOUNTAIN
PRESS

For Grandma and Mom

AUTHOR'S NOTE

I ALWAYS KNEW MY GRANDMA WAS SPECIAL. Her independence, tenacity, and love for people and animals made an impression on me. Since I was a little girl, I knew she had a challenging life as a young child growing up in what I called an orphanage in Columbus, Ohio. The Broadway musical *Annie*, the movie version with Carol Burnett, and the *Annie* soundtrack helped me imagine what my grandma's life was like. But her childhood was nothing like *Annie*. The reality was that my grandma had an astonishingly harder upbringing that wasn't accompanied by fun songs to sing along with. I didn't find out about the true history of her life until I was married with children of my own. After I moved from Ohio, I would sit for hours on the phone with my grandma. Our talks often led to her telling me about herself. In May 2009, my grandma sat for several days with my mom and recounted everything about her childhood while my mom rapidly typed up the details. The events my grandma spoke to her about weren't in any particular order, and the finished product wasn't what I would call a memoir. My mom named it *Memories of My Life*. It was nineteen pages, along with fourteen pages of photos. She printed it and gave my sisters and me a copy. After reading it, I remember thinking, *This should be turned into a book*; it was that chilling. I knew then, fifteen years ago, that someday I would be the one to turn it into a book. But I was a second grade teacher raising two young boys while my husband worked nights; who had the time? In 2023, I decided I had the time.

To write this book, I relied heavily on my grandma's keepsakes, the conversations I had with her, my copy of *Memories of My Life,* and I used my imagination to fill in the gaps. I knew I didn't want to write my grandma's story as a memoir or a biography, so I landed on fiction, which allowed me the freedom to add details to enhance the story. Character names were changed when writing this book, but most of the events, especially in Part 3, were actual circumstances my grandma experienced. I also researched Columbus, Ohio, where my grandma spent the first eighty-two years of her life, and I incorporated some local events from that time into the novel.

Writing this book was intense for me at times because I had to put myself in my grandma's shoes during some of the most difficult trials of her life. I debated whether to even include some of the events that happened to her because she was such a private person. But after discussing it with my mom, I decided to tell her entire story because it made her into the person she became; a strong and inspirational woman. When I was a teacher, I thought it was important for my students to read authentic literature about courageous people. I loved exposing them to brave individuals who made a mark in history, especially women. I couldn't help but think about my grandma while reading about those unique individuals. I hope this book gives her the homage she deserves.

PROLOGUE

IT TOOK ME OVER EIGHTY YEARS TO DISCUSS the truth about the horrible events in my childhood on Southwood Avenue. I tried telling my older brother, Charles, about the abuse I went through, but he refused to believe me. He didn't want to hear about things he didn't understand. He silenced me with the shame he made me feel that day. So, I held my secrets quietly inside of me as if they were someone else's, someone who had warned me never to tell a soul. But the secrets belonged to me, and they were mine to tell.

When I felt my daughter, Anna, was old enough to understand, I allowed her glimpses into some of the adversities I experienced as a child, but I never spoke about the true horror until one spring day in May. Sitting in her house, I released my hidden secrets. I sat with Anna and recounted the most terrifying times I faced during my childhood. While we began our conversation, the sounds of birds chirping outside distracted me. When I peered out the window, there were three cardinals flying around a maple tree like they were chasing each other. But then a hush passed over them, which oddly made me feel at peace, as if they were permitting me to release the pain I had held in for so long. My narrative took me down a dark path I thought I would never recount. It was difficult for Anna to keep her composure as I described how I was abandoned, starved, physically and emotionally abused, and molested before the age of ten.

My mother, Clara, left my family the day after I turned four years old. It was on a Tuesday night, April 13, 1920. Her decision to leave our family hurt us deeply. My older brothers, Bob and Charles, and my sister, Eleanor, and I were grief-stricken after she left. The year 1920 became horrific for my siblings and me. Her departure considerably altered the trajectory of my life. I don't know all the reasons why our mother abandoned us. My father never talked about it, even when we pressed him for information. He refused to speak about our mother, not even to say anything negative about her, even when my siblings and I begged him to tell us where she went and why she deserted us. "Florida," was all he could muster.

After my mother left, I had a horrible time falling asleep at night. I would lay awake in bed, wondering about Florida and what she was doing there. I wondered if she ever thought of us, if she ever thought of *me*. I wondered if she missed us. I wondered if she felt badly for leaving our family. I wondered about many things because all I could do was wonder. And the most pressing issue I wondered the most about was, *why me*.

Eleanor thought our mother left us because she couldn't handle or didn't want to raise four children. But I knew something that I never spoke about. I was there. I was with our mother the night she left our family. My mother and I were at our parents' bakery, waiting for a man to pick us up. I was scared because my mother was acting bizarrely. But then my father showed up with his best friend, Ed, a muscular, intimidating guy, standing six foot four. The rage and fury I saw in my father's eyes frightened me. I had never seen him look that way. When they found the bakery door locked, they kicked it in, shooting thousands of glass shards across the floor. My mother shielded me from the flying glass as she held me on her hip. She was crying as Ed grabbed me from my mother's arms and rushed me to the back seat of his vehicle. I was scared as I pressed my forehead against the window. I could hear my father's screams. I yelled, "Daddy! Mommy!" I didn't understand what was happening. I was cold as I sat in Ed's automobile. I heard my mother begging the two not to take me. I listened to my father's voice shouting. Then, the two jumped into Ed's vehicle and sped away with me. That was the last time I saw my mother.

Part 1

STELLA

Chapter 1

I WAS BORN ON AN UNSEASONABLY COLD and stormy Wednesday, April 12, 1916, in Columbus, Ohio. Because of the weather, the midwife my father hired never showed up. My mother was overdue with me and labored at home in terrible pain. She refused the help my brothers and sister offered, but they were probably too young to be of use anyway. Eleanor later told me she remembered being scared. She and Bob sat on the floor outside our parents' bedroom and listened to our mother's agonizing screams. Bob covered his ears and whimpered. Misty-eyed, Eleanor tucked her legs close to her chest and wrapped her arms tightly around her knees. "Charles, I'm scared. I think Mother is dying!"

"She's not," Charles reassured her. But my oldest brother was also worried and took off to retrieve our father.

Charles ran two miles to our father's jobsite downtown in the cold rain. Our father worked in construction and was helping to build the grand twelve-story Deshler Hotel in downtown Columbus. It sat on the northwest corner of Broad and High Streets and became one of Columbus's largest and most luxurious hotels. When they returned home, cold sweat ran from our father's flushed face as he rushed to our mother. Rainwater was dripping from his hat when he found her cradling me in her arms and weeping from exhaustion. "I'm too late," he breathlessly said. He embraced her. "I'm so sorry you were alone, Clara. Are you all right?"

"You're dripping wet all over me and the baby," she snapped as she shifted and slid away from him in her bed. "It's a girl."

"Can I hold her?" he asked after he removed his drenched hat and coat.

After he gently scooped me up from my mother's arms, she said, "Meet Stella Irene," before she rolled over and fell asleep.

My mother was a beautiful and intriguing woman. She was thin with long legs like a ballerina. She wore a nicely pressed skirt, matching blouse, and polished heels daily. It was essential for her always to look her best. Her blue eyes reminded me of a clear summer sky. She didn't wear much makeup, just a little lipstick, which brought out the natural rose color of her cheeks. Her brown curls lay perfectly around her pretty face. Even at a young age, I knew there was something different about my mother. She was an exceptionally independent and bold woman during a time when women weren't even allowed to vote. She ran our house like a military sergeant would. She didn't hug or play with us like my father did. She was very private and sometimes seemed cold. When I tried to snuggle next to her on our davenport, she would push me away, saying, "Stella, don't wrinkle my blouse, honey."

My brother Charles was six years older than me. He was blessed with our mother's piercing, sky-blue eyes and sharp appearance. He had thick, straight, dark, slicked-back hair. He used pomade to keep it in place, probably beeswax. Charles wore his nicest clothes to school and never had a wrinkle in his shirt. He thought his appearance was important and wanted to look his best, but he always wore a cross look, like he was ready for battle. He positioned his cap sideways on his head because he thought it made him look tough. But Charles was not a fighter like our sister Eleanor. When he was a baby, he was extremely frail, and then, as a toddler, he contracted poliomyelitis, an infectious disease that caused spinal and respiratory issues.

Polio paralyzed and killed many. Charles almost died once during a surgery to lengthen the muscle in his leg.

Eleanor was a year and a half younger than Charles but often acted and looked like his older sister. She was a tall, staunch girl with a pageboy haircut that cradled her face. Her brown hair was often tangled and unkempt. She did not inherit our mother's stunning blue eyes and rosy cheeks like the rest of us. Her eyes were a mystery and seemed to change color with her mood. Our mother bought Eleanor dresses she never wore. She wanted Eleanor to look pristine, but she didn't care about dresses or how she looked.

Children teased Charles at school because of how he walked. Since one of his legs was longer than the other, he limped. Kids called him names and mimicked him. The torture he received was relentless. Since Charles had a perfectionist personality, his disability was challenging for him to deal with. He loved sports and wanted to be the best athlete, but he wasn't. Eleanor felt sorry for Charles and pitied him because she was athletic and strong. She became overly protective of him. She threatened to beat up anyone who made fun of him. One day in the schoolyard, a boy taunted Charles and mocked him. Eleanor came out of nowhere and threw a hard punch to his nose without saying anything. The boy instantly fell to the ground with blood gushing everywhere. A crowd of children gathered around them, hooting and hollering as she stood over his body. She shouted so everyone could hear, "If anyone mocks my brother again, I won't be afraid to hit harder!" No one snitched on Eleanor about what happened that day in the schoolyard, and no child taunted Charles again. Later, our parents had a lift made for him to wear in one shoe. It was about three or four inches high, and it helped him immensely.

In 1918, when Charles turned eight, he started two paper routes to earn extra money. Two routes were hard on him. He had little sleep, and the pain he felt in his joints reminded him to be angry and resentful, especially toward our mother. He told her more than once that he wished he had never been born. He blamed her for his polio because he heard people call it infantile paralysis. He asked her why she allowed him to get such an awful disease as a baby. He told her it was her fault. He was mad that he wasn't like other children. Our mother had a hard time dealing with Charles's negative attitude. His cross demeanor irritated and annoyed her, so they fought a lot. She often reminded Charles that he should feel thankful to be alive. Our parents spent much time and money helping Charles with his condition, especially after his unsuccessful surgery. She may have resented their spending so much money and energy on Charles. There was no cure for polio, and Charles didn't seem to appreciate what they had done for him.

My other brother, Bob, and I were incredibly close. He was three years older, but he felt like an extension of me. It often felt like he could read my mind. He was funny, and his silly behavior was contagious; I always wanted to be near him. But Bob was much more outgoing than me. He was a risk-taker. He never said no to a challenge. He also had our mother's sky-blue eyes and rosy cheeks. He inherited an angelic face and blond hair from our father. His curls were constantly bouncing happily on his head. I rarely saw Bob without a smile on his face. He was small for his age, and we looked alike. Some thought we were twins, but my hair was dark and not curly. Bob taught me to roller skate when I was around three years old. He was astounded by how quickly I learned. Roller-skating on the brick road we lived on was difficult, but we still enjoyed the challenge of not falling. I loved playing with Bob and his friends in our neighborhood. Our favorite games were stickball, blindman's bluff, and hide-and-seek.

Chapter 2

OUR MOTHER EXPECTED US to help her with everything. We had to assist her with the cleaning, the laundry, and the cooking. Eleanor and Charles often argued about who would do what. Eleanor enjoyed lending a hand with the cooking, and Charles didn't mind cleaning the house, but neither wanted to help with the wash. I remember we had an old brass washboard to clean our clothes. Eleanor would scrub our garments against it furiously like she was fighting with the stains to come out. I tried to help her once, but she told me to stop because I was creating more work for her. She let me assist her in the kitchen, though. She loved an opportunity to boss me around. She ordered me to get this and that for her. I didn't mind because it made me feel good to be needed.

Eleanor and Charles were complete opposites, but they were also great allies. They often teamed up against Bob and me. They were relentless at times. Sometimes, the teasing got so ridiculous that we all laughed over the silly comments, but not always. Charles also tormented us until one of us, typically me, cried. He played awful tricks on me because I was younger and more vulnerable.

Charles took me on a walk one evening in 1920, about two weeks before my fourth birthday. He called it a mystery walk, which made me excited to go with him. I curiously wondered what the mystery was. I hummed the entire way, imagining what adventures we would encounter. We walked on an uneven old brick road. I had to look down to keep my ankles from turning because it was more unstable than the one we lived on. It was chilly that evening, and I soon regretted not wearing my coat. I was disappointed when we arrived at the end of the road. Charles said we were there. In front of us stood an old, abandoned, shabby house with boarded-up windows. It looked scary. I stared quizzically at Charles. He nudged me to go up the front porch steps.

"I don't want to. I want to go home now," I said to him.

But Charles just laughed and said everything was fine. "Let's explore the deserted house," he insisted. "This is our mystery, investigating this house."

I hesitated to walk in after he pushed the front door open. As we entered the house, a wash of dirty, musty air drifted through my nose. The flooring in the home had deteriorated, and every time I heard a creak from a floorboard, a cold shiver ran down my spine. Charles led me around the house. Fear continued to take over my body as Charles told me a terrifying story about the family who had once lived in the house. Charles's voice was a whisper when he spoke.

"In the late 1800s, a wealthy family from Franklinton moved into this house to escape persecution from an angry mob. They boarded up the windows in their old house and took refuge here. The oldest son was accused of killing young girls at night while they slept. Stockings and undergarments from the dead girls were found in the boy's trunk. The teenager denied any wrongdoing, but no one believed him because the evidence was irrefutable, so they escaped here."

"What does irrefutable mean?" I asked.

"Impossible to deny."

I wasn't sure what that meant either, but I didn't ask because he seemed irritated with my interruption. Charles was brilliant and had a vocabulary that I sometimes didn't understand.

"The night before the boy was to start his sentence at the old Ohio Penitentiary, his father somehow got him released from jail. They knew the police and townspeople would be looking for them. Something horrible happened in this cellar because they were prepared to fight back," Charles whispered.

We were now standing in front of the old, rickety cellar door.

"What happened in there?" I quietly asked. I had a pressing need to pee but hung onto every word Charles murmured.

"I'm not sure how many people died down there, but only the teenage boy survived. To this day, people report seeing him walking these grounds carrying girls' undergarments." Then I felt a sudden jolt. My knees buckled, and I fell forward. Charles had pushed me down the cellar steps and slammed the door shut. It was pitch-black as I stumbled down the stairs. I was terrified in the dark cellar. I couldn't see a thing, but it smelled horrendous. I turned around and darted up the steps, screaming.

"Charles! Charles!" I wailed. He did not respond. I banged on the cellar door and felt for the handle. As I pressed down, pee dribbled down my legs. I was relieved he had not locked me in. I could barely hear my cries for Charles over my thunderous breathing. I slammed the cellar door shut behind me and shouted his name again, but he didn't answer. I scurried to the front yard and screamed, "Charles!" There was still no answer. I was afraid I would see that teenage boy, so I quickly ran to the brick road, but then I tripped and fell. My knees were stained with blood as it ran down my legs to my urine-soaked socks. I felt miserable walking home in this condition. My knees ached, and I shivered the entire way.

When I finally reached our house, Charles was on the front porch reading a comic book with a sheepish grin on his face. I bolted past him to go inside without speaking to him. I was angry and didn't want him to see that I had peed myself. I let out stifled whimpers as I ran to my bedroom to change my clothes. I heard Charles yell my name, but I didn't answer him.

After I changed, I found Bob. I told him about the mystery walk Charles took me on. I cried while I told Bob about everything. "Charles took me to a scary house where a boy and his family hid from angry people because the boy killed girls. He told me something terrible happened in their cellar. He said people died in there, except for the boy who killed girls. Then he pushed me down the cellar's steps and shut the door. It was dark, and I was so scared. I thought he had locked me in, but he didn't. Charles was gone, so I had to walk home by myself. I was afraid because, at first, I couldn't remember the way home. Why is he mean to me?"

Bob shrugged his shoulders and let out a sigh. "I don't know, Stella."

I told Bob I was going to tell our father. He warned me not to squeal because Charles would only figure out another way to be meaner to me out of spite for snitching. But I wanted our father to know. I wanted Charles to get in trouble.

"I thought Charles was being nice. I was excited to go on a mystery walk with him," I said, my tears growing stronger as I cried.

"You can't trust him. Especially when you think he's being nice."

After that day, I had nightmares about that teenage boy from Franklinton sneaking into my bedroom to murder me while I slept. And in my nightmares, I yelled for Charles to save me, but he never did. I was often soaked with sweat and anxious when I woke up from those dreams. It wasn't easy to go back to sleep. I would lay awake beside Eleanor's sleeping body and wonder why Charles was so mean to me. Why didn't he like me?

Chapter 3

I WAS SOMEWHAT OF A TOMBOY because all my friends were boys, and I enjoyed playing with Bob and participating in what he and his friends were doing. Like Charles, I often wore a boy's hat and positioned it sideways on my head. I wanted to look tough too. But I also loved exploring my mother's closet and dresser drawers when she was not home. I put on her lipstick and clothing, pretending to be her. She had a lot of dresses and skirts. I didn't have a favorite one, but I particularly loved wearing her silk slips. I pranced around her bedroom and admired myself in the mirror she had in the corner of her room. I had to do this in secret because my mother would not be happy with me if she caught me. My aunt Lucille often told me I looked like my mother. She told me I had a pretty profile, just like my mother. I used my mother's hand mirror to examine my profile when I was in her bedroom playing dress-up.

Even though my family was not wealthy, my father worked hard to provide a good life for us. The only days he had off were Sundays. I loved Sundays because he would take us places as a family. Our favorite places to visit were Olentangy Park and Indianola Park near downtown Columbus. We rode the carousel, screamed on the roller coasters, played in the enormous pool, and picnicked in the vast, beautiful park area. It was the only time I saw my parents get along.

One afternoon, Bob and I were at a park near our house. I saw an elderly man pushing a little girl on a swing. As she glided through the air with every push, I noticed the man was missing a hand. For whatever reason, it scared me. I don't know why seeing a missing hand frightened me. Bob told me not to be scared because he had probably lost his hand in an accident. My brother always made me feel better when I needed reassurance, but I was afraid I would see that man again. I was still scared of being killed in my sleep by that murderous teenage boy Charles told me about from Franklinton and now by this man. I feared he would sneak into my bedroom and cut one of my hands off. I don't know why I would think that, but I started hiding my hands under my blankets when I slept. I pulled my blankets up under my chin or sometimes to my nose. I hid my hands between my knees. I felt a little safer doing that. I tried not to think about the teenage boy or the handless man before falling asleep at night, but it was hard not to. Since I shared a bedroom with Eleanor, I tried talking to her about things to distract my thoughts, but she would shush me and tell me to sleep. I sang nursery rhymes while hiding my hands under the covers. My singing annoyed Eleanor, so I had to sing them in my head. My favorites were "Rock-a-Bye Baby," "London Bridge Is Falling Down," and "Baa, Baa, Black Sheep."

I remember being lonely at home when my siblings were at school because my mother didn't play with me. I taught myself how to read when I was three years old. I learned to make my own food and entertain myself. I played with an old military radio to occupy my time while I waited for Bob to come home. We had a grandfather clock in our living room, and even though I couldn't tell the time, I counted the chimes until his arrival. Our mother often vanished like a ghost when my siblings got home from school. It was an enigma to us. We didn't know where she went, but we knew better than to ask her where she had been when she returned. We also learned to keep her secrets from our father. Mother often warned us not to report to our father that she left us alone. It was only for a few hours and not every day. Sometimes, she looked a little disheveled and smelled of cigarettes when she returned home. We watched with curiosity as she climbed up the stairway to her bedroom to change her clothes and freshen up before our father got home from work. He was working late nights then, at least that's what we thought. I often wondered why she smelled of cigarette smoke and what she was doing in her bedroom after she got home. I would peer through the crack in her bedroom door and watch her. Eleanor would hiss at me to stop spying. She knew Mother would not be happy with me if she caught me. We had strict rules in our house, and privacy was one of them.

Chapter 4

I LOVED GOING TO THE GENERAL STORE with my mother to pick up items and supplies. I wasn't always allowed to go with her, so it was a big treat for me when I did. She allowed me to pick one piece of candy at the store if I was good for her. I adored candy and didn't get it often, so I was always on my best behavior. I liked rock candy, but caramel was my favorite. I loved the texture of it and the different shapes it came in. I would let it sit in my mouth and melt so I could enjoy the taste of it longer.

One spring morning, while we were at the store, my mother quietly asked the druggist if she could get Charles's expenses "on loan" for a short time. He was in constant need of pain medication, replacement splints, or new shoe lifts. I didn't know what "on loan" meant, but I quickly noticed the look on my mother's face. Fury took it over when the druggist said no. Her jaw clenched, and her eyes darkened to an ominous shade of dark blue. She promptly turned us around, grabbed my hand, and we left the store without buying anything.

She said nothing as we trudged home, but I could tell she was angry by how she walked. Her stride was brisk, and her footsteps were louder than usual. When we got home, she put me down for a nap, which confused me because I wasn't napping anymore. I asked her if she was mad at me because she seemed angry. Her brows were pulled together, and her lips were turned down. She said no, she wasn't upset with me. "Then why do you look mad?" She didn't respond. She clicked her tongue and removed my black button boots. "Mommy, why am I taking a nap? I'm not tired."

"Because you are," my mother shot me a look and pursed her lips.

"Mommy, what does 'on loan' mean?"

"It's when somebody loans or gives you something until you have the money to repay them."

"Why did the man behind the counter say no to you?" She pulled my dress off before helping me into bed.

"You're asking too many questions. Now go to sleep and don't worry about that man from behind the counter. He's a rude man, and I'm not going to waste my time trying to explain why," she said as she tucked my covers under my chin. I nodded and lifted my head for a kiss, but my mother was already walking away.

Later that day, my mother ordered me to wear a nice dress because we were going out again. I quickly found my favorite pale-blue sailor dress and black button shoes. I knew she would approve of my choice when I entered her bedroom. But my heart skipped a beat when I saw her snatch my father's pistol from the top drawer of his wardrobe and then place it in her brown leather shoulder bag. She didn't know I was in her bedroom watching her when she turned around.

"Damn it, Stella, you scared me!" she gasped. "How many times must I tell you to knock before entering?" She glared at me.

"I'm sorry. Where are we going?" I asked while walking backward out of her bedroom. She didn't respond. Instead, she gave me a quick smack on my rear end and hurried me out the front door like we were running late to be somewhere.

After we left our house, I ran to keep up with my mother's long strides. The rage on her face made me feel scared. It reminded me of how Eleanor looked before she threw a punch. Whenever I heard the pistol knock against the inside of her shoulder bag, I quivered. Our walk was familiar, so I knew we were returning to the general store. Then I forgot about the pistol and grew excited because I thought we were returning for the piece of candy I hadn't gotten earlier that day. Once we entered the store, my mother marched us to the back. I remember it was unusually crowded with more shoppers, and we waited in a long line. When we reached the front of the line, my mother laid her bag on the counter. She cleared her throat, discreetly took out the pistol, and pointed it at the druggist behind the counter. She used her bag to shield it from the other shoppers. "I'm here for that loan we discussed earlier," she said quietly.

"Okay," the druggist raised his hand. "Please put the pistol away, ma'am," he whispered. He turned and gathered medications and things for Charles from a tall shelf behind the counter.

My mother cleared her throat again, and I pulled on her skirt. "Mommy, what's going on?" I noticed her hands slightly shook when she shoved the pistol back into her handbag. She looked around the store nervously.

"Nothing. Everything is fine," she hissed. Then she gave me a sharp look, tucked a lock of her hair behind her ear, and ran her hands down her brown bell-shaped skirt that flared at the bottom. She thanked the man with an unapologetic smile when he handed her the bag of supplies. As we turned to leave, she handed the bag to me and grabbed my free hand. "Let's go, Stella. We don't have time for candy today," she said as she drifted out of the store like nothing had happened.

As we walked home, she warned me not to tell anyone about what had happened in the store. I felt like I was being scolded for something I had done. My eyes grew large when she bent at her waist, grabbed my chin, and looked into my eyes, her eyes narrowing. "If you breathe a word about this, about the pistol or the loan, we will not celebrate your birthday as planned." My face puckered, and I urgently nodded my head up and down to show her that I understood. Then we walked home in complete silence. My eyes were mostly downcast, but I felt jittery, and thoughts were spinning through my mind. I was scared about what had occurred. I was scared of not celebrating my birthday. I was scared of the pistol in my mother's shoulder bag. I had never seen my mother use my father's pistol to get what she wanted. I thought about my father and wondered what he would say if he knew. It felt like we stole from the druggist. My father disapproved of stealing. He often reminded us, "It's not worth having if it needs to be stolen."

Chapter 5

LATER THAT EVENING, my father received word about what had transpired at the general store with my mother and the druggist. I am unsure who told him, but when I heard my parents fighting, I hid behind the curtains in the parlor and listened. I wondered if Bob was going to join me from behind the curtain. I wondered if Charles and Eleanor were also spying. A tear slid down my face when I heard their hushed voices become louder and louder.

"Damn it, Clara, what were you thinking? Things could have gone wrong, very wrong. And with my gun, for that matter! I can't believe you did that! And Stella was with you! You probably scared her to death!" My father paced in front of my mother. "What has gotten into you?" he asked in disbelief. His voice sounded exasperated. She was sitting at our kitchen table, holding her forehead. "You haven't been the same for years now. What's going on with you? Please talk to me," he pleaded.

"I'm fine! Stella's fine! Just drop it, Frank! Nobody even saw me with your pistol. It's not that big of a deal, Frank. We'll pay the store back. That's why I said, 'on loan' to the druggist," she paused. "And truthfully, I'm nervous about our finances. The bakery isn't making the money it once did. We're spending more than we're bringing in now that you're making me stay home with the kids." My stomach fluttered with every high-pitched remark.

"*I'm* not making you stay home. If I remember correctly, you're the one who said raising four children and working in the bakery was too much for you. You're the one who wants to sell the bakery. You're the one that's upset about money; I'm not." I heard my father breathe out a heavy sigh. My body grew stiff. I hated hearing my parents fight; they seemed to argue over everything.

"Well, you should be!" she snapped. My eyebrows wrinkled, and more tears crawled down my face when I heard the loud clicks of my mother's heels walking away.

"You can come out now," my father said to my shadow from behind the curtains in the living room.

"Daddy, don't be mad at Mommy," I begged as I ran to hug him. "We got everything on loan, and when you get things on loan, you pay them back." I leaned into him and held my hands around his neck. My father kissed my forehead and wiped my tears away. His cheeks were flushed, and his brows knitted together.

"Sweetheart, that's not how our family does things." Then he released our hug and told me to get changed for bed. I slowly walked to the steps that led upstairs. I wasn't ready to go to bed. I wondered why my father wanted me in bed so early. I glanced back at him several times to see what he was doing. Each time, he waved at me with a forced smile. I saw Bob, Eleanor, and Charles sitting on the steps when I walked upstairs. They were each on a separate step with their chins resting in the palms of their hands, looking forlorn. But Charles had a different look than the other two. By the scowl on his face, he looked like he was stewing over something.

The next day, our father reimbursed the druggist with money from Mother's weekly allowance, and he apologized for her behavior. When she found out, she was outraged that he used her allowance money. Our house grew tenser, and our mother didn't speak much after that. The scowl she wore on her face looked like Charles's scowl the night I saw him sitting on the steps. She was brewing over something too. It made me anxious and nervous. I didn't like the silent treatment she was giving to everyone. I wondered what she was intensely thinking about so much. My fourth birthday was rapidly approaching, and I feared we wouldn't celebrate it. *I didn't tell. I didn't do anything*, I thought. *Why would we not celebrate my birthday?* I worried she wouldn't make my favorite cake. But when the day arrived, she made a sponge cake with extra cream and fruit.

"Happy fourth birthday, Stella," she said as she kissed the top of my head. Bob and I were licking the bowl of leftover cream.

"Thank you, Mommy," I said, licking my fingers. It was the first time she had spoken since the evening we got Charles's supplies on loan. She ran her hand through my brown hair and looked at me wistfully. It made an impression on me. "What's wrong, Mommy?"

"Nothing, dear. I just can't believe how big you're getting. Let's get washed up for dinner."

Part 2
CLARA

Chapter **6**

EIGHTEEN-YEAR-OLD CLARA BAKER'S stomach ached while she watched her mother pack all her belongings into a suitcase one afternoon. *This can't be real*, Clara thought to herself as she sat on her mother's bed. Her heartbeat was gaining speed, her breathing became heavy, and her brows furrowed. "Mama, please don't leave! You can't go!" Hot tears welled up even though Clara tried to push them down. She hated crying. But they streamed down Clara's pale face as she pleaded with her mother.

"I'm sorry, Clara, but I'm moving to Grandma and Grandpa's. It would be best for you to stay here and finish high school. I don't want you dropping out like your sister did. You only have a few months left before you graduate, and then you can join me. But I can't stay in this house anymore!" Clara noticed her eyes were sunken in. They were bloodshot from crying. Her mother blew her nose into a handkerchief and choked down her sniffles. "The stress and the rumors of that possible labor dispute have affected your father. I can't handle it! I can't handle him!" she said as she walked around her bed, placing more items into her suitcase. We have debts we cannot afford to pay because he's gambling and drinking all our money away!"

"But Mama, what about me? You expect me to stay here with *him*? He's not even my real father!" Clara stomped her foot on the floor and grabbed her mother's shoulders. "Mama, don't do this to me! Don't just leave me here with him!" Clara fretted breathlessly. She grabbed the dresses and hats from her mother's suitcase and threw them on the floor with as much force as her tiny frame could manage. Before Clara knew it, her mother had already picked up her belongings and packed them back into her suitcase.

"I don't expect you to stay here with him. I already told you to move in with your sister and John. They would love the help."

Clara's parents were Irene and Owen Baker. Her father died when Clara and her sister were young children. Irene quickly married Owen after that. They were a thriving couple who people once admired in the community they lived in. Owen had a successful job that he enjoyed. He worked at a factory called the Columbus Buggy Company. It was an early buggy and automotive manufacturing company. Owen quickly advanced with his shrewd business sense and charm. When his role in the factory changed, he feared losing his job. As he poured himself a bourbon one evening, he told his wife that the daily stress from work was getting to him. "I can't lose this job, Irene. Since we've been married, I've worked hard and given them much of my time. I don't want to start over now." Owen started drinking more in the evenings when he got home from work. And then, his drinking became a big problem. His actions and words became reckless. He turned into a person Irene didn't recognize. He took his frustrations out on her with his cruel words. Irene didn't like it, so she often went to bed early to avoid him. And then the ugliness started. Owen began sneaking into Clara and Lucille's bedroom after their mother fell asleep. Lucille was Clara's older sister. When Lucille thought she was pregnant, she knew it was her father's baby. She was terrified of what to do because she kept what he did to her a secret. Only Clara knew because they shared a room. Lucille felt much relief when she found she was not pregnant, but she knew she could no longer take the abuse. When she turned sixteen, she dropped out of high school and ran away from home to work as a nanny for a wealthy family outside of the city. She remained friends with a boy she knew from school. His name was John. He was a few years older than Lucille. After graduating high school, he secured a job at a bank in downtown Columbus. John and Lucille got married soon after. She wasn't in love with John, but she knew he would provide a good life for her. Things were finally better for Lucille but worsened for Clara. The first time her father entered Clara's bedroom after her sister ran away, she knew to fight back. She kicked and screamed and hollered. She threatened she would tell her mother.

Then, he lost his job at the Buggy Corporation. Owen found a new job working as a streetcar motorman in downtown Columbus. He was underpaid and worked long hours. He was unhappy working as a motorman. He thought it was beneath him. Later, his coworkers threatened to strike. When the buzz of a possible labor dispute erupted, he took his frustrations out on his wife again, but the abuse turned physical. Clara often heard her parents fighting and clawing at each other. Her mother tried to hide her bruises, but she couldn't hide a black eye. Clara hated her environment. It was slowly changing her into a different person. She felt like she was in constant survival mode. She often escaped out her bedroom window when her father came home drunk.

Thinking about living alone with her father made Clara's stomach turn inside out. She was confident he would focus his violent outbursts, or worse, on her, which made her heart throb in her chest. She grabbed her mother and hugged her tightly. She thought her mother would change her mind if she pleaded enough. She pressed her face into her mother's shoulder, wondering if her mother could hear her heart pounding. "Please stay," she said through tight lips. "Maybe we can get him to change. Maybe we can help him with his problems. Why can't Grandma and Grandpa come here and visit us? He'll behave in front of them. I don't want you to move, and I don't want to move in with Lucille and John. They just had a baby. Lucille won't have any time for me other than bossing me around. They live too far from school. They live too far from Richard."

"Honey, I'm sorry, but I've already made my decision, and my train is leaving soon," her mother said as she pulled out of Clara's hold. She turned from her daughter to finish packing. When Clara saw her mother putting her last few items in her suitcase, she stormed out of the bedroom and hurried down the stairs. She grabbed her coat, swung open the front door, and ran. Her mother begged Clara to return from the top of the steps, but Clara ignored her pleas. Her legs felt like rubber as she pulled her coat over her shoulders. She felt like she was running blindly to her boyfriend Richard's house.

Chapter 7

WHEN SHE FINALLY ARRIVED at his house, she was panting so loudly that Richard could hear her from a half-open window in his kitchen. He stopped washing the dishes and went outside, where Clara stood shivering in his backyard. She looked anxious and tense.

"What's wrong?" he asked.

"Richard, I need you. I need help," she gasped and grabbed his hands. She told him about her mother moving to Cincinnati and how she didn't want to live with her father or Lucille. She was talking so fast, making it difficult for him to comprehend everything she said.

He raised an eyebrow at her. "Slow down, slow down." He hugged her and whispered, "Everything will be okay."

Her eyes narrowed, and rage rushed through her veins. "Everything will be okay! How can you say that to me?" she asked incredulously. "You know *him*! You know how he is! How do you expect me to live *alone* with him?" Clara snapped as she pushed herself out of his hold and shoved him away. Richard stumbled backward. "I'm sorry," she said as she clutched her chest. "I'm just distraught and don't know what to do. My mother told me to move in with my sister and her husband, but I don't want to. They just had their baby, and ... well, I don't want to. Her house is too far away from everything." She choked back tears and looked at the sky when she heard thunder in the distance. She noticed storm clouds were moving in. The way they looked reminded Clara of how she was feeling, swirling heavy and gray and full of anger.

Richard grabbed Clara's hands. They were cold and shaking when he held them to his lips and kissed them. Her eyes pleaded with him to make things better. "Please don't panic," he said. He pulled her against him and embraced her tighter as he rubbed the small of her back. "I have an idea," Richard murmured, "but I need to talk to my parents first."

He kissed her forehead, breathed her in, and hugged her again. He wanted to help her in the worst way. "Stay here while I talk to my mom and dad." Clara nodded and wiped her nose.

"What is your idea?" she pressed for more information.

"I don't want to tell you yet. Stay here and wait until I get back."

"Please don't take too long," Clara urged as she shoved her hands inside her coat pockets. "It's getting colder out here, and it looks like it's going to rain." Richard gave her a reassuring look and nodded his head. After he turned, Clara surveyed the backyard. She didn't see anyone, so she pulled out a pack of cigarettes she had stolen from her father. She struck a match and lit one while sitting on a black iron chair. She felt nervous since she wasn't sure what Richard had planned to talk to his parents about. She smoked another cigarette after she put the first one out. Her lips quivered as she puffed on the cigarette, waiting for Richard to return.

Richard smelled the cigarette smoke when he walked inside the kitchen. He sighed heavily and looked out the window. His brow creased when he saw Clara smoking. He didn't want her to smoke, especially at his house. He knew his parents would disapprove and find it unladylike. He heard music playing and found them reading the paper and drinking tea in their parlor, which worked in his favor because you couldn't see the backyard from there.

"Mom, Dad, can I talk to you?" Richard's parents nodded their heads. He let out a nervous laugh as he turned down their phonograph. "Sorry. I don't mean to be rude, it's just loud." He cleared his throat. "So, I want to talk to you about Clara. I want to know if she can move in with us until I start college, or at least until we finish high school," he nervously waved his hand through his hair.

"What? Why?" his mother blurted in disbelief as she set her cup of tea down. Richard explained Clara's situation. "I don't understand why she needs to move in with us. Why are you asking us this?" Her eyebrows furrowed with confusion.

"Because Clara doesn't want to live with her stepfather. Mom, please, it's hard to explain."

"Well, you need to. Why doesn't she want to live with her stepfather?"

A bead of sweat crawled down Richard's face as he shifted his stance. His palms grew clammy when he spoke. "He's not stable. He's been drinking a lot, and then he has violent outbursts and hits her mother. She can't take the abuse anymore, and that's why she's moving to her parents' house in Cincinnati. Clara fears he'll start taking everything out on her if she lives alone with him."

Richard's dad put his hand up to stop him from saying more. His expression mirrored his wife's. "Then why isn't she taking Clara with her?" he asked. "I don't understand why her mother would leave her behind with an abusive and unstable man."

"She wants Clara to finish high school here since we're almost done. Then I think she's hoping Clara will move there, but Clara doesn't want to. Like I said, it's complicated. You don't have to say yes, but please consider it. She could stay in Mary's old bedroom." That comment stung. His sister, Mary, died a few years earlier of pneumonia. His mom's expression suddenly changed. Her eyes were downcast, and she pressed her lips together when she grabbed her husband's hand. "I'm sorry, Mom. I didn't mean to upset you. But we do have a room for her."

"Doesn't she have a sister she can live with?" his father asked.

"Yes, but her sister just had a baby. Clara doesn't want to be a burden. And they live too far away from here and from school. Please think about it. Should I leave so you can talk?"

His father shook his head back and forth, shifted in his chair, and uncrossed his legs. He looked at his wife with deliberation. They leaned into each other and quietly whispered. Richard ran his hand through his hair again. He tried to hear what they were saying, but his father used his newspaper to mask their voices. Richard moved from one foot to the other. He rubbed his forehead and pressed his lips. He stuck his hands in his pockets while he waited with anticipation.

His mom cleared her throat and was the first to speak. "Yes, she can move in for a short period of time to finish school. Then, we'll need to reassess the situation. What does she plan on doing after high school anyway? Will she be attending Ohio State with you?"

"I'm not sure yet. But we'll figure it out," Richard reassured them. He let out a huge sigh. "Thank you." He cupped his hands around his mouth and exhaled. He was anxious to tell Clara. "She's actually in the backyard waiting for me. Do you mind if I leave to tell her the news?"

"Go ahead," his mother waved him on with her hand. "But I expect her to help around the house while she's here," she added quietly as Richard ran out. His parents looked at each other sharply. "Do you think this is a mistake?" his mother asked.

"I don't know." His father let out a profound breath, rubbed his forehead, and crossed his legs. "I guess we'll find out," he murmured.

Chapter 8

IT WAS DRIZZLING WHEN CLARA stomped out her last cigarette. Annoyed, Richard picked up the cigarette butts that were on the ground. "I wish you wouldn't smoke. You know I don't like it. And you'll have to stop smoking while you're living here!"

"What? You asked your parents if I could live here? Did they say yes?" Richard smiled and nodded his head.

"Oh my, I can't believe they said yes! Thank you! Thank you! I love you!" She kissed him. "I want to make it home and pack before the rain falls harder."

"Wait, I'm not sure if they meant tonight," Richard yelled as she ran from him. But Clara was already too far away to hear him. He walked back into the kitchen and hid the cigarette butts in the garbage. "Mom, we need to get Mary's bedroom ready now," he said. "She'll be back soon with her stuff."

When she returned to her house to retrieve her belongings, Clara was damp from the rain but didn't care. She wanted to pack before her father returned home. She had no idea when that would be, so time was of the essence. She jammed as much as she could into two suitcases. She realized her mother had already left when she noticed a letter sitting on her nightstand. Clara grabbed the letter and placed it into one of her suitcases. She wasn't ready to read it yet.

To Clara's dismay, she heard the front door slam and the sound of heavy boots stumbling up the steps before she could snap her last suitcase shut. She looked up as her father slipped into her bedroom. A cold shiver went through Clara's spine. He was drunk, and he wobbled when he asked, "Where the hell is your mother, and what the hell are you doing?" Clara ignored his questions. She closed the last suitcase and grabbed the other one. She had a suitcase in each hand as she started to walk out of her bedroom. But he pulled the back of her hair and swung her around. "Where the hell do you think you're going, girl? Answer me, damn it."

Clara smelled a mixture of sweat, cigars, and alcohol as she managed to turn away from him and run with both suitcases down the stairs. Her father leaped after her, and he was faster than she expected. He slammed his hand on the front door so she could not open it. Then he pushed her against the door and put his hands against Clara's shoulders, pinning her against it. He looked like a wild beast and yelled, "Girl, if you leave here, I will end you. Do you hear? I WILL END YOU!" Angry spit flew out of his mouth and landed on Clara's cheek as he yelled. She quickly wiped the spit away. His breath was hot and smelled vile. Her heart was racing, and her breathing was heavy. She desperately wanted to be out of his grasp. Clara closed her eyes and thought for a second. Then pure rage overtook her.

She pulled herself up onto her tiptoes, leaned close to his ear, and whispered, "You ended me a long time ago, Daddy." She felt the prickly stubble from his face. He removed one of his hands from her shoulders to scratch his chin. He sighed and squinted at her, then rubbed his hand through his dark, wet hair. He breathed deeply, and a revolting smell seeped from his mouth again. Clara strained to keep herself from shaking. She didn't want her father to see her fear. Then she slowly pulled out of his hold and turned around.

He opened the front door and said, "Go ahead and leave, you ungrateful girl. Daddy ain't gonna take care of you no more!" Clara quickly grabbed her coat and suitcases. As she did, she felt a hard slap to her backside. She fell forward and stumbled down the porch steps, landing on her face. She immediately felt pain, and her lower lip was bleeding. One of her suitcases opened, and all her clothes flew out, covering the lawn. She heard her father laugh behind her when he slammed the front door shut.

Clara moved quickly as she shoved the clothes back into the suitcase. When she got up, she noticed her stockings were ripped, and both knees were bleeding, but she didn't care even though they were her best pair. Her face was throbbing, but she didn't care about that either. She could only think about one thing: returning to Richard's house before the rain fell harder. Holding two suitcases and walking in the rain was more challenging than she anticipated. Then, an automobile pulled beside her. A couple was in an expensive, brand-new Ford Model T. They looked to be her parents' age. The woman in the passenger seat seemed concerned when she asked, "Honey, can we drive you somewhere? We're just on our way home to Franklinton, you won't be a burden. You shouldn't be walking in this rain, especially with those heavy suitcases." Clara didn't like others helping her. Her first thought was to say no thank you, but she quickly changed her mind.

"Yes, ma'am, I would appreciate a ride. It's not too far from here."

"Well, get in before you catch a cold."

"Thank you so much," Clara said as she slid into the back seat. The rain was growing harder, and her suitcases were unbearably heavy. She tried to swallow the lump in her throat as the car ground into gear and continued on into the night.

Chapter **9**

RICHARD RILEY WAS DANGEROUSLY HANDSOME with a tall, muscular frame and an award-winning smile. He had an irresistible grin that melted most girls. He was not just good-looking but athletic and intelligent. Richard excelled at anything he put his mind to. But he was humble and didn't brag about his accomplishments, which made him one of the most popular boys in school and sought after by many girls. He grew up in an upper- to middle-class family. After his older sister, Mary, died of pneumonia, he became an only child, causing his family immeasurable grief. His parents put all their energy into raising him to be an exceptional person. Clara often wondered how she managed to get a boy like Richard. The fact is, she didn't have the best reputation at school. She didn't do anything to earn a bad one, but many of her classmates disliked her due to her father's public intoxication and ill repute. When she set her sights on Richard, she knew she would not settle until he was hers. Richard admired Clara's attitude and overall demeanor. She was independent, fierce, and quick-witted. And her beautiful appearance made her even more attractive.

When Clara moved in that evening, his parents gave her his sister's bedroom. Since Mary's death, the room hadn't been used. Clara walked around her room, studying everything she saw. Mary loved flowers, so her wallpaper and bedding were decorated with them. Clara thought it was a little much, but she knew better than to voice judgments. She wanted to open the boxes in her closet but restrained herself. She didn't know Mary well and was curious about her. At first, Clara was uncomfortable moving into her room. It felt like a museum with signs that read, "Do Not Touch" everywhere. She didn't want to displace anything because she could tell they kept it the same after Mary died. Clara unpacked her belongings and carefully placed her things in Mary's dresser drawers. She noticed the unopened letter from her mother in one of her suitcases. It unnerved her to open it, so she put it aside. After she finished unpacking, she decided to read it. Clara smelled the envelope before she opened it. She thought she could smell her mother's scent. Tears swelled in her eyes when she smelled it again. She sat stiffly on Mary's bed and tore the envelope open. It gave her a small paper cut. Clara sighed heavily and sucked the blood from her right finger. She wasn't sure why she felt nervous to read it. She was feeling a mix of emotions.

My Dearest Clara,

This is the most challenging letter I have written. It was heartbreaking for me to leave you today, but I had to. My father managed to get me a job working at his company. As I explained earlier, our debts must be paid so the Debt Collectors don't come after us. Then I am cutting ties with your father. He doesn't deserve us. He can no longer be in our lives. That's why I want you to live in Cincinnati after you graduate.

Please move in with Lucille and John. I don't want you living with your father, and they are more than happy to have you. I know they don't live as close as you would like, but I'm sure John will help drive you places when he can.

I know you were angry with me today, and I am sorry I left without a proper goodbye. I hope one day you will understand my actions. Life has been hard on me, and now I need a fresh start. Maybe you need one too. I love you, and I will think about you every day.

Love,

Mother

After she read the letter, Clara's chest rose heavily as she sat quietly on Mary's bed. She felt the corners of her mouth being pulled downward, and her eyebrows furrowed. She couldn't force a single tear out, even if she wanted to. She understood why her mother wanted to leave, but she still felt angry. She was angry with both her parents. She hated her father for betraying their family the way he had. For creating a rebellion in her own home. She thought about all the fighting. *I will never be like my mother,* Clara thought. *I will never allow a man to control me to the point I must leave my family. To the point I leave my children behind!* Clara carefully folded the letter up the way her mother had folded it. She smelled it for the last time. She placed it back into the envelope and put it in one of the drawers where she put her undergarments. She heard a soft knock at the door. Richard's mom peered in and asked her if she needed anything. "Everything is perfect, Mrs. Riley. Thank you again for allowing me to stay here. I promise I won't be a burden. And I will help around the house with whatever you like."

Mrs. Riley smiled, and then she stared at Clara for a second. Her eyes were dark and unreadable. She glanced around her daughter's bedroom, her eyes sweeping over every surface until they landed upon a picture in a gold frame sitting on the dresser. A picture of Mary. Richard's mother's eyes turned wistful, and the corner of her lips curled downward. She cleared her throat and forced a welcoming smile. "Dinner will be ready in ten minutes, dear."

Chapter 10

CLARA SOON REALIZED that life at Richard's house was wonderful, and she adored being with his family. It felt like a good dream you didn't want to wake from. She no longer heard fighting. She felt safe in her new environment. She quickly developed a bond with Richard's mother. Her favorite thing to do with her was to shop. They dressed in their finest clothing when they went to downtown Columbus. They loved the Lazarus Department Store. It was in a six-story building with many different departments. Their favorite ones were women's apparel, jewelry, and shoes. Richard's mother often showered Clara with things she bought from the store. They ate lunch at different cafés. Clara loved the attention, and Richard's mom enjoyed having a girl in the house again. And, with Clara living under the same roof as Richard, it also allowed them more time together. Time when Richard's parents weren't always around to supervise.

A week after they graduated from high school, Clara realized something she wasn't expecting. "I'm pregnant, Richard."

Richard lowered his face and raised his eyebrows. He felt stunned by the news. His stomach tightened, and his mouth went dry, "Are you sure?"

"Yes, I'm certain." Clara felt irritated and disappointed by Richard's expression and the tone he used when he asked her if she was sure. She sat at the kitchen table and rested her head on her hands.

Richard paced the kitchen floor, breathing in and out loudly. His head was down, and Clara could tell he was deep in thought. She wondered what he was thinking about and started to feel worried. An impalpable, cold, damp feeling in the air surrounded her.

"Richard, are you going to say something?"

"Clara, I don't know what to say. I'm not ready to tell my parents. I don't think they'll react well. Maybe we should marry first, and then we'll tell them about the baby." His perfectly chiseled features suddenly looked not so perfect. "I'll find a place for us to rent. And I think you should get a job, like at that department store you go to so much. Even though my parents are paying my tuition, we'll still need money. I'll work part-time somewhere when I'm not in school." He ran his hands through his dark hair and continued to pace. Clara thought his face looked white and clammy. For the first time, she felt insecure with Richard. He wasn't hugging her and telling her everything would be okay.

She looked at him pointedly. "Okay, I'll apply for a job at Lazarus tomorrow. Are you okay?"

"This is not what I expected before starting college," he sighed, and an inauspicious cloud followed behind him as he left the room.

Richard found an affordable place for them to rent. It was a small brick house with two bedrooms. He drove Clara to the house to show her one rainy afternoon. "It's wonderful, Richard! It looks so cute," she gushed. "We'll be happy in that little brick house with our baby!" When she lunged forward to hug Richard, she felt him pull away. Clara winced. It was only for a split second, but in that split second, her stomach turned. She knew something felt wrong. They drove home in silence. Clara stared at the windshield wipers dancing back and forth in front of her. She didn't like the chill in the air. She wanted to be celebrating with Richard, but instead, she felt alone.

In late June, Clara had a miscarriage and lost their baby. She didn't know what had caused the miscarriage, but she felt like the stress she was feeling over Richard may have contributed. She wasn't sure; all she knew was she was devastated and depressed. She feared he wouldn't marry her if he knew the truth so kept the miscarriage a secret. She still wanted to get married and live together like they had planned. Richard started sensing something was wrong. "What's going on with you? You haven't been yourself this past month."

"I'm fine. Maybe it's just pregnancy. I'm working long hours at Lazarus and I'm tired." Clara felt guilty for lying, but she wasn't ready to tell him the truth about the baby. She was working and grieving at the same time. She didn't realize how much she wanted a baby until it was taken away from her.

But Richard continued to see a change in Clara. She wasn't behaving as usual; he knew it was more than just the pregnancy.

After some time, it got to the point where she knew she couldn't keep avoiding his questions, so Clara finally told Richard the truth. "I'm heartbroken," she cried. "I feel empty inside. I miss the baby, and I've been grieving every day. But I still want to get married like we planned. Maybe we can try to have another one once we get settled in our rental."

"Try for another one! Are you serious? I can't believe you knew for a month before telling me! To be honest, I'm relieved you lost the baby. I don't mean to be hurtful, but I'm not ready to be a father. I'm glad we're not married yet. We were only getting married because of the baby. I can't believe you kept this from me! Were you waiting to tell me after the marriage?" Richard hissed. He stood up so fast and hard that his chair tipped over and fell onto the floor. He didn't pick it up when he stormed out of the kitchen. He didn't want to hear her response. She had already broken his trust.

"Richard!" Clara screamed. "What are you saying? You ARE being hurtful! You're being cruel!" she yelled, chasing him from the kitchen.

Clara felt an odd sensation in her chest. "You're not sad about the baby?" she cried. "Not even a little? I'm sorry I didn't tell you sooner. I needed time to process. Don't just walk away!" she yelled as he slammed his bedroom door shut. The sound of the door slamming made her wince, and her heart skipped a beat. She banged on the door. "Richard, come out here and talk to me!" She pressed her face against the door. "Richard! Please, open the door and talk to me," she sobbed. It was silent on the other side of the door. She knew he wasn't coming out. Clara's tears streamed down her hot face as she ran to her bedroom and slammed the door shut. She threw her bedcover back and flung her body on the bed. Her body was shaking; she felt nauseous. She felt like the rug had just been ripped from under her. She grabbed her pillow and sobbed Richard's name into it. She pushed her face deeper into the pillow and cried. "Why? Why?" she screamed into her tear-soaked pillow until the spent rage left her body.

After that day, Richard was cold and distant toward Clara. She was in shock and numb to the overwhelming sense of loss. Her body felt flooded with sadness. She had a persistent knot in her stomach daily. She had difficulty focusing at work after spending sleepless nights wondering why Richard had suddenly changed. It was early August, and she was supposed to be pregnant; they were supposed to be married, moving into the little brick house together.

Richard's parents felt the tension between their son and Clara. She often felt his mother staring at her like she wanted to say something but didn't. After a week of that, Clara told them she was moving out. She felt angry that Richard didn't tell them about their breakup. She was embarrassed that the news came from her. Richard's mother's jaw hung open when Clara told her about the pregnancy, the proposed marriage, the miscarriage, and then how Richard behaved when she told him she lost the baby. She knew Richard would be mad as hell that she did that, but Clara didn't care.

She felt disrespected and angry and rejected, and she wanted his mother to know what her son did. *Her perfect son wasn't so perfect after all*, she thought.

Richard's mom's disbelief was written all over her face. "I'm utterly speechless. I'm so sorry. What are you going to do? You can stay here for as long as you need, dear." But Clara sensed the unassertive tone in her voice. And she didn't want to feel she had to hide her sadness anymore. "Thank you, Mrs. Riley. That's kind, but I should move out soon."

Clara moved into a small apartment off High Street in early August. It was not a nice place, and she had to share a washroom with other tenants, but it was all she could afford with the money she had saved. Clara became obsessed and fixated, thinking about Richard and the little brick house they were supposed to live in together. She knew the address and walked by it several times a day before Richard moved in. She was still angry with Richard but still loved him even though she felt scorned. A young man always watched her from a few houses down, so she couldn't peek inside the windows for a better look inside the house when he was around. Clara didn't want to appear suspicious and quickly grew annoyed with this person staring at her. He was interfering with her spying.

Soon after Richard started college, he met an exquisite woman. They met when Richard accidentally bumped into her while walking into class. Her name was Helen. There was an instant attraction between them. He felt his heart pound as he apologized for his clumsy behavior. Helen was tall and thin with delicate features. She had soft green eyes and a wide, radiant smile. Her face reminded Richard of an angel. Her curly, sun-kissed blonde hair hung at her shoulders. Richard couldn't keep his eyes off Helen while sitting beside her. After class, they walked together, exchanging pleasantries. He liked the way she carried herself. She had a maturity about her he'd never seen in a girl before. It made sense when he found out Helen was a few years older than him. He couldn't keep his mind off her the day he met her. They made plans to see each other daily. Their relationship progressed rather quickly, and they started courting. Richard was in love.

Helen grew up in Franklinton, just west of downtown Columbus. Her family was from old family money. They loved Richard the minute they met him. Richard enjoyed the lifestyle Helen's parents represented. They took them to theaters and entertained them at excellent restaurants. Helen's father often took Richard to the Columbus Country Club to play golf. When it opened in 1903, it was a horseman's club, but then a golf course was established there in 1907. It made Richard feel special when he was at the club. His parents were not poor, but they could not offer Richard the same type of lifestyle that Helen's parents could. He enjoyed the attention he received from them. Even though Richard and Helen only knew each other briefly, they fell in love and knew they would marry someday.

Chapter 11

ONE AFTERNOON, while Clara was walking on High Street, she saw Richard walking hand in hand with a tall, beautiful blonde woman. The way the sun landed on her made her hair glow. Her blonde curls bobbed on her shoulders as they strolled down High Street. It was the first time she had seen Richard since she moved out of his house. It took her breath away. *Who is that woman,* she wondered. Her eyes felt as big as saucers. Her jaw tightened, and she felt jittery and stunned at the same time. She crossed to the other side of the street. Her stomach clenched as she watched them. Her mouth grew dry, and she felt herself sweating through her blouse. She stayed behind them but not close enough for them to see her. She shuddered at their chatter and laughter but couldn't hear what they were saying due to the traffic. When Richard put his arm around the blonde woman and kissed her, raw anger settled deep within Clara's body. She followed them until she saw Richard hop into the passenger seat of a brand-new Ford Model T. It looked exactly like the one that drove her to Richard's house the night she moved in with his family. She flinched as the car turned the corner. Clara tried to block the sun from her eyes as she followed where it was heading but then jumped and lost sight of it when she heard a blaring horn honking behind her. With no traffic signals, walking could be dangerous in Columbus.

The policeman at the center of the intersection directing traffic blew his whistle and yelled, "You better watch where you walk, lady. You could have been hit!" She hadn't realized she was in the street until then. Clara felt disoriented. She hugged her clutch against her chest and continued walking. She found herself walking toward the little brick house. When she arrived, she spotted the Model T parked near the home she was supposed to be living in. Clara froze, but this time instead of anger, sadness rose heavily in her chest. Her breathing started to quicken, and she felt her heart beating in her throat. She pulled a cigarette out of her clutch. She felt like she was being watched again as she lit it. She looked up and noticed the same young man from two houses down peering over at her. He waved, but Clara didn't wave back. She felt annoyed that the man noticed her again. She quickly turned around and walked away, feeling like she was pushing her way through a fog. Her mouth clenched as her eyes welled up. Tears slid down her rosy cheeks.

Clara fumbled inside her clutch to find the key to her unit. Once she made it inside, she screamed, "Why?" Her mind buzzed with questions. *Who was that woman? Are they serious? How serious are they?* Clara felt a heavier pit forming in her stomach. She clutched her belly and thought of the baby she had lost. *Why did I have to lose that child,* she thought. *Richard would still be with me if I didn't lose the baby.* Clara's mind was racing. She paced the floor and exhaled her cigarette smoke with heavy breaths. Her stomach turned, and she stomped her cigarette before it was finished. She felt saliva forming in her mouth, the kind one tastes before throwing up. She ran to the water closet she shared with other tenants. She hastily knocked on the door before she entered. She rested her arms around the basin and heaved into it while vomiting what little was left in her stomach from earlier that day. When she finished, she glared at her reflection in the mirror. She didn't recognize herself. "Who are you?" she asked the girl with the bloodshot eyes and tear-streaked face looking back at her. Her dry lips were quivering, and her hands were shaking. She hated the reflection she saw. "Who are you?" she asked again. She shook her head several times and then slapped her face. She noticed a man's straight-edge razor on the shelf beside the basin. Her hand shook as she picked up the shiny razor. She stared at it for so long it began to blur. She slowly ran it down her red cheek to the bottom of her neck. She turned her left wrist over and carefully studied how her purple-blue veins looked under her pale skin. They reminded her of tree roots. She began to shake more when she pressed the razor to her left wrist. Suddenly, someone banged on the door, asking how long she planned to cry in there. Clara was startled, and she dropped the razor. It fell on the dirty tile floor. She hurriedly picked it up and put it back on the shelf where she found it. When she opened the door, Clara kept her head down. She didn't want to make eye contact with the man. She was embarrassed to interact with her rude neighbor.

That night, Clara lay on her makeshift bed and thought of Richard and that woman. So many thoughts raced through her mind. She missed Richard and seeing him with her was a painful surprise. She remembered how she and Richard walked hand in hand and laughed together, just as she had seen him do with the pretty blonde woman earlier that day. She remembered the good times they shared, but her thoughts changed to questions again. She wondered how they met. She wondered how long they had known each other. She wondered if they were intimate with each other. She wondered if they were in love. Clara's questions flew through her mind so fast it made her brain hurt. She was annoyed that she didn't have the answers to her questions, and her mind tingled. She knew she needed sleep but couldn't get her mind to shut down. Her questions agitated her. She tossed and turned so much that her blankets twisted around her. She couldn't get comfortable and became increasingly frantic as more questions popped into her head.

Clara thought about the Model T she had seen that afternoon. The couple who had picked her up in the rain and drove her to Richard's house drove the same kind of car. Clara remembered they told her they had a daughter who attended Ohio State. *Could that couple have been her parents?* she wondered. She remembered the mother was a pretty blonde lady. Clara thought the woman resembled the girl Richard was with. She tossed and turned and huffed loudly. Her brain hurt and felt heavy inside her head. She put a pillow over her face and screamed into it. She couldn't fall asleep, so she fetched her purse and pulled out a cigarette. Clara was lucky enough to have a unit with a window. She lifted the windowpane and breathed in the fall air. The streets were still busy, and Clara could hear the hustle of people walking, cars honking, and streetcars coming and going as she exhaled her cigarette smoke. She wondered if her father was running one of them now as she blew her cigarette smoke out the window. Clara rubbed her forehead and closed her eyes.

Chapter **12**

WHEN CLARA WASN'T WORKING at Lazarus, she walked by the little brick house hoping to run into Richard or spy on what he was doing. She wasn't sure if she wanted to see him or just snoop, but she made a routine of it. She knew it was a wild thing to do, but she couldn't stop herself. She hid behind large trees that lined the street across from the house. She peered through the windows when she felt nobody would catch her. During one of her visits, she noticed the same young man watching her again. When they exchanged glances, he whistled and waved his hand, motioning for Clara to come over. She didn't. He irritated her, so she ignored him. Her blood was boiling when she pulled out a cigarette and sat down on the front steps of the brick house. She struck a match and inhaled the cigarette. She thought about the times she smoked in Richard's backyard when she exhaled the smoke. Richard hated her smoking. She wondered if the blonde woman smoked. She wondered many things about the blonde woman. Suddenly, she realized the man was standing before her. He startled Clara and interrupted her wondering.

"Hi. Is everything okay?" he asked. He removed his hat and tucked it under his arm. Clara nodded yes but didn't speak to him. She was annoyed and embarrassed. She wanted him to leave. "Do you know the couple living in this house?" Clara stood up, nodded yes again, and quickly left the man behind.

The couple living in the house! echoed in her head. *The couple living in the house!* Oh no, Clara thought. "I am the one that should be living in that house. Richard and I are the couple who should be living in that house," she muttered from under her breath as she pulled her hat down over her ears. Anger grew inside Clara as her strides grew faster. She thought about the life she was supposed to be living with Richard. She thought of the baby she was supposed to be having. She thought of the happiness she and Richard once shared. They were supposed to be married. They were supposed to be the couple living in that house. A tear streamed down and stung her face.

The next evening, Clara decided to walk by Richard's house again after her shift at Lazarus was over. It was cold and breezy outside, so she wrapped herself in her wool coat. The Ford was parked in front of the house, but no lights were on. It looked dark and uninviting. Something bizarre overcame Clara as she glared at the house. She walked to the front door and felt the door handle. She was surprised to find it unlocked, and without much thought, she gently opened the door and listened. She didn't hear any voices; she didn't hear anything. She quietly walked inside the home. She felt as if she were in a trance. She stood still and studied every detail of the house. She couldn't help critiquing the decor. It was decorated in a way that surprised Clara. It didn't remind her of Richard's taste at all. There were throw pillows on the couch and chairs. They had flowers on them. Richard didn't like flowers. They reminded him of his dead sister.

Clara sat on the sofa and smelled one of the throw pillows. She hoped to smell Richard, but she didn't. Instead, she smelled the scent of light lilac perfume. She made a face and threw the pillow back on the sofa. She got up from the couch and explored the house some more. She found the kitchen and turned on a small lamp. She saw Richard's coat hanging off one of the kitchen chairs. She pulled the coat off the chair and pressed it against her face. She smelled him. *It feels so good to smell him again.* Then she noticed a photograph of Richard and that woman smiling happily. She snatched it from the counter and studied it. A tear crawled down her face. Her throat went dry as she stared at it. Then she slid the photo into her coat pocket. Her face felt hot under her hat, and she was sweating under her coat. She noticed two glasses of half-drunk wine. She ran her finger around the glass rim with no lipstick print. She removed that glass from the counter and drank the last bit of wine. She tasted Richard. She missed kissing him. She missed hugging him. She missed being with him. She placed the glass back on the counter, leaned against it, and stared at the black-and-white checkered floor, contemplating what she would do next. Her jaw tensed as she found herself at the bottom of the stairs. She slowly walked up the narrow steps to the second level. She felt relieved when they didn't creak. There were two bedrooms upstairs, but she knew that. No one was in the first bedroom. It was filled with moving boxes and clothes that didn't belong to Richard. They were women's clothing. Clara imagined it as their baby's room, though. She pictured a wooden rocking chair next to a beautiful cream-colored crib. She saw herself rocking the baby in the chair and then putting the sleeping infant in the crib. She felt Richard beside her with his arm touching the small of her back, smiling at their baby.

A palpable urge to kick all the boxes over interrupted Clara's thoughts of the baby. She wandered out of the bedroom toward the second one. Her breathing felt heavier when she saw the door was closed. She put her hand on the door handle, which creaked when she slowly pushed it open. She put her hand over her mouth to stifle a loud gasp when she saw Richard with that woman sleeping next to him. Her face burned. A terrifying jolt ran through her body. Clara's heart pounded as the shocking revelation hung over her head. It had become real to her now. She stepped closer to get a better look at them. At that moment, Richard stirred and shifted in his bed. Clara quickly turned to leave. She darted down the narrow steps as hurriedly as she could. She thought she heard footsteps behind her but didn't look back. She thought she heard someone call her name, but she wasn't sure since her heart was thumping loudly in her ears. She reached the front door and slipped outside as fast as she could. She quietly shut the front door behind her, turned on her heels, and ran down the steps of the front stoop into the street. She only glanced back once to see if anyone was standing at the front door, but no one was.

As Clara slowed her pace, she started to walk. Tears streamed down her cheeks and stung her face in the cold darkness of the night. She couldn't get the sight of them out of her mind. She put her hands in her coat pockets and suddenly felt the photograph. She pulled it out and ripped it into small pieces as she walked, slowly throwing them on the street like she was leaving breadcrumbs behind. Then she realized she was being watched again. She turned around and saw the same young man from the day before leaning against a light pole. He waved his hand and yelled hello to her. Clara was wearing a black cloche hat. She pulled the bell shape of it down over her eyes. She crossed to the other side of the street and sped up, praying the footsteps she heard from behind her didn't belong to him. But they grew closer and louder.

"Miss, miss," the man called from behind her. "Do you remember me? Miss, it's not safe to be out this late by yourself. Would you like me to escort you home?"

Clara mumbled a "no thank you" under her breath, but that didn't stop him. He was now walking alongside her. "I see you around a lot. We sort of met yesterday at Richard's house. You said you knew him. How do you know him?"

Clara ignored his question and started walking faster, but the man continued to trail behind her. He caught up with her again. "I live two houses down from Richard." Clara remained silent but slowed her pace down. The stranger had an excited rush to his voice that Clara found annoying, but she wanted to know more about him since he must know Richard. "I've seen you many times outside his house. I'm sorry, I know it's none of my business, but I must ask why, why do you hide behind the trees across the street like you are spying on them if you know them?"

Clara swallowed hard and choked down her breath. She couldn't believe the audacity he had in questioning her. She was growing more and more irritated by the minute. She stopped walking, pulled a cigarette from her handbag, lit it, and blew smoke near his face. She stared at him for a second. "I don't have time for this," she ever so quietly muttered from under her breath as she turned. She wondered if he had heard her, but she knew he was not giving up so easily when she heard his footsteps behind her again. She debated whether to run or allow the man to walk with her.

"Miss, with all due respect, a pretty girl like you shouldn't be walking this late by yourself ... or be smoking." He meekly said the last part to himself rather than to her. "May I please escort you somewhere?" he nervously coaxed.

But Clara heard everything. She stopped, spun around, and blew her cigarette smoke into his face. He winced, yet he smiled at her while she eyeballed him. They were standing under a streetlight now. As the light shone over him, she observed him differently, noting things she liked about him. He had blonde, thick, curly hair that he tried to slick back, but a few curls dangled down. She admired his strong jawline, full lips, and hazel eyes. He had trusting eyes. And she liked the way he dressed. He had a neat and clean appearance, more like a sophisticated man than a teenage boy. Clara immediately felt oddly attracted to him, even though he annoyed her.

"With all due respect, it looks like *you* are the one spying on *me*," she jabbed back and took another puff. She blew the smoke into his face again and cleared her throat. She hesitated for a moment, waiting to hear his rebuke.

The handsome stranger laughed and said, "Touché." Clara stood awkwardly as she flicked her cigarette on the sidewalk and put it out with the heel of her shoe. She wasn't sure how to respond. She had never heard that word before. She crossed her arms around her chest and gave him a quizzical look. An uncomfortable silence rose between them, but the handsome stranger broke it. "I'm sorry. I don't want to make you angry. I just really wanted to talk to you. To meet you. I met Richard the day he moved in, that's all. I'm curious how you know him."

"You've only talked to Richard when he was moving in?"

"Yes, we haven't had a chance to get to know each other because he's with that young lady a lot, and now she moved in with him." The tips of Clara's ears burned. They grew hotter, and she feared he could see them turning red.

"Well, I know him quite well," she said, rearranging her hat over her ears. "We have a history, and I'm the one who is supposed to be living in that house with him. Not that blonde floozy."

"Who, Helen? I wouldn't call her a floozy. She seems like a classy dame if you ask me. So, you and Richard were a thing?"

Clara ignored his question. "I don't mean any harm, so please don't say anything to them. And I would appreciate it if you would stop watching me constantly." She pulled another cigarette from her handbag, but he blocked it from her lips.

"I'm sorry. But I can't let you light that."

Clara bit down on her lower lip, wondering what he would say next. Before she knew it, he reached for Clara's hand. To her surprise, she shook hands with the handsome stranger. They were cold and rough, but his touch felt good. Her attraction to him quickened her breathing, and her stomach fluttered.

"Hello, my name is Frank Miller. I'm a simple fellow but a good, hard-working man. And yes, I've been spying on you, but with good reason."

Clara and Frank were still shaking hands when he paused before saying, "And if I may say so, you are the most beautiful woman I've ever seen. I fell hard for you the first moment I saw you peering through Richard's windows. That's why I've been watching you. I hope you will give me the honor of your company and go out with me sometime."

A small smile crept onto Clara's face.

Chapter 13

CLARA ACCEPTED FRANK'S OFFER. She agreed to have lunch with him at Goodale Park. Frank was ecstatic. He packed a picnic basket full of food and purchased a new blanket for them to sit on. He wanted the day to be perfect and feared Clara would cancel if the weather didn't cooperate. But on their picnic day, the sun shone bright, and the air felt warm even though it was breezy. Frank was relieved that everything was falling into place while he set up a spot under a tall, beautiful tree for them. Red leaves swarmed around and danced above them, welcoming them.

"Clara, I am so happy you agreed! Thank you again for coming here with me," Frank said while beaming from ear to ear as he positioned himself next to her on the blanket. Frank's bright smile was infectious, and Clara started smiling along with him. Frank liked Clara's smile. It seemed genuine. "You look stunning today, truly stunning." Clara felt her face become warm and blushed. Her natural rosy cheeks turned rosier. I can't believe you put all this together on your own. I'm impressed! Your mother taught you well."

"I never knew my mother," Frank replied quietly.

"Oh, I'm so sorry to hear that. I hope I didn't upset you." Her playful smile turned down, and her forehead creased.

Frank Miller was born in Canton, Ohio. His mother died from complications during his childbirth. He had an older sister, Elizabeth, who was five. Their father's sister, Alice, moved in to care for Frank and Elizabeth after their mother died. Frank's father was devastated after his wife passed away and took to the bottle to escape from his grief and loneliness. Alice worried about her brother's drinking, but she couldn't do anything to stop it.

"No, you didn't upset me. How would you have known? My aunt Alice raised my sister and me until I was ten years old. Then, my aunt died from an infection of some kind. My dad had a hard time after she died. He quickly married a woman he barely knew, and she was not nice to us. They met at a bar. I'll just say her behavior was challenging."

One day, while walking home from school, Frank saw his father's new wife climbing out of an open window at a neighbor's house. The man who owned the home fought in the Great Sioux War. He lost one of his legs during the last battle. Frank could hear a woman screaming and cursing from inside the house. He stopped and stared as he watched his father's wife scurrying down a trellis from under the open window. Then, a prosthetic leg was thrown out of the same window she escaped from. It landed only a few inches from her. Frank heard a woman scream, "Buzz off, you floozy!" and the window slammed shut. His father's wife gave Frank a quick glance. Then she smoothed her black hair behind her ears and rearranged herself inside her white dress. She looked at Frank again and gave him a sheepish smile as she hopped over the prosthetic leg where it fell in the grass. Frank stood in amazement while he watched her saunter down the street like nothing had happened.

"So, I started working at a young age, maybe ten, to help support my father's income. He worked in construction, but most of his earnings were spent at the bar where he met his wife. I delivered newspapers and worked at a bakery as a dishwasher. Once I became a teenager, I worked with my father at his construction sites when I wasn't in school."

Frank's teachers helped him apply for college scholarships in high school. He loved Ohio State University and dreamed of attending college there. Frank was excited when he was accepted. He was ready to leave Canton for good.

"After graduating high school, I moved here and started college. I recently graduated this past summer. I work in construction, but I'm also trying to obtain a steady job. I don't talk to my father anymore. I don't even know if he's still with the same woman. My sister lives in Springfield, but we don't talk much," Frank said as he removed his hat, covered his eyes from the sun, and laid back on the blanket. Clara felt a connection to Frank. She knew what it was like not speaking to family. She carefully removed her hat and rested her head on his shoulder.

"Frank, I think we are more alike than I thought," she murmured in his ear as she ran her finger down his face. Then, she did something that surprised her. She gently kissed him on the cheek. "I'm sorry, that was forward of me." She quickly sat up. Clara placed her hand over her mouth, hiding her embarrassment.

Frank sat up beside her. "Don't be sorry." He rested his hand on her knee with a pleased grin like a kid on Christmas morning. "I'm happy you're here with me. I'm happy that you look happy. Sitting with you under this radiant tree on such a beautiful day is wonderful! It's much better than having cigarette smoke blown in your face," Frank chuckled, and Clara laughed uncomfortably.

"I know, I'm so sorry about that. My behavior was horrible. You must have thought I was extremely rude."

"Nah, don't sweat it," Frank said. "Shall I unpack the picnic basket now? We could eat and then take a walk around this lovely park."

"That sounds swell," Clara said as she gave him an approving smile. She felt bubbly, which surprised her. She liked being with Frank. She wanted to get to know him better. She didn't feel as attracted to Frank as when she first met Richard. He wasn't as tall as she would have liked, but he dressed nicely, which was essential to Clara. She liked a well-dressed man who smelled good.

Frank carefully took out the items he packed in the basket and laid them on the blanket. With every item he removed, he glanced at Clara's expression. He was delighted that she seemed to approve of all his choices. Then he removed a glass flask and a thermos. "I'm not a big drinker, but I heard about this drink called an Old Fashioned. I probably didn't make it right, so I also brought some tea." Clara grabbed the flask, sipped the whiskey, and immediately shook her head.

"Oh my, that's strong," she grimaced, wiping her mouth with the back of her hand. Frank shook with laughter and said he was sorry. "It's not bad. It's just a little strong for me," Clara coughed. Her eyes welled up a little. Frank took out his handkerchief and dabbed it under her eyes, which were slightly watering. Clara's moist lips pressed together but turned upward. She liked the attention he gave her. "Let's eat because I'm anxious to go on our walk. You're right, this park is beautiful," she said while biting into a sandwich. Frank didn't eat as much as Clara did. He couldn't keep his eyes off her. He studied every gesture she made when she ate and talked. He studied her soft lips and rosy cheeks. He thought she had the prettiest profile he had ever seen. He was in love.

"Tell me about yourself, Clara. I'm curious why you think we are more alike than you had thought." She cleared her throat and repositioned herself on the blanket.

"Well," she sighed as she sipped from the flask of whiskey again. It made her feel more relaxed, but it burned her nose. "I'm pretty much on my own too." She handed Frank the flask and he took a drink from it. She laughed when he grimaced and coughed up a little whiskey. He shook his head, wiped his nose, and apologized. Clara giggled, "Don't be sorry." Then continued, "I have an older sister who lives nearby. Her name is Lucille, and she's married to a man named John. They had a baby not too long ago. His name is Norman. My mother lives with her parents in Cincinnati. She moved out of our house before I graduated from high school. My parents didn't have the best marriage. I don't speak to my father either. He's not my real dad, and he's not a nice man, but I don't want to talk about him," she mumbled before taking another bite of her sandwich. "I wanted to attend college but couldn't afford to, so I work at Lazarus. And now, as you know, I enjoy being watched by a mysterious stranger as I walk by my old beau's house." Frank snorted and coughed more whiskey up. He slightly shook his head with a knowing smile on his face. Clara liked how his soft lips curved upward, and his strong jawline appeared wider. She noticed he had a tiny dimple under his right cheek.

"Why are we drinking this? It tastes awful," Frank said as he closed the cap over the flask. Then he and Clara locked eyes and giggled again. He put his hand on her hand. Clara felt a wave of excitement with his touch. She blushed and felt her face turning red. She turned her hand over and placed it in Frank's hand.

"Let's put this food away and go on that walk now," she said. Her sky-blue eyes peered up at him with an irresistible smile. Frank's lips curled upward.

Chapter **14**

CLARA BAKER BECAME Mrs. Frank Miller three months after their date in the park. They didn't court each other for long. Their wedding wasn't the type of wedding Clara dreamed of having with Richard. Only her sister, Lucille, went to the justice of the peace with them.

"I don't even have a suitable dress to wear," Clara fretted to her sister earlier that day. "I think I should call it off. Am I making a horrible mistake? Tell me I'm making a mistake."

"No," Lucille answered. "The dress you are wearing is beautiful. You look perfect. Let's not forget you're pregnant with Frank's baby. I don't think you have a choice anymore. Do you love him?" her voice was tight.

"I think," Clara said as she bit her lower lip.

"You think? Well, that's not the answer I was hoping for," Lucille grunted. "But you will learn to love him with time. Frank seems like a good man, just like John. And I bet you will feel a deeper connection with him after the baby is born. It happened to John and me after we had Norman. Trust me, you're doing the right thing."

Clara looked at herself in a mirror while her sister combed through her hair. She studied the reflection that was looking back at her. She saw a familiar scowl. She couldn't help herself from thinking about Richard. Her chest hurt. She was nervous about marrying Frank, but as her sister said, she knew it was the right thing to do.

Frank and Clara had their first child, Charles, in the summer of 1910 when Columbus held its first Industrial Exposition, honoring locally made products. Frank was at the parade so was not present for the birth. After their marriage, he obtained a job with Bell Telephone Company. He drove one of the decorated automobiles that served as a float in the parade. It was covered in flowers with a bell hanging over his head. Frank didn't know Clara was in labor since she wasn't due yet. Only Lucille, her friend Nora, and a midwife were with her when Charles was born. He was considered a premature baby. Nora and Lucille were worried that Clara or the baby wouldn't survive the birth. Nora remained calm and helped the midwife with everything she requested, but Lucille was a wreck. She cried while she was holding Clara's hand. She remembered that Frank's mother died while giving birth to him. She remembered how hard it was for her to have a child due to all her previous miscarriages. She whispered a prayer in Clara's ear.

"I'm getting this baby out of me and never having another one," Clara announced. "I'm not dying, and neither will the baby, so quit your fussing, Lucille. You're making things worse for me with all your crying and worrying. Go pray outside!" Clara screamed as she bit down on a wooden spoon and pushed her first child out of her womb.

"He's a boy!" the midwife announced. "He's small, but he's breathing on his own."

Tears gushed from Lucille's eyes. Nora and the midwife tended to the baby before they swaddled him and laid him on Clara's chest.

"He's a fussy little fellow," Clara soothed. He had brown hair and blue eyes, like Clara's. Lucille sat next to Clara and held a cold cloth on her forehead. She looked more drained than Clara. "I'm naming him Charles, after our dead brother," she proclaimed. Clara never spoke about her twin brother, who was stillborn. Her mother named him Charles before they buried him. Nora put her hand over her mouth and let out a gasp.

"I never knew you had a twin," she said.

"I never knew him, so I never had much to say about him." But deep inside, Clara blamed herself for Charles not surviving the birth. She felt like somehow it was her fault. Lucille grabbed baby Charles from Clara and held him to her face.

"He's beautiful," she sobbed. "He looks a little like Norman, don't you think?"

"He looks like our mother," Clara said flatly. She was now overwhelmed by the birth and Charles's fussiness. She felt drained and had a hard time nursing him as Frank waved to the crowd cheering in the streets.

Frank felt horrible that he missed his son's birth. "It's fine," Clara reassured him. She didn't understand why he was so upset. "You wouldn't have done any good other than calm Lucille down. I'm the one that did all the work. I had Nora and the midwife, that's all that mattered." Her response didn't make him feel any better. It made him feel insignificant. He thought about his father and how he must have felt when his mother died. It was important to Frank to be present for the birth of his first child.

"He's so small," Frank said as he held Charles's little hand. "Are you sure he's okay? What did the midwife say about having a baby this early?"

"I don't remember, but he'll be fine." Clara handed him the baby. "Here, take him so I can sleep." Exhaustion had settled deep into her body, and she wasn't in the mood to talk. Frank rocked Charles's tiny body in his arms as he strolled from room to room, thinking about Clara and Charles. He was figuring out a plan to surprise her now that they were a family. He ran into Lucille in the kitchen while he was cuddling Charles. She was sitting at the table drinking a cup of tea.

"Would you like me to pour you a cup?" she asked.

"No, I don't want to put Charles down, but thank you. Clara would never discuss names with me when we found out she was pregnant. Why do you think she picked the name Charles?"

"Clara never told you?" Lucille looked surprised.

"No, what?"

"Clara had a twin brother who died. His name was Charles. He was what people called a stillborn. He died in our mother's womb after Clara came out."

Frank fell silent for a moment. He stared at Charles and wondered why Clara never told him she had a twin brother. "Sometimes your sister is a mystery to me," he murmured. "She's loud and vivacious at times, and then she retreats into this invisible shell and doesn't talk. It's almost like she's living two separate lives. One with me and then one on her private island, and she won't allow anyone to join her." Lucille took a sip of her tea and didn't respond. She sat awkwardly with an uneasy look on her face.

Frank took out a loan from Huntington Bank after Charles was born and bought a small bakery in a busy part of Columbus as a present for Clara. He knew about bakeries since he worked at one when he was younger. He couldn't believe his luck when he saw it was selling at such a great price because Columbus was starting to boom. After the purchase, Frank changed the bakery's name to Baker's Bakery, after Clara's maiden name. He spent countless hours getting the bakery ready for Clara while working at Bell Telephone. Clara was restless with Frank's absence. She didn't know why he was coming home from work late and working weekends. She was miserable being home alone so much. Once Frank was ready to surprise Clara with his purchase, he could hardly wait to show her.

"Frank, you didn't!" Clara exclaimed when he removed the blind-fold covering her eyes. "This is mine! All mine?" she asked excitedly as she held Charles against her chest. "You even named it after me! I love it!" Clara kissed Frank and handed him the baby before running to the bakery's front door.

Life was finally good again for Clara, especially as Charles grew stronger and she had the bakery. She worked long hours there while he slept in a bassinet in the storage room in the back. She enjoyed the responsibility of working and owning their own business. Clara felt a sense of fulfillment. She thought about what her sister said about growing in love with Frank while she fed Charles in the storage room one day. As she laid Charles against her chest and patted his back, Clara couldn't help but smile. "You were a right, big sister," Clara said out loud. "I do believe I love Frank now." Then she cradled Charles in her arms before placing him into his bassinet.

Frank and Clara had their second child, Eleanor, a year and a half later. It soon became difficult for Clara to work in the bakery with a newborn and a small child. Frank also noticed this when he entered the bakery one day and found Clara frustrated and screaming at Charles for waking Eleanor.

"I think it's time for you to stay home with the children," Frank informed Clara. "I will hire someone to manage the store for you."

"What?" Clara asked. "What?" she demanded. Annoyed, she glared at Frank with her jaw hanging open. "What I need is for you to hire a nanny to watch the children while I work," she exclaimed. Frank shifted in his stance and put his hands in his pockets. Clara knew what he was about to say. She crossed her arms around her chest and pointedly looked at him for his reply. She looked exasperated, but Frank didn't want to rock the boat.

"Clara," Frank calmly said as he sighed and slid his hand down her arm. "Don't do this. Don't make this more complicated than it already is. You know I love you, but we must do what's right for the children."

"Don't do this? You say … don't make this more difficult … don't do this to *me*, Frank! Don't take away the one thing that makes me happy," she said incredulously as she scooped Eleanor out of her bassinet to hush her cries. She blew a strand of her hair off her face and breathed heavily as she bounced Eleanor in her arms. "You're right, I can't take care of the children while working here. Obviously, this is not the right environment for Charles. He needs to be at home. But it doesn't need to be with me. We're making enough money to afford a nanny."

"But a nanny won't care for the children like their mother would. It makes more sense to use our money to hire someone to run the bakery," Frank protested as he tried to embrace Clara, but she pushed him away and laid Eleanor back in her bassinet.

"But a person running the bakery won't run it the same way the owner would. It will just create more problems for us, for *me*!" Clara shouted. "You know, when we were courting, you were never this bullheaded. You were a risk-taker, a pleaser. Now, you're just linear, Frank. You're consumed with yourself and your own beliefs. You don't want to understand anyone else's ideas or thoughts but your own."

"What do you mean, "I'm linear"? You know what, never mind." Frank shook his head in disbelief and ran his hands through his blond curls. You've spoken your piece, and I've spoken mine," Frank said in a softer voice when he saw Charles standing in the doorway to the backroom with a sad look on his face.

"So, the discussion is over?" she asked.

Frank lowered his voice to a whisper when he spoke in Clara's ear. "The children need their mother, Clara, not a nanny. The bakery will be fine in someone else's hands. I'll find a good manager, so don't worry about that. Why don't you take them home now? It's been a long day. I'll stay here to finish up. Did you get the flour and sugar we ordered?"

"Yes," Clara huffed as she shoved Charles's arms into his coat sleeves and pulled it closed. She hastily gathered her bag and coat and placed Eleanor in her carriage. After covering her with a blanket, Clara glanced at Frank before leaving the bakery with their children. Frank thought he noticed a flash of hatred in her eyes. She left without kissing him goodbye. He leaned against the counter and shook his head. He wished he would have told her what he really thought. He didn't want his kids to be raised by a nanny because he always wished he had had a mother. Even though his aunt loved him like her own, it wasn't the same in Frank's eyes. Growing up, he never felt truly loved by anyone. There always seemed to be a dark cloud hovering over his house. His aunt was constantly worrying about his father's drinking, his sister was older and kept to herself, and his dad wasn't around much. He always felt jealous of his friends who had a close family, with a mother and a father at home interacting with their children. Frank rubbed his forehead and closed his eyes. He often wondered if his father blamed him for his mother's death because he was the reason she died while giving birth.

Clara was angry with Frank's decision, especially when he quickly hired a manager without allowing Clara to participate. Frank's determination to keep Clara at home made Clara grow resentful. She didn't enjoy staying home with the children. Frank also picked up a second job working construction while maintaining his job at Bell Telephone. Clara didn't like that either. She felt more alone, and she missed running the bakery.

Frank noticed Clara slowly changing into a woman he didn't recognize. Their marriage wasn't what it once was, and he wanted to change that. He was saving money to buy land on Buckeye Lake and build a cottage for Clara. He thought that she would love it, and he wanted to surprise her with that since purchasing the bakery ended up causing problems between them. He wanted a special place to spend holidays and vacations with his family. He thought it was important that his children spend time together boating, fishing, and hiking. He wanted to give them the life he never had growing up.

Chapter **15**

IN 1913, TEN INCHES OF RAIN caused both the Scioto and Olentangy Rivers to overflow. Clara and Frank's third child was born on March 27, two days after the break in the levee protecting Franklinton. A massive amount of water flowed south through the community. Over four thousand houses were damaged or destroyed. Because of the flood, transportation was difficult, so Clara gave birth to Bob in city hall on State Street. It was being used as a shelter for flood survivors. After Clara gave birth to Bob, she spotted a recognizable, tall, thin woman with curly blonde hair tending to an elderly couple from across the room. Clara noticed immediately it was Richard's Helen. Her throat narrowed. *The girl who ruined my life*, Clara thought as she slid down her cot. A familiar ache settled in Clara's stomach. Then she froze, and her heart quickened when she saw Richard walking to Helen. She didn't want him to see her, especially in her present condition. She sunk farther under her blanket and rubbed Bob's back to keep him from crying. Then, Richard disappeared as quickly as he appeared. She hadn't thought about Richard and Helen for years. Now, they were all she could think about. She remembered seeing them walking hand in hand for the first time. She remembered how she felt afterward, and her stomach turned. She remembered the time she saw Helen and him in bed together at the house she was supposed to live in. Clara grew agitated with those thoughts swimming in her mind again. But then Frank appeared. He rushed to Clara's side and gently took the baby from her arms.

"He's perfect, Clara," Frank said as he kissed Bob. Clara turned her back to him. She was no longer in the mood to celebrate Bob's birth. Her heart felt heavy.

"Are you feeling okay? What's wrong?" Frank asked. Clara noticed the concern in her husband's voice, but she didn't care. She couldn't stop thinking about Richard and Helen. Jealousy and sadness ran through her veins again, just like before. She ignored Frank and slid farther down in her cot with her blanket covering her face.

"Please don't be mad at me. Ed told me Nora was watching the children. You must have been scared. How did you make it to city hall by yourself? Are you okay? Is Robert okay?"

"Yes," Clara sneered from under the covers. "I'm very tired. Please take the baby for a bit. I just fed him, so he should be fine. Oh, and I thought we agreed to call him Bob," Clara spat under her breath.

"We did," Frank said as he turned away with their baby in his arms. He chose to ignore Clara's abrupt behavior and her last comment. He smiled and said, "Hello, Bob," as he tickled his chin. "Oh my, you're such a handsome boy." Frank snuggled his face against Bob's cheek. "You look like me," he whispered. Frank walked outside with Bob in his arms as he watched the chaos that was happening in the streets.

Clara grew restless again, being home with three children. Charles had developed polio, which was extremely hard for Clara to deal with while Frank worked long hours. She also found herself crying at the littlest things. She felt confused and concerned about her emotions. She could not get out of bed most days until she had to. She had never experienced feeling so paralyzed that she had to force herself to do the ordinary things she was used to. She wondered what was happening to her, but her helplessness took over. She felt she was in a fog every time she visited the doctor with Charles. When Frank came home in the evenings, she had little to say. Sometimes, she was still in her bathrobe with her hair unkept, but Frank never questioned her. He knew Clara was struggling and didn't want to worsen matters. But what he didn't know was that she could not stop thinking about Richard and the life they were supposed to have had together. She had terrible thoughts and depression. She had horrible notions of ending her life. She imagined driving her husband's car through the little brick house she was supposed to live in.

Frank snuck up behind Clara one evening and wrapped his arms around her waist. She was washing dishes and was annoyed when she felt his hands around her. But after he whispered into her ear, "Your sister is here to watch the children because I have a great surprise for you," a rush of excitement ran through her body. Clara dried her hands on her apron and whisked around with curiosity as Frank led her out the front door. Her sister smiled at her while she was holding Bob. Clara raised her eyebrows and gave her sister a questionable stare as she walked to her husband's car.

"What's going on?" Where are we going?" she asked as she slid into the front seat. Clara felt tense when she realized they were driving to the bakery. "Did the flood affect the bakery? It looks different. Frank, did the flood damage the bakery?" Clara asked as he pulled the car over and parked it.

"Not too bad. But it needed some work anyway," Frank said as he unlocked the bakery door and turned the lights on.

Clara smacked Frank on the back of his head. His blonde curls cascaded forward. "Why didn't you tell me?"

"Because of all the stress you've been under. I didn't want to add more. The damage wasn't too bad, and I wanted to surprise you with the upgrade. How do you like it?"

"It looks great, Frank. It looks really good." Clara ran her hand down the new countertop. She admired the new containers and bowls. The new design was better than before. She felt her stomach flutter. "Don't you think it's time for me to return to work? At least for just a few hours a day."

"Why are you in such a rush to get back to running this place?"

"Because I liked running it. It felt good to have a purpose in life. You bought the bakery for me, and then you took it away. That wasn't fair. You're not being fair."

"I know. I bought the bakery because the sale was a good price, and I wanted to make you happy. I envisioned us both running the store together. I didn't think things through well enough. I'm sorry."

"Don't say you're sorry. Just agree that we can afford a nanny so I can go back to work. How do you expect me not to now? It looks beautiful!"

"How about part-time?" Frank said. He rubbed his hands through his thick, blond hair. "Just in the mornings, and we'll see how that goes." He pressed his lips and squinted his eyes. Clara screamed with excitement and hugged Frank.

"Thank you, thank you, thank you!" She kissed Frank. "This is the best news! You won't regret this, I promise."

Chapter 16

CLARA WAS STARTING TO FEEL BETTER, like her old self again, even though she missed running the bakery full time. After they hired a nanny, Clara returned to the bakery in the mornings alongside the manager Frank had hired. That gave her flexibility with Charles because sometimes she couldn't work. He was hard to care for, and the nanny sometimes complained that she needed help. Clara hated when the nanny griped how difficult Charles was. She knew he was difficult, so she didn't need a nanny to remind her of it.

One morning, someone walked into the bakery, and Clara's life was never the same. Clara heard the bell rattle, signaling someone had entered the store. She stopped taking inventory and turned around to see who was there. A wash of disbelief overcame her. Her face flushed, and she licked her lips and pressed them together. She suddenly felt self-conscious and unkept as she slid her hair behind her ears. "Richard, what are you doing here? I mean, hello, it's nice to see you," Clara sputtered as she ran her hands down her face and wiped her forehead clean of any flour. She couldn't believe he was standing in front of her.

"Clara," Richard cleared his throat. "Hello, it's wonderful to see you. You look great! How are you?" But before Clara could answer, he asked, "Do you own this? I noticed the name outside. It's named after your last name."

"My maiden name, and yes, I do. But I'm Clara Miller now."

Richard raised an eyebrow. "Oh, when did you get married?"

"In January of 1910. How about you? Are you married?"

"Engaged, well, I was engaged. My fiancé, Helen, passed away after the flood. We lost her parent's house, and then I lost her. She had cancer that we weren't aware of. Her parents died shortly after she did. Helen was their only child," his voice ran off like he was thinking about something he couldn't quite explain. "Do you have any children?"

"Yes, I have three. Two boys and a girl," Clara replied. "Do you?"

"No."

Clara felt her heart skip a beat, and a nervous excitement spread through her body. She could hardly concentrate on what they were speaking about. *She passed away* was distracting her. She felt guilty for feeling happy and carefully hid her genuine emotions. She forced them down, trying not to change the expression on her face. She felt the weight of Richard's eyes eyeing her up and down. She wished she had worn a nicer dress. "I'm sorry to hear about your fiancé and her parents. That must have been difficult."

"Yes, it was. Please excuse me, I didn't come in to buy anything. Curiosity got the better of me when I noticed the bakery's name. And I guess I was right. It was great seeing you today, Clara. Really great, but I must get going." Clara was disappointed that he was leaving the store so soon, but she also didn't want their manager to hear them talking. She felt like an awkward teenager when saying goodbye to him. But when he hugged her, she felt the same thrilling excitement burn through her body as when they were teenagers.

Stella Irene Miller was born a year later, on April 12, 1916. The birth wiped Clara out for weeks. She felt exhausted from caring for four children. Their nanny stopped working for them when Stella was only a few months old. She couldn't deal with Clara's mood swings and the constant arguments she witnessed Frank and Clara having. Frank knew without someone to help, Clara would become more unbearable. So, he contacted Clara's sister for support. Lucille only had one child, Norman. Clara wondered why Lucille and her son started showing up unexpectedly to help when Clara's children returned home from school. Lucille had always hoped to have a daughter. She couldn't help herself when she went shopping. She bought the frilliest dresses and the cutest bonnets she could find for Stella. She loved caring for her while Clara dealt with the other children. Lucille would immediately change Stella from her sleeping jumper and dress her in one of the dresses and bonnets she bought. She played with her on the floor and took her for walks in her carriage. It annoyed Clara. It reminded her of a child playing dress-up with a baby doll.

Clara was furious when she found out Frank had solicited Lucille's help without discussing it with her first. It reminded her of when he sent her home from the bakery and then hired a manager without her input.

"How dare you do this to me, Frank," Clara shouted one evening after Lucille and Norman left. "You know I can take care of myself. I don't need Lucille's help. And Norman just makes things more difficult. He teases the boys, and he gets on Eleanor's nerves. And, you know I like to do things on my own. I feel controlled when my sister is around. She thinks she's helping, but she's not. Now you put me in a position where I must ask her not to come around as often."

"I'm sorry, Clara. I thought I was helping. You seem so different since Stella was born. I know Charles has been difficult, and you're under a lot of stress." Frank rubbed his forehead and tired eyes, and sat down in his leather chair. He was tired of fighting with Clara. "I thought you'd appreciate a little help, but I guess I was wrong. I'll tell Lucille you are handling things fine on your own."

"No, you won't!" Clara shrieked. "I am capable of telling my sister that. You will just make things worse. You know how sensitive Lucille is. I'll handle it on my own."

Clara continued to fight with Frank over the smallest things. Their marriage was suffering worse than before, and Frank felt helpless. He hated how much they were fighting in front of the children. He knew it wasn't healthy for them to watch their parents fight constantly. But he couldn't control Clara's rants. No matter what he did or said, the fighting grew worse, and her yelling grew louder.

"Stop ignoring my needs!" Clara screamed one evening as she threw a fork at Frank while they cleaned the dishes after dinner. "I have needs too. I hate the way you dismiss me. You always seem to ignore what I want! You only care about the kids. The children need this, the children need that. The children need their mom. But what about what I need, Frank? What about me?" she challenged.

Frank didn't know how to answer. He had stopped working at Bell Telephone to be home more, but Clara didn't like that either. When he worked two jobs, they had more money, and she saw him less. She told Frank to take on more construction jobs, so he did. He worked his way up to lead superintendent. That made Clara happy, but they still argued over money. Eventually, Frank started visiting the local tavern called The Bar after work to avoid Clara's nightly rants. He wasn't a drinker but liked to smoke cigars and play poker to keep his mind off his troubles.

Chapter **17**

FRANK WASN'T FEELING WELL the evening after Stella's fourth birthday, so he skipped the tavern and came home early. "Hello?" he called out, hanging his hat and jacket up. No one answered. He walked around the house looking for Clara and the children. He had an odd feeling in his stomach that something was wrong. Then Bob rushed through the front door, red in the face.

"I can't find them anywhere! I was playing outside, and when I came home, they were gone. I don't know where they are!" He was out of breath and panting loudly.

"Who's they?" his father put his hands on Bob's shoulders, trying to calm him.

"Mother and Stella! We've been looking for them! They're gone!"

"We can't find them anywhere, Dad," Charles reported, walking in with Eleanor.

Frank's first thought was to phone his friend Ed Chaplin because Clara's best and only friend was Nora, Ed's wife. Clara and Stella visited Nora sometimes when their kids were in school. Nora said she had not seen Clara all day. Frank then phoned Lucille, and she reported the same thing.

Later that evening, Nora paced the kitchen, nervous and ridden with anxiety. "What's wrong with you, Nora? You're acting strange."

"Ed, sit down. I need to tell you something important, but please don't be mad at me." Nora informed Ed that Clara had told her she was planning to leave Frank. While playing cards together a few months earlier, Clara confided the details to Nora. She was saving her money and was planning to move to Florida with her ex-boyfriend, Richard Riley. She wanted Stella to go with them. "I thought she was joking at first. We were drinking a bit, and I assumed she was getting a rise out of me because it sounded so outlandish. But then she swore me to secrecy, and she started crying. You know how Clara is; she doesn't cry easily. She told me about her past with Richard. She told me he was her only true love and that she would miss her children, but the love she felt for Richard was more important. That's when I figured she was telling the truth. She said she wanted out of her marriage to Frank but didn't know how. She said she didn't like raising four kids alone, especially with a man she no longer loves. I was shocked, Ed, completely shocked. How could she have been having an affair with this Richard for five years without me knowing? I'm her best friend!"

Ed rubbed his head and then shook it with disgust. "Why are you just now telling me this? Frank will be devastated."

"Because I didn't think she would go through with it. And because it's not my business to tell. She's my friend too, you know. Just like Frank is your friend."

"Do you think tonight is the night she plans to leave? It makes sense, especially if Frank can't find Clara and Stella." Ed stood and spun around on his heels before Nora could answer. "I must tell him before it's too late!"

He grabbed his jacket from the coat stand and kissed Nora's forehead before he turned to leave. "Try the bakery," Nora yelled as she watched him climb into his car.

Ed raced to Frank's house. When he pulled up, Frank was smoking a cigar on the front porch. He typically only smoked when playing cards at

The Bar, but tonight was different. He knew in his bones something felt wrong. The thumping sensation in his chest told him so. Ed didn't even turn the car off when he yelled from his open window, "Frank, it's not good. You better get in."

Ed proceeded to repeat everything Nora had told him earlier. Frank listened silently as he heard about Clara, her ex-boyfriend Richard, and their plans to take Stella to Florida. "Richard Riley? I know that man," was all Frank said.

Frank hardly moved an inch in Ed's car. He was overwhelmed and stunned by the news he had just heard. Frank remembered that Richard and Clara were in love once, and that she had difficulty getting over their breakup. That's how he met Clara. Frank's mind was spinning. "Where are we going?" he finally asked Ed.

"To your bakery. Nora suggested we check there."

It was a breezy and chilly Tuesday night when Clara and Stella walked to the bakery to meet a man her mother called Richard. Stella did not know who Richard was and why they were going to the bakery so late. It was closed, but she could hear her mother's keys rattling in her handbag. Clara unlocked the front door and rushed Stella inside. Stella didn't understand why her mother didn't turn on any lights. She told her to sit behind the counter and be still. Stella did not do what she was told because she was scared. She tugged on her mother's coat and asked, "Mommy, why are we here so late? What are we doing? Why are the lights off? It's dark." Clara told her to shush, and she ignored her questions as she nervously paced the black-and-white checkered flooring, waiting for Richard to arrive. Clara gazed at the floor, reminding her of the kitchen in the house she never lived in with Richard. She pulled out a pack of cigarettes from her handbag. She hastily lit one and exhaled the smoke. Stella's eyes grew wide when she saw what her mother did.

"Mommy, are you smoking?"

"Stella, stop asking so many questions. I told you to stay quiet and do what you're told. Now get behind that counter and sit still." Stella went behind the counter and sat down on a chair with a frown on her face. She watched her mother puff on the cigarette while looking out the front window. She had never seen her mother smoke before. She immediately hated the smell. She knew something didn't feel right. Her mother looked worried.

"Mommy, what's wrong? What are we doing here? Where is everyone? Why did we leave Bob at the house?" Stella asked, but her mother did not answer her. She continued to pace the checkered flooring. "Mommy!" Stella urged.

Clara snapped her fingers and hissed, "Damn it, Stella, hush! Hush now!" She paced in front of the bakery's door.

Chapter 18

EARLIER THAT EVENING, Clara found herself hastily walking to Richard's house. He had moved a few streets from Clara after their affair started. When she reached his front door, he was already standing under a dim light in his doorway. He kissed her on the cheek, and they went inside. A fierce, loving feeling had grown inside Clara and Richard again. She marveled at the fact that Richard did not have children with Helen. He was single and unattached. Their affair started quickly because Clara had always loved Richard, and Richard fell back in love with Clara after he saw her at her bakery.

"I can't take it any longer, Richard. I want us to leave for Florida tonight. I know you said to wait a little longer, but I can't. I already bought our train tickets with the money I saved. Please come with me, Richard. We will have a good life together. We'll start a new family there. Please, let's get out of Columbus tonight!"

Richard was quiet and kept his head down. His elbows were resting on his knees. He rubbed his hands together and breathed in and out intensely. He shifted his position a few times in his chair. Then he looked deeply into Clara's sky-blue eyes. He loved how beautiful her eyes were. He loved her tenacity. He took her soft hands into his hands and rubbed them against his face. He loved her again. He loved her more than anything but was unsure it was a good idea. He didn't have all his affairs in order to move so suddenly.

Then, he said, "Okay. But I still think you should divorce Frank and do this the right way."

Clara raised her eyebrows, grunted, and said there was no right way. "If I divorced Frank, things would get messy. I don't like messy. He probably wouldn't agree to one. Plus, I would have to take all the children, and there is no way Frank would allow me to take them to Florida." Clara reassured Richard that running away was the only option. He agreed to meet later that evening at the bakery.

Now, Clara nervously walked back and forth in the front of the bakery, waiting for Richard, smoking a cigarette. Stella asked more questions, but Clara silenced her again and again. Stella started to cry. Clara's anxiety took over. She walked around the counter and grabbed Stella's shoulders. She shook them harder than she had intended. "Stella, you need to stop asking so many questions and stop crying. Do you understand me? Stop asking questions!" Stella sniffled and said okay, but she continued to weep, unnerving Clara. "Do you want to know a secret?" Stella stopped weeping and looked at her mother with curiosity. Clara kneeled and took Stella's hands into hers. She was desperate to stop her crying. Without much thought, she said, "You are about to meet your father, your real father! Isn't that wonderful?"

"What do you mean?" Stella asked, confused. Then, Clara noticed automobile lights approaching the bakery. She was so relieved that Richard had finally shown up. But it was not Richard.

Clara quickly turned around to scoop up Stella. She rushed to the front door to unlock it, and that's when Clara and Frank locked eyes through the glass door. Clara immediately started crying. Frank did not even try to open the door. He and Ed kicked through the door, with glass shattering everywhere. Clara turned her body to shield Stella from the shards of glass.

Ed snatched Stella from her arms before Clara could react. He then placed Stella in the back seat of his car. Stella heard her father yell to her mother, "I can't believe you, Clara! Go ahead and leave with him, but Stella is not going with you. It would have to be over my dead body."

Frank and Ed were quiet during the car ride back to Frank's house. Stella whimpered in the back seat while Frank stared out his window. He knew he needed to regain his composure. Stella was confused, and her mind was spinning with questions. "Daddy, what's happening? I'm scared."

"Everything is going to be fine, sweetheart. Now, don't cry, everything is okay," he said vaguely.

Then, Stella's whimpers turned to wails. She could hardly get her words out when she cried, "Why is Mommy leaving with that man she called my father?" Frank's eyes twitched and darkened. His face grew white as he lowered his hat and repositioned himself in his seat. His chest rose heavily.

"I don't know, sweetheart, but we'll be home soon. Try not to worry about your mother. She's going away for a little while." Ed said nothing and kept his eyes on the road.

Now that Clara was gone, Frank panicked about what to do with his children while he was working. Clara's sister offered to help. Lucille watched Stella during the day while the other children attended school. But then Norman got diphtheria and died. He was only eleven years old. It was a terrible loss for Lucille and John. The grief and stress they experienced from losing a child put a hardship on their marriage. Lucille struggled the worst. Then she disappeared one day. She didn't even leave a note. No one knew where she went.

One afternoon, Eleanor saw a postcard in the mail from their aunt Lucille. "Who's Richard?" Eleanor asked her father when he came home from work.

"What, why? How do you know that name?"

"We got a postcard from Aunt Lucille today. She said she was sorry for leaving us so abruptly. She said she's grieving every day over Norman, so she wanted to be near her sister. She said she's living in Tampa, Florida, near Mother and Richard. Who's Richard? Why did she say, 'near your mother and Richard'?"

"I don't know," he muttered as he left the room. Frank didn't have the energy to explain everything because he knew that would only lead to more questions. Questions he didn't have answers for. They had already asked many questions about their mother that Frank didn't want to talk about. He was upset that Eleanor read the postcard before he had a chance to get the mail. Eleanor put the postcard in her pocket and ran off to find Charles.

Frank received word that neighbors were talking about social services getting involved now that the children were home alone when he worked. Frank was nervous his children would be taken from him, and he knew he needed to make a change.

While looking through *The Columbus Dispatch* one evening, he cursed Clara's name for doing this to him. It was the first time he had said her name out loud since she left. Frank was angry with Clara but also heartbroken. He missed her, but he didn't miss the Clara she turned into after Stella was born. He wanted to shield his children from his mixed emotions. They missed their mother too, and he didn't want to paint a negative picture of her. He sat in his leather chair and skimmed the newspaper. He wasn't sure what he was looking for, but he knew he needed to keep his mind off his true emotions. He was scared that social services would try to take his children. He worried the most about Stella because she was young and not in school. He thought about what she said the night in Ed's car. "Why is Mommy leaving with that man she called my father?" kept him up at night. He did the math over and over again in his mind. He and Clara were intimate around the time Stella could have been conceived. But if she was also having an affair with Richard Riley, then any hope of knowing the truth went out the window. Frank sighed profoundly and reached for one of his cigars. He smoked in his house for the first time.

Frank searched the newspaper and found an advertisement for a boarding house on Southwood Avenue that provided rooms to rent and childcare. It was called Spangler Boarding House. It was farther south of Columbus than he liked, but he didn't feel he had much of a choice at this point. He needed to make a change, and he felt pressured to do so fast. He needed childcare, and it pained him to know that. The advertisement noted it was a two-and-a-half-story house with indoor plumbing and room for storage. Frank thought it sounded too good to be true.

Part 3
STELLA

Chapter **19**

IN THE SUMMER OF 1920, I cried while sitting on the parlor floor when my father informed us that we were selling our house and moving into the Spangler Boarding House. I didn't know what a boarding house was. It sounded scary.

"Please don't cry, Stella. It will be all right. Daddy's moving too, you won't be alone," he explained.

My siblings and I didn't want to leave the only home we knew. We wanted our mother back, living with us in our house. But our father didn't. He never spoke poorly about our mother, but we got the sense he didn't want to be reminded of her. He quickly sold the bakery after she left. And then he put our house up for sale.

"Dad, we're fine on our own. We don't need to move to Southwood Avenue," Charles pleaded. "How far is it anyway? I've never heard of that street before. I don't think we should move. Eleanor and I can take care of Bob and Stella. We're used to it because Mother always left us home alone."

"What? She did? Where did she go?"

"I don't know. We weren't supposed to talk about it, especially to you." Our father's expression changed. He looked like somebody had just punched him in the gut.

"Well, that was the past. I know you're turning ten soon, but Stella just turned four and Bob is only seven. They aren't old enough to stay home alone, and you and Eleanor need to be kids, not caretakers. I told you city hall would get involved, and they already have. I can't risk losing any of you. We must make this change. I'm sorry, but it has to be this way. I'm trying to handle the selling of our house and work two different construction jobs at the same time. I know you and Eleanor act like you can take care of yourselves, but you're still children, and Bob and Stella need someone who will care for them. Truth be told, Charles, so do you and Eleanor. Try having a good attitude, you may end up liking it there!"

The boarding house was a tall, skinny structure with two triangular-shaped roofs, one sitting higher above the other. It reminded me of a birdhouse. The shorter roof that covered the front porch had three white pillars holding it up. The pillars were dirty. The house was a dingy gray color with peeling white trim. It looked unwelcoming. When we walked up the steps for the first time, I felt like we were trespassing on someone else's property.

"When was this house built?" Charles whispered to our father as we stood on the porch.

"About seven years ago, why?"

"Because it looks older than that. Hasn't had much upkeep on it." The diamond pattern lattice skirting under the porch was splintering and ripped with holes. The wooden flooring on the front porch needed to be repaired. The paint on the house looked like it was sliding away. The grass was unkempt, and the bushes were dead or needed trimming.

"Don't be rude, Charles," our father said as the door opened.

Margaret Spangler, the woman who ran the boarding house, was a lanky German lady who smelled of cheap vanilla perfume and cigarettes. She had dark hair pulled tightly into a low bun. Her clothing looked worn, just like her face. She appeared older than she was. She had the blackest brown eyes

I had ever seen. The brown of her eyes blended in with her pupils. She had a mole on her left cheek, and her skin was ashen. She reminded me of a witch. When she smiled, her yellow, stained, crooked teeth showed. It was an ugly smile. Her laughter also sounded wicked, and she scared me.

Her family immigrated to the United States in the late 1800s from Germany. Once established in America, they settled in Columbus, Ohio, when she was pregnant with her son, Albert. In December of 1915, her husband died when Albert was eleven years old. It was on Christmas Day. She told people he died of tuberculosis, but suicide was the actual cause of death. After waking up on Christmas morning, Margaret found a kitchen chair kicked over and her husband dangling from a rope in the doorway. She never remarried. Her husband left her their house and some money, but not enough for her and Albert to live on. So, she turned their home into Spangler Boarding House.

"Well, hello! You must be the Millers."

"Yes, we are," my father said as he removed his hat and greeted Mrs. Spangler with a warm smile. "And these are my children I told you about." My father introduced each one of us to her, but she didn't seem to care. She was too busy eyeing him.

After walking into the boarding house on Southwood Avenue, we immediately hated it. It was nothing like our old home. Not much sunlight came in because the curtains were pulled shut. It felt dark and dingy. I immediately saw wooden steps leading to an upper level. Then, I noticed the living room to the left of me. A brick fireplace stood against the side wall, a sofa sat against the back wall, and two oversized chairs were in front of the window with a round table between them. A radio sat on the table with an ashtray filled with cigarette butts. The furniture was stained and looked old. The house held a rotten egg aroma, along with the smell of cigarette smoke. There weren't any pictures hanging. Ripped wallpaper dangled from a wall in the front room that separated it from the kitchen, where the sofa sat. It didn't feel pretty like our old house. My mother was a great decorator, and our home was bright, smelled nice, and was spotless. Our father could tell by our sour faces we were disappointed and unhappy. "Daddy, it's so dark in here. Why is it so dark?" I asked after I grabbed his hand. Before my father could answer, Mrs. Spangler threw the curtains open that hung over the front window. Sunlight exploded into the room, and dust particles swarmed everywhere. It looked like it was snowing.

"Gee whiz!" Charles and Eleanor both said, covering their heads, and started to cough. My father gave them a hard stare to silence their rudeness.

"I close the curtains to keep the house cool in the summer. The sun hits this room the worst during this time of day," Mrs. Spangler explained.

"My last tenants just moved out, so I haven't had time to do much cleaning. But I'm sure the kids can help me with that," Mrs. Spangler said as she took us on a tour of the house. Charles and Eleanor winced at that comment. Their noses wrinkled up, and their lips were turned down. I didn't let go of my father's hand. Bob anxiously followed behind Mrs. Spangler. Her bottom half didn't synchronize with her top half when she walked. It looked funny and reminded me of a duck waddling. The shoes she wore also made a loud squeaking noise when she walked. Bob pointed to the back of her and to her shoes and laughed when he looked at me. My father put his hand around Bob's neck and squeezed it, sending him a nonverbal cue to stop. He covered his mouth with his hand and bit the area between his thumb and his forefinger to keep his giggles in.

"Let's go upstairs so I can show you where you'll stay." I heard the sound of loud footsteps stampeding above me. Then, a door slammed shut, and a lock clicked. I felt scared. I looked at my father for reassurance and winced at the booming noise the door made.

"Don't mind him. That's my son, and he's probably in one of his moods. If you ask me, sixteen-year-olds can be worse than toddlers," she teased. We followed Mrs. Spangler up the staircase to the second level. I noticed four doors. Only two were open.

"This first bedroom will be for Charles, Eleanor, and Bob. The bigger bed is for the boys, and of course, Eleanor, you will have the smaller bed." She stretched her arm in the doorway and motioned for us to enter like we were about to see something remarkable. But the room was modest and virtually empty. The beds took up most of the space. There was hardly any room to walk around. A tall chest stood between the two beds. A long, narrow dresser lay against the other side of the wall. A jagged, diagonal crack sliced through the mirror above the dresser. It made you look distorted when you looked at yourself in it. "The last tenants in this bedroom left it a mess all the time. It was a mother with two sons. The boys made that crack in the mirror. They liked to roughhouse in here, so I had to kick them out. I expect no roughhousing and for you to keep this room in tip-top shape while you're here." She eyed the boys with a critical look on her face and then gave Eleanor a stern stare as if it was her job to keep the room clean. "I'm sure you'll be comfortable here." Then she turned to our father and gave him a gnarly smile.

I grimaced when I saw her ugly teeth and quickly asked, "Where's my bedroom?"

She ignored me. "Frank, let me show you where you'll be staying. It's one of our nicest bedrooms, right next to mine." She grabbed his arm and tucked it around her as she led him to it. It's small, but I think you'll find it comfortable. The mattress is brand new!" She gave our father a half-flirty, half-sinister smile.

I tugged on my father's hand. "Daddy, where am I staying?"

"I'm sure somewhere grand," he reassured me as Mrs. Spangler opened the door to our father's bedroom.

"The interesting thing about this room is that it connects to my bedroom with this door. Of course, I'm a lady, so I will keep the door locked." Mrs. Spangler could hardly keep from smiling when she said that with a light chuckle. "Currently, I have three siblings staying with me until they get placed with a family. Their parents were killed in a car accident. I heard it was a terrible wreck. When the accident happened, their parents were driving to pick them up from a relative's house. They are twins named Molly and Ellen and their younger brother, Samuel. Stella, the twins are a little older than you. Luckily, they're not identical," Mrs. Spangler said with a snicker. "That would have made things difficult for me. You'll be staying with them. You all will get along magnificently. I'll show you where later, now, I must show your father the rest of the house. Oh, and let's not forget, I have indoor plumbing! Here's the washroom. But we must share it, so let's keep our primping to a minimum, okay Charles," she said pointedly.

She displayed her ugly smile again and snickered over her third dumb joke. Charles didn't appreciate the joke. He shoved his hands in his trouser pockets and glared at her. Our father let out an uncomfortable laugh. Mrs. Spangler pushed by Charles, ignoring the look on his face. Then, she took my father by the arm and ushered him downstairs and throughout the rest of the house. Bob followed behind them again, but I shadowed Eleanor and Charles in their bedroom. I sat on Eleanor's bed. When I did, it sank, and dust particles shot up.

"Where's my bedroom?" I asked again. Charles was putting his belongings away. His face was scrunched up, and he looked agitated as he put his clothing in different drawers. Eleanor shrugged her shoulders while she was unpacking her suitcase.

"I counted," I said, "and there are only four bedrooms. I tried to open one of the doors, but it was locked. Do you think that's where I'll stay with the other children? When I peeked in the other door, it looked like her bedroom."

I found the other children playing outside in the backyard. The twins were riding tricycles that were too small for them. Their knees were tucked in tight and rose higher than they should. One twin was slightly taller than the other. She was having the most difficulty on the tricycle. Samuel was trying to climb a tree but kept slipping from the branches. The girls were dressed nicely but looked unhappy. Samuel's sad eyes reminded me of a lost child. He was dirty and tired-looking. He had blond hair, like Bob, but it was a lighter blond and straight. I tried to interact with them, but they ignored me like I wasn't there. That made me sad because I wanted to be friends. I wanted Molly and Ellen to like me, but they were quiet and didn't seem interested in me. "I think I'll be sleeping with you in your bedroom," I announced to the girls. They looked at me with blank stares. They didn't respond and kept circling the backyard on their tricycles.

Once I found out where I would be sleeping, I bit my lower lip and tried not to cry while I followed Mrs. Spangler up a dark, narrow staircase that stood next to the washroom. Eleanor was trailing close behind me. It went to an attic above the other bedrooms on the second floor. The stairs didn't have a railing. When I got to the top, I practically fell into the room. It was dark, and the wooden floorboards creaked. Cobwebs were dangling from the wooden ceiling, the beams, and the room's corners. It was filled with old stick mattresses that were used as beds. There were six lined up against the left side wall. Each bed had a small wooden trunk at the foot of it. There were also old wooden wardrobes that were falling apart. They were scattered on the opposite side of the room but not pushed up against the wall because some stood taller than the wall. There were old clocks and wash bins on the wardrobes. A vase had fallen over, and broken chards of glass lay in a heap where someone had swept them up and pushed them to the corner. Old, silver and gold picture frames of people who looked sad and ominous leaned against the wall behind the wardrobes. Some were turned around with a blanket covering them. I wondered why those were turned around.

"Here's where you'll be sleeping, Stella. You'll be with the twins and their brother. That bed over there is yours." She pointed to the stick mattress that was near the window. It was the only window in the attic. It was on a pentagon-shaped wall that overlooked the front yard. The walls were short, and the slanted ceilings seemed odd to me. I had never been in an attic before. The stick mattress she pointed at looked like a heap of old brown straw. It had one pillow and a blanket on it. "Find an empty wardrobe and unpack your belongings," she said.

My heart sank as I looked around. I felt like I was being banished to a dungeon, and I started crying. Eleanor helped me unpack my things. "At least you're not up here alone. Please don't cry. You'll make friends with the twins once you get to know each other," she assured me.

"Why am I up here, and everyone else is downstairs? I want to be with you." Eleanor pondered for a second and then shrugged her shoulders.

"I don't know, Stella. The room I'm sharing with the boys is pretty small. Maybe there are more younger kids moving in, so she does it by age. It'll be okay. Be a big girl."

The first night I slept on my stick mattress, it made awful noises when I moved around. The twins and Samuel complained about the noises I made. The quilt I had was small and too thin. The pillow I slept on smelled musty. I had a hard time finding a comfortable position. I also had difficulty hiding my hands when I slept because I didn't have enough blankets. I had a horrible dream the first night. In my dream, mice were scurrying around in the attic. They jumped on my bed and were biting me. I screamed for help, but only the handless man from the park appeared. I woke up screaming, which roused the twins and Samuel. My screams scared him and he started crying. The girls gave me a dirty look when they soothed him. I felt jealous when I watched them being kind to their brother. I wanted them to soothe me too. I wanted them to talk to me and tell me everything was okay, but they didn't. I felt a little like the character Cinderella. I hated the dreary attic. I hated the boarding house. I hated that the twins wouldn't talk to me. I wondered again why I wasn't with my siblings, sleeping with them on the second floor. But I was too scared to complain to my father about my sleeping conditions. I didn't want him to get angry with me. The next day, I tried telling Charles how miserable I was in the attic. I showed it to him. I wanted him to tell our father and make things better for me, but he didn't.

"Stop your nonsense, Stella," he rebuked with clenched fists. "Stop your crying and stop complaining. You should be thankful you have a bed to sleep in. It could be worse. Who knows where you would be sleeping if social services were involved? You'd be taken away from us, so stop complaining!" He pushed the back of my shoulders when he left the attic room. My knees buckled and hit the hard wooden floor first, then I rolled over to my back. I heard Charles say a bad word under his breath as he stomped down the wooden steps. I started crying as I stared at the cobwebs floating from the ceiling. I knew cobwebs meant spiders. I was scared of spiders. The twins and Samuel popped their heads up from the steps and looked at me. I rolled over with a tear-streaked face, and I asked them to help me up. I told them I was hurt. Then the twins were gone. I no longer saw their curious faces at the top of the steps. I heard them scurrying away. Only Samuel stayed.

"Samuel, will you help me?" But he just stared at me with his sad, lost eyes while I lay on the attic floor crying.

Chapter 20

AFTER MOVING INTO THE BOARDING HOUSE on Southwood Avenue, Mrs. Spangler developed a liking for our father. She smiled only at him. Her voice rose several octaves when he was around. Her flirting was relentless and inappropriate, and it clearly made him uncomfortable. Once, he found her wearing only her brassiere and stockings with a cigarette dangling from her mouth while cooking dinner! When he entered the kitchen, he was startled by such an odd sight, so the air he gulped down made a noise. It startled Mrs. Spangler, and her cigarette fell into the stew she was stirring. My father helped her fetch the cigarette out of the stew. "Without sounding too rude, do you mind putting on some clothes?" he politely asked. "The children will be coming in to eat soon."

Charles laughed at that part when he recounted the story to us. He witnessed the odd event, unbeknownst to her and our father until Charles started chuckling. But Charles also shared something that upset us.

"Mrs. Spangler is trying to get close to Dad. She tries to slip into bed with him. He told me she's behaving in a way that he finds unacceptable. He also told me he's asked her to stop, but she hasn't. He doesn't like living here with her. He told me he found a house on Frebis Avenue, about a mile from here, that he would like to purchase. But we have to stay here for a while longer."

"Why can't we go with Dad?" Eleanor asked.

"Because of Bob and Stella. He doesn't want them here alone. He wants to keep us together."

"What do you mean 'get close to Dad'? I don't understand what you're saying," I started crying. "You can't leave me here. Please don't leave me." I bit down on my bottom lip.

"We won't. It doesn't sound like we have a choice right now anyway," Eleanor spat.

Our father bought the house on Frebis Avenue in October. Mrs. Spangler became bitter once she learned he was moving out at the end of the month and stopped speaking to him. "I know you're upset with me, but may I talk with you about something?" he asked while she was cooking in the kitchen one evening. We were hiding in the living room with our ears pressed against the wall, listening.

"What?" she snapped. It was the first time we heard her sound rude to him. At first, she wasn't interested in hearing his proposal. We could tell by how she stomped around in the kitchen while opening cabinets and collecting utensils. But when our father mentioned the word money, she stopped making so much noise. Her voice grew high and flirty again. My body moved up and down with every word they spoke.

"I'll pay extra rent if you agree to a few things. First, I would like Stella to move into my bedroom. She seems scared in the attic. She'll feel better being closer to you and her siblings. I've also noticed that you offer the same, limited food options. With the extra money I'm willing to spend, I expect you to provide some different ones. Fresh fruit and vegetables would be nice too. And last, since Sunday is my only day off, I would like to visit my children every Sunday and stay for dinner." Now Mrs. Spangler liked that idea. They agreed on the conditions my father proposed.

But those conditions never happened. If we ate breakfast, it was always the same. It was typically warm, mushy oatmeal or cold oatmeal. I'm not sure which one tasted worse. They both tasted horrible in their own ways. The mushy oatmeal stuck to the roof of my mouth, and the cold oatmeal stuck to my teeth. I got one slice of bread with some fruit jam smeared on top for lunch. Sometimes, the bread was moldy. I could tell when I turned it over. I thought about my siblings and how they were eating school lunch. I was sad that I didn't eat school lunch. They never knew what I ate. I was too afraid to tattle on Mrs. Spangler. She often warned me I would get the rod if I complained. Our dinners weren't any good either. Our only decent meals were on Sundays when our father visited. We never received any of the fresh fruit and vegetables our father wanted us to have during the week. Eleanor knew our father was paying extra to have better meal options that we never got.

"This food tastes like garbage!" We can't eat like this all the time. I'm going to tell my father what you're feeding us!" When Eleanor forcefully slid her plate away from her, a piece of bread with gravy on top fell to the floor. An icy chill went through the air. Eleanor sat at the table with her arms crossed and glared at Mrs. Spangler. She had warned us that we would get the rod if we complained about anything, especially to our father. She had the rod hanging from a hook in the kitchen to remind us to behave. Mrs. Spangler looked at Eleanor, disgusted, as she sprung from the table and reached for the rod that dangled above us.

"Uncross those arms and get over here, you ungrateful girl." She wasn't afraid to sass Mrs. Spangler and so was the first to receive the rod. It upset me to hear the rod hitting Eleanor's bottom so many times, so I scurried out of the room. "Get back here!" she demanded. Mrs. Spangler made us watch as if it were entertainment for us, but it wasn't. I returned to the table and put my head down. Smack, smack, smack rang in my ears. My body shuddered and tensed with every whip, and I closed my eyes. I could feel the uneasiness of everyone in the kitchen. Eleanor was determined not to let Mrs. Spangler break her, but Mrs. Spangler was committed to stealing her tenacity.

"Stop, please stop!" Charles stammered. Eleanor didn't let out a scream until the last hit.

After that day, Eleanor said, "If you ever get the rod, cry after the first spank. If you don't cry out at the beginning, Mrs. Spangler will make each hit harder and harder until you do."

After our father moved out, we weren't allowed to use the wash tub inside. Mrs. Spangler had an old wooden barrel that she filled with water from the hose in her backyard. She made each of us take turns washing ourselves in it. Standing in line with the other kids waiting for our turn was humiliating. Charles always went first, and then Eleanor. Somehow, Samuel and I were always last. She never emptied the barrel between baths. We all used the same water, so if you were the last one, you bathed in dirty water. Bathing in the winter was the worst. My bones shivered, and I feared getting frostbite, especially if snow was on the ground. We always took our baths very fast, but in the winter, we went faster. I heard her neighbors complaining to Mrs. Spangler about it one day. It sounded like an argument. I heard Mrs. Spangler tell them to mind their own goddamn business when she walked away from the fence. She moved the barrel to the opposite side of her house after that.

Sundays were the only days she made Eleanor wear a dress. She told us to wear our nicest and cleanest clothes on Sundays when we saw our father. That didn't bother Charles, but Eleanor hated it. My clothes were often dirty, so wearing clean dresses made me feel good. I also looked forward to seeing my father and eating normal dinners. But we couldn't eat too fast. If we did, our bellies hurt afterward. We sat in the living room, talked, and listened to the radio. I usually sat on my father's lap and snuggled with him. Mrs. Spangler seemed annoyed with the attention he gave me. My father loved to make Bob and me laugh by tickling us. He acted like his arm was a crane, and his hand was the claw, scooping us up to a tickle frenzy. Charles and Eleanor weren't any fun with that game. They rolled their eyes when our father tried to get them involved. He often played cards with Eleanor and Charles during his visits. Bob and I loved to watch Charles get angry if he wasn't winning.

Chapter 21

WHILE MY SIBLINGS AND THE TWINS attended school, I stayed home with Samuel. Sometimes, Mrs. Spangler babysat other children during the day. It was typically two brothers around my age and their baby sister. They lived down the street from the boarding house. The boys became friends with Samuel, and they played together when they came over. Their baby sister's name was Rose. I helped Mrs. Spangler with her. She was great entertainment for me. But one day, I heard Mrs. Spangler arguing with their mother outside on the front porch. It had something to do with money and improper care. After Mrs. Spangler slammed the front door shut, I heard her hiss to herself that she wasn't babysitting infants any longer. Those siblings stopped coming over after that. I liked playing with Rose, and I missed her. It was like having a real-life baby doll.

As winter arrived during our first year living on Southwood Avenue, Mrs. Spangler became more unbearable and sterner. She spoke in the meanest voice I have ever heard. It was low and gruff. I felt intimidated and frightened every time she spoke. No matter how hard I tried to please her, she never changed the tone of her voice. I felt like she only used her angry tone with me. She wasn't as aggressive with Samuel as she was with me during the day when we were the only ones home. Christmas was coming, and she told me I was on Santa's naughty list and wouldn't receive any gifts from him when I asked her for a cup of milk. I felt confused. "Why?" I asked her.

"Because you're spoiled rotten." she pursed her lips. "And spoiled rotten children don't deserve anything more!" she bellowed in her low, mean witch voice. I ran out of the kitchen as she poured herself a drink and lit a cigarette. Whiskey was her choice of drink in December. I hid in the attic until my siblings arrived home from school. Bob was the first to find me. I was crying in the corner behind a wardrobe. He grabbed my hand and led me to the room he shared with Charles and Eleanor.

"I found Stella crying upstairs. She said she was on Santa's naughty list. She's scared here while we're in school. Mrs. Spangler is different. She's meaner to her, and I don't know why." Charles's eyebrows arched upward, and Eleanor sighed.

"Stella, you are not on Santa's naughty list. Don't listen to her. She's a strange lady. We'll be back with Dad soon." Eleanor rubbed my back and smoothed my hair behind my ears.

"I think we should tell Dad," Bob said. "He'll let us move home now if we tell him how unhappy we are living here."

"No, he won't. You know how Dad is. He'll just tell us to behave and not to complain. Dad doesn't seem the same, and I don't trust Mrs. Spangler. I think we'll make things worse for ourselves if we complain to Dad because he'll say something to her, thinking he's helping our situation." Charles walked in circles around the room while deep in thought when he spoke. "I think it's best if we say as little as possible and mind ourselves. She pays no attention to those twins and their brother. We need to act like them."

But I couldn't behave like the twins and Samuel. They didn't speak to anyone and kept to themselves. I was naturally a timid girl, but I was a curious girl with a lot on my mind. I liked to ask questions and learn new things. I liked being around other people. I didn't want to be like the twins and Samuel because I didn't want to feel more alone than I already did. The loneliness I felt at the boarding house during the day was different from the loneliness I felt at home with my mother. I didn't feel scared of my mother. I didn't feel scared of my surroundings. I didn't feel unsafe.

One brisk Saturday, I rode a tricycle in the basement while Mrs. Spangler hung laundry. It was my first time down there because I was afraid of the basement. The twins had moved the tricycles there after Thanksgiving. I wanted to sing Christmas songs, but I didn't know the words to any, so I sang my favorite songs while riding around the perimeter of the basement. "Stop your singing, Stella," she said. But I didn't hear her. As I started my third tune, "Rock-a-Bye Baby," Mrs. Spangler popped me on the head to get my attention and demanded that I stop singing. "Shut up, shut up, shut up, you irritating little shit! I can't handle your singing, so you *Rock-a-Bye* your way out of here," she yelled before she poured hot, soapy wash water over me. The water felt unbearably hot as it stung my body. I started to cry hysterically. My screams were deafening, which aggravated Mrs. Spangler even more. She grabbed my chin and pressed her nails into my cheeks when she said, "I told you to shut up, and you didn't. This is what happens when you don't listen to me. Now stop your crying and go upstairs!" She then spanked me with an open hand before I could run away. Bob heard the commotion and approached me before I reached the attic to hide from her. He took one look at me and hurried me into his bedroom. Charles's jaw hung open as he looked at me.

Eleanor rushed into the bedroom and put her hands over her mouth. "Stella, what happened?" she asked breathlessly. "You're all wet!" I was crying too hard to talk. I was sitting on her bed with Charles and Bob sitting in front of me on their bed. Eleanor sat next to me and put her arm around my shoulders. "Hush, it'll be okay. Don't let Mrs. Spangler hear you. What happened?" she whispered to Bob.

"Mrs. Spangler poured hot wash water over Stella!" he blurted.

"Shhh, you don't want her to hear us. How hot was the water?"

"I don't know, but it must have been pretty hot."

"I was just singing," I managed to tell them as I gulped for air between cries.

Eleanor examined my arms and back. Red marks were forming. Charles told them he didn't think my burns were severe enough to cause much damage. Then, he remembered a potted aloe plant Mrs. Spangler kept near the kitchen window. Charles grabbed the plant and brought it back to the bedroom. "The gel inside will help cool her burns," he instructed as he rubbed aloe on me. That was the first nice thing Charles did for me. He made me feel good and loved for the first time. I looked at him while he rubbed the aloe on my arms. I wanted him to hug me, but he didn't. Bob squeezed some aloe from the plant and started helping Charles. Eleanor sat uncomfortably next to me.

"I'm not sure if this is a good idea. I think I hear her," she said. Mrs. Spangler stomped into the bedroom with a cigarette hanging from her mouth. We froze after eyeing the crazy look on her face. She quickly exhaled her smoke and flicked the cigarette butt at us. Eleanor picked me up from her bed, and we shuddered as we defensively stood against the back wall.

"You're wasting your time with that plant. It's mine! I got it as a gift from a previous tenant, and I'm sure it cost a lot. You don't see aloe plants around here," she shouted before she picked up the plant to examine it. "You ruined it!" she yelled, launching it against the wall above our heads. The pot exploded into a million pieces. We weren't prepared to move out of the way or shield ourselves. Dirt waterfalled down the wall and landed in a heap around us. "Now look what you made me do! Dirty, Dirty, Dirty! Dirt is everywhere, you dirty little shits! Clean this mess," she snarled. "Then go to the backyard!" She slammed the bedroom door shut.

Eleanor and Charles quickly retrieved a broom and cleaned up the dirt. "Why did she say that?" Bob asked as he bent down to help. "Why did she say go to the backyard? It's snowing outside. I don't understand why she said that." Eleanor and Charles didn't respond. I saw panic in their eyes. Their chests rose in and out heavily, and their breathing was labored.

"I'm scared. I don't wanna go to the backyard. My hair is wet. It's cold," I whined while gulping down air. My cheeks were red and tear-stained.

The air was frigid as we walked outside. A shiver settled in my body, and I couldn't stop shaking. I started crying again. Bob hushed me and held my hand, but it didn't make me feel better. I could feel his hand tremble around mine. I felt scared when Mrs. Spangler marched outside. The boots she was wearing sounded loud and angry.

"Strip down and line up." She stomped to the side of her house. We all looked at each other in disbelief.

"Did she just say strip down?" Eleanor gulped.

"Yes," Charles said. "She did." I could hear the fear in his wavering voice. Bob started to sob. Everything became too overwhelming for me. I didn't understand what was about to happen.

"Why? I'm not doing that. I'm not!" blurted Eleanor.

"Just keep your eyes straight ahead, and do what she says," Charles warned. "I don't want her to get angrier."

We stripped down to our undergarments and stood in a straight line. When I went to remove my undergarments, Eleanor hissed at me. "No! Stop, Stella," she snapped and then looked straight ahead like Charles said.

"Take your shoes off. I don't want you to track snow inside," we heard Mrs. Spangler yell from the side of her house. We kicked off our shoes. I swallowed freezing cold tears as I stood shaking. I wondered what was going to happen. But Charles and Eleanor already suspected what she was planning. Mrs. Spangler came around her house holding her rubber garden hose as it trailed behind her. Water was gushing out of it. She looked like a crazy person rushing to put out a fire. "Stand still!" she yelled. She stood before us and sprayed our shivering bodies with the icy water. It felt like needles prickling my body. "Quit your crying, Stella! You're all little dirty shits, but I'll clean you up. You hear me? I'll clean you up! I won't have dirty and thieving children living in my house. You stole my precious plant and then ruined it!" Eleanor started to whimper for the first time. "Oh, poor little

Eleanor. I guess you don't like this?" Mrs. Spangler taunted as she focused the hose on her face. "You're not as tough as you act, you bratty child." Water sprayed all over her face. She looked like someone who had just been slapped. She winced and shut her eyes. Bob and I were gripping hands. My toes felt numb sinking into the snow on the ground, and the cold water felt like ice, sending shivers down my spine. Mrs. Spangler continued to squirt all of us one by one. "Go on and clean yourselves, you dirty little shits."

The cold air mixed with the water shocked my system and took my breath away. The wind was blowing as I gasped for breath. I felt like I was drowning as I held tightly onto Bob's hand. Charles stood still like a soldier with his hands covering himself. Then Eleanor suddenly moved behind Charles while taking Bob and me with her. She pushed us behind her body. I sunk my head into Bob's back.

"We're clean now, Mrs. Spangler! Stop, please stop!" Charles yelled. "We learned our lesson!" Then he noticed a figure looking out the window from the house next door. Another one appeared. He yelled, "Hey, your neighbors are watching! They will snitch on you! They will tell our father!"

Mrs. Spangler sprung around and saw the outline of two people looking out their back window. She quickly dropped the hose and rushed us inside through the kitchen door. We watched her through the window as she darted back to the yard to see if the neighbors were still watching. She looked like a crazy beast searching for its prey. She sprung to the side of the house, and we heard her turn off the water. She yelled something derogatory toward her neighbor's house as she walked back inside.

Mrs. Spangler's sixteen-year-old son, Albert, lived with her. He reminded me of Charles. He had every hair slicked back, but it was thicker and sat taller on his head. He also wore a cross look on his face. But he wasn't as attractive as Charles. His eyes were dark like his mother's, and his ears looked a little too large. His bedroom was the one I found locked when we first moved in. Albert was eating at the kitchen table when we stumbled in from outside. He gawked at us weirdly. He didn't say anything; he just stared at our shivering, wet, half-naked bodies. "Albert, when did you get home?" his mother asked. Her cheeks were flushed, and her forehead was damp with sweat.

Eleanor and Charles took that as a cue to leave. They hurried Bob and me out of the kitchen to their bedroom. Charles grabbed new drawers for him and Bob while Eleanor retrieved a towel. Everything became a blur as I stood with my cold, wet bloomers sticking to my body like glue. I felt Eleanor pat me dry. Our hair was dripping and puddling on the floor. She led me to the attic.

The twins and Samuel were there. They were pretending to be napping. Probably because they were scared. I shivered all over when Eleanor checked my burns before dressing me. "It will be okay, Stella," she whispered. "What Mrs. Spangler did was awful, but I think the cold water could have helped your burns." Eleanor hugged me when she spoke. I held onto her and didn't want to let go. I pressed my face into her cold, wet hair. She soothed my cries the way the twins soothed Samuel's the first night I slept in the attic with them. "Come, Stella, let's dry our hair. I don't want you getting sick."

"I'm afraid to go downstairs."

"I know you're scared, but you can't be afraid, Stella. You need to be a big girl." Eleanor paused and sucked in a breath. "Pretend this never happened. Go to sleep tonight and wake up tomorrow morning with no memory of today." She wiped tears off my cheek with the back of her hand. "Do you understand? Pretend this never happened. This was all just a bad dream. This never happened, okay." And that's what we all did. We went to sleep that night and pretended it never happened.

I liked the attention Eleanor gave me while living in the boarding house. She was nicer to me there than before we moved in, but it didn't make living there any easier for me. I missed my father terribly. I missed our old home. I wanted my old life back. I wanted my mother to come home. I hated the boarding house and Southwood Avenue. I hated how Mrs. Spangler treated me. Every day, I felt nauseous, like getting on a roller coaster that I feared. One that you never wanted to ride but were forced to. And then it doesn't stop, and you can't get off. It just keeps going and going and you don't know when it will end, so you shut your eyes and pray that you'll be on safe ground soon.

Chapter 22

WE NEVER SPOKE ABOUT THAT NIGHT TO ANYONE, not even to each other. We never told our father. Telling him would make it real. I did exactly what Eleanor told me. I went to bed that night thinking it was just a bad dream, but that's not to say I didn't have nightmares about it. I woke from cold sweats sometimes. I didn't understand how I could shiver and be hot at the same time.

I cried almost every day. Mrs. Spangler's unpredictable behavior scared me. All my crying caused Charles to lose his patience with me. He often shook me or hit me out of frustration; we were all miserable there, but Charles took his anger out on me. "Stop crying all the time and stop acting so scared. She'll target you more if you keep acting like a crybaby. Remember, I told you to act more like Samuel and the twins."

One time, he left a dark black-and-blue bruise that looked like finger-prints on my upper arm from squeezing it too tightly. Even Mrs. Spangler asked about it, but I didn't tell her the truth. I didn't want Charles to get into trouble or get the rod. I said that I ran into a door handle. "That doesn't look like a bruise from a door handle," she breathed out while her cigarette smoke circled in the air in front of me. But then, she snorted and said I probably deserved it, whatever it was from.

Mrs. Spangler's erratic behavior grew worse as Christmas drew near. Our first Christmas with her was on a Saturday, a few weeks after the back-yard incident that the neighbors witnessed. On Christmas Eve night, I dreamed I got a beautiful baby doll. She had blue eyes, brown hair, and a fancy lace bonnet. She wore a pretty pink dress trimmed in lace that matched her bonnet. The doll came in a carriage that I could push her in. When I woke up on Christmas morning, I ran to find it, and once I realized it was not there, I started to cry. Our father visited us on Christmas Day, but we weren't our usual selves. We were somber. The next-door neighbors, the Hendersons, were getting into their car with presents in their hands when our father arrived. We watched from the doorway as he spoke with them. I was still in my nightwear and I ran barefoot to him. The cold ground felt like it was biting my feet as snow began to fall. I jumped into his arms and sunk my head into his neck. He held me tightly and rubbed my back as we approached the front porch. "What's wrong, sweetheart?" But I didn't say anything because I noticed Mrs. Spangler's ugly face spying from the front window. She looked like an irritated detective trying to unwrap a clue with no leads. I hid my face back on my father's shoulder.

"What were you talking to them about?" Mrs. Spangler demanded as we entered the house.

"Who? Your neighbors? Nothing much. Just wishing them a Merry Christmas and exchanging pleasantries."

"Oh, well, they're terrible neighbors. They are nosy, and I don't care for them. They're always snooping in my backyard for no reason. I caught the lady stealing clothes off my line once. Can you believe that? Who would do something like that? They can't be trusted."

We knew Mrs. Spangler was lying, but we didn't say anything to our father to prove her wrong. The Hendersons may have played an essential part in our lives since they always watched out the window facing her backyard. Looking back, I think things could have been worse if it hadn't been for them watching all the time. I don't think Mrs. Spangler knew their names. She only referred to her neighbor as "Nosy Bitch." Mrs. Spangler repeatedly yelled from her backyard, "I see you watching, you nosy bitch. Mind your own goddamn business, you nosy bitch." But Nosy Bitch and her husband kept watching.

Christmas Day was disappointing for my siblings and me. Since it was on a Saturday, our father had to work overtime and couldn't stay long. The atmosphere in the house was stifling. Mrs. Spangler's son made a brief appearance with a grouchy look on his face when he grabbed his only present that lay against the fireplace. It was wrapped in green paper with a beautiful red bow. We each were given a small toy wagon with an orange in it from Mrs. Spangler. We didn't have a tree. Only stockings hung on the mantel, filled with little presents and trinkets from our father. Our "big gift" was saved for birthdays.

I received the rod for the first time on a Saturday in early February of 1921 when I refused to eat the moldy bread under the questionable jam. She caught me when I threw it in the garbage.

"You just wasted a fine piece of bread, you little shit! Get it out of the garbage and eat it."

"No!" I shouted back.

"Then get your ass to the attic and stay there until I come up!" She still had me sleeping in the attic. She said my room wasn't ready yet.

"No! I don't like it up there. You told my father I could move to his room, and I haven't." I felt my eyebrows scrunch together, and my heart pounded. I said no to Mrs. Spangler for the first time. Her face flushed a deep red shade, and her expression changed. Her nostrils flared like a hippo, and her furrowed brows lowered. A streak of hatred went through her eyes when she smacked me across the face. Then she grabbed the moldy bread from the garbage and shoved it in my mouth.

"No!" I cried while spitting the bread out.

Mrs. Spangler's lips tightened when she grabbed the rod that hung on the kitchen wall. She yanked my body over her lap and spanked me with it. I remember what Eleanor had once told us, so I screamed on the first whip, but that didn't matter. She continued spanking me. The intense burning stung my bottom. It was pain I had never felt before, like I was being attacked by a thousand hornets. My sobs caught everyone's attention at the boarding house. I heard the rapid pitter-patter of Samuel and the twins' feet running up the steps to the attic. Then I recognized the shoes that entered the kitchen.

"Mrs. Spangler, stop! She's sorry, please stop!" Bob shrieked.

At that moment, the kitchen door that led outside flew open and slammed against the wall. It was Eleanor. She reached for the rod that swung through the air. It caught Mrs. Spangler off guard. She suddenly sprung around and stood up. I fell to the floor like a rag doll. Mrs. Spangler had a crazy look in her dark eyes. She and Eleanor both had their hands on the rod in a game of tug of war. Bob pulled me off the floor and yelled, "Eleanor, stop!"

Eleanor's jaws were clenched, and she and Mrs. Spangler locked eyes with anticipation. Eleanor stood taller and gripped the rod so hard that her knuckles turned white. Determination covered her face. You could smell the sweat sliding down Mrs. Spangler's flushed face and feel the adrenaline rush taking over Eleanor. When Charles entered the kitchen, Mrs. Spangler flinched and let go of the rod. Eleanor stood with the rod in her hands. We all watched expectantly, and then nervously, waiting for Mrs. Spangler's next move. But she did something that surprised us. She sat down on the wooden kitchen chair and started crying. She rested her sweaty forehead in her hand, and she wailed.

"Everybody leave! The show is over, you hear? Leave, leave me alone!"

I'm not sure where Charles and Eleanor went. I ran with Bob, hand in hand. We scrambled around the backyard, searching for a place to hide. "Stella, let's hide behind the shed near the Hendersons house," Bob whispered. I found myself crouching under a fir tree behind the shed. Bob had his arm on my shaking body. The needles were prickling me. My cries grew softer until they were just little gulps of air. We noticed the next-door neighbor's outline appear through the window. Bob was uncertain what to do next. He quietly spoke in my ear that they were watching. We lay under the tree and watched them watching us while I sniffled. It felt like hours under the fir tree, but it was only a few minutes.

"Come out from under the tree," Charles commanded. "She went to her bedroom. I can hear her crying in there. I think we're okay. We just need to stay out of her earshot."

Bob and I pulled ourselves out from under the tree. I felt sticky sap on my body and smelled the woodsy fragrance it made as we walked back inside the boarding house. Charles trailed behind us. When he tapped on Mrs. Spangler's bedroom door and asked if she wanted cigarettes, Bob and I gave each other a tense look. We knew what we were going to do next.

Mrs. Spangler smoked Lucky Strike cigarettes. She liked to send Bob and me to fetch her a pack of Luckies at the store near her home. She never gave us money to pay for them. She expected us to steal them. Bob and I knew stealing was wrong, but we had no choice, fearing we'd get the rod or something worse. The man who owned the store, Mr. Jackson, caught me putting a pack into my coat pocket.

"Are you a smoker, young lady?"

His question startled me. My heart began to race as I replied, "No, no sir."

"Then why are you stealing cigarettes from me?" I was speechless, and my lips quivered.

Bob quickly jumped in and rescued me. "Mister, if we don't come home with these Lucky Strikes, my sister and I will get the rod so hard we won't be able to sit for a week." Bob's lips quivered too. "We don't have money to pay for them, but I will work for you if you let us take them. I can sweep floors and stock shelves. Please, mister, don't get us into trouble." Bob paced the floor with his hands in his pockets. His eyebrows were pulled together.

His voice was anxious when he spoke. "We don't like stealing. That's not how our father raised us. But we don't live with him now. We live with this mean old lady who smokes too much and is cruel." Bob could barely finish his last sentence. He wiped back a tear.

Mr. Jackson looked Bob over. I fidgeted with the pack of cigarettes in my pocket, waiting for his reply. His eyebrows arched upward when he gave each of us long stares. I chewed on my lower lip while I looked around the store. I was too scared to look at Mr. Jackson, but Bob wasn't. He shifted his weight from one side to the other and cleared his throat. He looked Mr. Jackson in the eye. Then, the store owner shook hands with Bob. "Son, I think we have ourselves a deal." He told Bob to come back the next afternoon. Then he did something that shocked Bob and me. Mr. Jackson put another pack of cigarettes into my other coat pocket.

He kneeled, looked me in the eye, and said, "I'm not sure who this mean old lady is, but if you need help, I want you to know you can trust me." I gave him a nod and then put my head down, but then he hugged me. It felt like hugging my father. I sunk my head closer into his neck and smelled his shaving cream. He smelled like my father. I didn't want to let go of him. But Bob grabbed my hand and pulled me away.

"Thank you, sir! I'll see you tomorrow." He wanted to return to the boarding house with the cigarettes before Charles looked for us. Bob smiled at me as we exited the store like we had accomplished a considerable feat. "Shoot, we needed help a long time ago!"

Charles was standing on the front porch when we arrived. "I was about to go look for you," he said. "What took you so long?"

"I got a job there," Bob proudly said as he handed Charles the two packs. "We ain't stealing for her anymore."

The next day, after Bob returned home from Mr. Jackson's store, he had a wonderful surprise for us. It was a bag of Conversation Hearts! I had never seen candy with words on it before, but Eleanor and Charles knew what they were. "It's for Valentine's Day," Charles said as he popped one in his mouth.

"Yeah, you give one to your sweetie!" laughed Bob. "Who's your sweetie, Charles?"

I started laughing too. "Hey Eleanor, who are you going to give one to?"

"To myself!" she popped another one into her mouth and smiled. That made me laugh even harder. We sat on the front porch and giggled while reading the Conversation Hearts. We ate every single heart until the bag was empty.

In March of that year, Bob came home with the best gift! It was a set of Lincoln Logs the Jacksons gave him for his birthday. It was a toy construction set of little wooden logs that you used to create cabins, forts, or buildings. We were over the moon with excitement with that set. "Dad is going to be impressed with this. I'll show him I can build things too!" Bob exclaimed. I looked forward to playing with that set and designing different homes with Bob after school every day until one day it went missing. We never knew where it went. It just disappeared.

Chapter 23

WINTER HAD TURNED INTO SPRING, and it was April. I was excited about my fifth birthday coming up, even though we had been living in misery on Southwood Avenue for almost a year. Now that it was warmer, we snuck outside the smoky, musty house to play whenever possible. It felt like playing hide-and-seek but from Mrs. Spangler. One Sunday morning, she caught me conversing with her nosy neighbor, Mrs. Henderson. We were just talking about how warm the day was for a spring morning when Mrs. Spangler lurched outside, grabbed my arm, and shoved me inside her kitchen. "What were you doing outside? Why were you speaking to her? What did you say? You know that Nosy Bitch isn't your friend. She will only get you into trouble!" Mrs. Spangler's words spewed out of her like hot lava as I sat on a kitchen chair.

"Nothing," I said. I felt my stomach quiver and put my hands under my bottom. She lit a Lucky Strike while she sat on a chair across from me. With every exhale, she snarled. "What am I going to do with you, Stella? Should I tell your father what a bad girl you've been when he visits today?" Then, a crooked smile slowly appeared on her wicked face. She laughed when she announced that my father wasn't visiting today. He had to work overtime to complete one of his jobs. "I know what will teach you a lesson," Mrs. Spangler sneered as she flicked her cigarette ash into the ashtray. Then, she took a long drag of it while staring coldly at me. I nervously glanced around the room and swayed in my chair, avoiding eye contact with her. She let out a heavy exhale of her cigarette before smashing it into her ashtray. I felt sad when I heard my father wasn't visiting, but I was more tense and scared about what Mrs. Spangler had said to me. *What will teach me a lesson?* I wondered. My hands felt sweaty under my bottom. My stomach quivered again. Then, she grabbed me from under my armpits and pulled me off the chair. She dragged me over to the basement. She opened the rickety door, shoved me down the steps, and locked the door. I blindly stumbled down the dark steps and quickly felt my way back up. I stood at the closed door, shaking from head to toe.

"No, no, please don't!" I pleaded as I banged my fists against the wooden door. "Please let me out! I promise not to speak to her anymore. I promise never to do anything bad again." I sobbed as I pressed my face against the cold door. "Let me out!" Panic pounded on my chest when I heard Mrs. Spangler's loud footsteps walk away. I pressed my forehead against the door. She turned a deaf ear to me. I knew I was trapped as I lowered myself onto the top step. I was locked in the cold, damp basement, where she hung laundry in the wintertime. It smelled of wet dirt. My fists throbbed from my banging, so I cradled them against my chest as I rocked back and forth, wondering when I would be let out. I couldn't see anything other than a small crack of light that shone from under the basement door.

Suddenly, fear pricked my body as I heard geese squawking up the basement steps. They made awful noises and pecked at my feet. There were two of them. I kicked and kicked my feet as hard as I could. "Get off me!" I screamed, "Get off me!" I didn't want to hurt them, but I was scared. I didn't understand why they were in the basement. Then they squawked back down the steps. I shot upright, and I banged my throbbing fists on the basement door again, begging to be let out. "There are geese down here, please let me out!" I put my ear against the door and banged with one fist, but my pleas were ignored. I fell back down to the top wooden step. I clutched my chest. "Why are there geese down here?" I whimpered. I was too afraid to go farther down now that the geese had returned to the basement. It felt like I was sitting on pins and needles as I wondered what to do.

I remembered the time when Charles pushed me down the old cellar steps during our mystery walk, and I started crying. *Was the murderous teenage boy hiding in this basement now? Would he murder me too?* A wave of fear settled into my body and didn't leave. Hours passed by, but I had no real sense of time. *Am I going to be forgotten about? Will I die down here?* I clenched my body, trying to hold my pee in. I pressed my cheek against the cold door, whimpering. I felt spent from all my screaming and crying. Then, I couldn't do it anymore, so I fell asleep.

My back was aching when I woke in complete darkness. There was no light escaping from under the door. It was pitch-black, so black that my eyes had difficulty getting used to the dark. I knew I had soiled myself. My undergarments stuck to my legs, wet with pee that soaked the top step. My bottom felt numb from under me, I felt like I was glued to the step. I wanted out of the basement in the worst way, but I felt like I couldn't move. I'm not sure how long I sat cemented to that top step. Thinking about the dangers that could be lurking around in the basement scared me. I was more scared without the sliver of light. I hugged my knees and rested my head on them. A whiff of strong ammonia lingered inside my nose. I felt depleted. I felt powerless. I sensed it was nighttime, so I went back to sleep. At least when I slept, I didn't feel scared.

In the morning, I woke to the patter of small footsteps above me. I could tell they weren't Mrs. Spangler by how they sounded. Hers were loud and clunky. I heard lighter footsteps that sounded barefoot. I wondered who it was. I knew they had to belong to a child, but which one? I could hear someone shuffling in the kitchen. I lowered myself and tried to peer through the open space under the door. But then I saw fingers appear. They were waving to me from under the door. "Who's there?" I asked.

"Stella," Bob whispered. My heart raced, and I touched his fingers. I was so happy to hear his voice. He slid crackers under the door. He lay on the floor and whispered through the crack, "Are you okay?" I shoved the crackers into my mouth and told him I was thirsty. "I don't know how to give you any water," he said. He waved his fingers under the door again, and I touched them. Touching his fingers gave me comfort.

"I'm scared. Don't leave. There are geese down here. Why does she have geese in the basement?"

"I don't know. Oh no. Hush, she's coming!" And then I heard his soft footsteps run across the ceiling above me.

I sat all day on the cold, urine-stained top stair and waited for Bob to return. The longer I sat, the more my legs shook. I sat with my cheek pressed against the basement door and waited. I felt like all I did was wait. When I didn't hear the heavy sounds of Mrs. Spangler's steps, I would whisper Bob's name, hoping he would come, and I waited. I waited to hear the sound of the lock click. I wondered if she planned on feeding me. I waited for food. I waited for water. And then I slept.

When I woke, there was a plate of bread with jam smeared over it and a glass of water sitting next to me. I grabbed the glass and put it to my dry lips. I felt like I couldn't get enough. I drank it down so fast it hurt my belly. I scooped up the piece of bread and shoved it in my mouth. I didn't look for any mold. That didn't seem to matter to me anymore. I wanted more water, but there wasn't any. I picked up the glass and tried shaking droplets into my mouth. I tried licking the inside of the glass, but my tongue couldn't reach the bottom.

When I needed to move my bowels, I banged on the door for a long time. Finally, Mrs. Spangler opened it. A flood of light entered and blinded my eyes. I told her I needed to go to the water closet with my hand covering my eyes from the light. "You smell terrible. Stop peeing yourself. There are buckets downstairs you can go in," she said, then slammed the door shut and locked it. I had to go so badly that I eventually slid down the wooden stairs on my bottom. The geese squawked and circled me as I entered their arena. I couldn't see any buckets because it was so dark. I only had the crack of light that shone on the steps. My jaw quivered as I fell to my knees and crawled, feeling my way around. The floor was hard and cold; it felt dirty, covered in goose droppings. I waved my hands before me, hoping not to bump into anything. I may have scared the geese away with all my searching because they squawked to the corner. I wondered if they could see me. I wondered if they had given up on me. I tried to remember what the basement looked like but couldn't. I never returned there after Mrs. Spangler poured the hot wash water on me. I felt lost, searching through the black abyss I was in. My head knocked into a pole and sharp pain radiated my forehead. I rubbed my head and checked for any blood. I didn't feel anything other than a bump forming. I wanted to cry, but I held my tears back. I blindly crawled around some more, and then I came to a wooden table. I slid my hands up the table legs and pulled myself up. I immediately felt the sharp sting of a splinter. I put my finger in my mouth. I thought I could bite that splinter out, but I couldn't. I stretched my arms in front of me and felt the things on the table. None of them were buckets. I slid back down on my hands and knees and searched again. I finally found a set of empty buckets. They were under the table the whole time. I grabbed two and took them back to the steps, where I could see just a tiny bit. When I lowered my undergarments, my bottom felt like it was bleeding. It was numb and raw. I left the buckets at the bottom of the steps and crawled back to the top step. I put my face against the door and whispered Bob's name. He didn't come. I slumped down and tried looking under the door. I couldn't see anything but dim light. I put my fingers under the door and waved them, but no one touched them. I cried again, and my nose ran. I wiped my nose with my fingers and felt the splinter with my thumb. I wondered how I would remove it when my finger started to throb. I tried digging it out with my nail, but it was dull and not sharp enough. I felt helpless and scared. I sat on the top step and rocked my body back and forth.

I lost all track of time in the basement. I only knew when it was day or night by the light that shone from under the door. Mrs. Spangler gave me a blanket and just enough food and water to keep me alive while I was in her prison. I only saw a quick sight of the kitchen when she opened the door and put a plate of food and a cup of water on the step. Then the door slammed, and I heard the lock click. I tried to keep my mind busy thinking about things that made me happy. I thought about spending Sundays with my father and playing hide-and-seek with my friends. For entertainment, I marched up and down the steps, and I counted each one, there were eleven. I named all the steps and became friends with them, well not all of them. I disliked the bottom two steps. I named them Earl and Pearl. "You stink, Earl and Pearl! Bad steps!" I scolded them. My buckets sat on Earl and Pearl. But then I felt sorry for them. I felt bad for not liking them, but I didn't like them as much as I did the other ones. I played blindman's bluff with the steps. I won every time. I sang to the steps as I moved up and down each one and patted their backs. And I waited and waited. I waited for Bob's fingers to wave from under the door.

I turned five years old while I was in the basement. I didn't know it was my birthday until Bob slid a piece of candy and a beautiful picture under the door that he colored for me at school. I could tell it was a picture of us roller-skating from the crack of light that highlighted it. Tears crawled down my cheeks and rested under my chin.

"Happy Birthday, Stella," he whispered.

"Is today my birthday?"

"Yes, it's Tuesday. She can't keep you here for too much longer. Father will find out."

"Where is everybody? I don't hear any noises above me except for Mrs. Spangler."

"She's keeping us away from the first floor, especially the kitchen. We eat in our bedrooms. She doesn't want anyone trying to let you out. She said it would be our turn next if we did." Then I heard a clop of loud, clunky footsteps from above. Bob's fingers disappeared, and I heard the pitter-patter of his feet as he ran away.

Bob visited me when he could. I don't remember how many times he did, but it felt like at least once a day. I loved it when I saw his fingers waving up at me. I grabbed them and didn't want to let go. He tried to console me when I cried, which I did often. He would slide crackers under the door when he could. "How long have, have I been here now?" I stuttered during one visit. I felt hopeless, alone, and weak.

"Six days, but I heard her tell Eleanor she was letting you out soon." Bob's words were a comfort. I rocked back and forth on the top step, waiting to hear the sound of the lock open and for Mrs. Spangler's wicked voice. But I didn't. My tailbone was sore from rocking so much. I didn't understand why I felt so weak, especially since I wasn't doing much other than sitting and sleeping. I wasn't in the mood to talk to the steps or play with them anymore. I wanted out. I missed the attic. I missed my stick mattress. I missed the twins who wouldn't talk to me. I missed my father. It felt like forever before I heard the lock rattle. When the door opened wide, a horrible smell escaped. When my stink reached Mrs. Spangler's nose, she winced.

"Stella, you smell appalling! Get up! Come on, get up here. It's time to go upstairs, wash yourself, and put a clean dress on. Use my washroom. Your father may come this evening if he can get off work early, but he'll be here tomorrow for his Sunday visit for sure." It was the first time I felt relieved to hear her wretched voice. I felt sluggish and exhausted when I climbed the steps. The light from the kitchen blinded my eyes. I closed them and hugged my body. I couldn't move. She pushed me out of the kitchen and practically dragged me to the front room. My skinny legs could hardly get me up the stairs to her washroom. Mrs. Spangler screamed for Eleanor to help me. She was immediately at my side, ushering me up the stairs to the second level. My eyes were shut, but I felt the stares from the other children watching every move we made. When we entered the washroom, I fell into Eleanor's body and cried when she shut the door. Charles and Bob put their ears against it. I could hear Bob crying from the other side.

"She's okay," Eleanor hissed at the door. I'll take care of her. Go to the attic and get clean clothes I can dress her in."

Eleanor helped me scrub under my fingernails, but we couldn't get them entirely clean. She was able to remove the splinter that ached in my finger. The light that shone through the bathroom window hurt my eyes, so I kept them closed while Eleanor washed me. She sang "Rock-a-Bye Baby" while pouring water over my skinny body. She could hardly look at me with my ribs protruding out. The water wasn't very warm, so she tried to be as quick as possible. The cool water didn't bother me, though. The song she sang bothered me more. It made me think about the time when Mrs. Spangler poured the hot wash water over my head because I was singing that song.

As I crawled up the attic steps to lie on my straw mattress, it felt good for the first time. It was Saturday afternoon, and I slept in the attic for the rest of the day. I dreamed of my mother for the first time. We were shopping at the store, and she bought me a huge bundle of caramel. Then, she held my hand when we walked home. We were singing together, and before I knew it, we were cuddling on the davenport, and I read to her. She was extremely impressed with how good of a reader I was. She kissed and hugged me. She told me she loved me.

Then I awoke in a panic when I heard Mrs. Spangler screaming, "It will be your turn next if you speak to your father about this! You hear me, Eleanor?"

I stood in the doorway to my siblings' room and sniffled the next morning. I looked like a lost dog. Eleanor washed me again because I had soiled myself while I was sleeping in the attic. I watched the water drip from my hair. I could hardly hold the wet cloth Eleanor handed me. "Why me?" I asked her. Eleanor didn't say anything. I don't think she knew what to say.

She sang to me instead. I closed my eyes and pretended she was my mother. I snapped out of my thoughts when I heard the front door close.

"Stella, he's here. Dry off quickly and put this dress on," she said before running downstairs.

As I slowly walked down the steps to greet my father, I automatically counted each one. "Happy Birthday, Stella!" he cried with excitement. He had a fresh-cut bouquet of daisies and a box wrapped with brown paper in his hands. "I hated missing your birthday, sweetheart. Daddy worked long hours these past few weeks. Since city hall caught on fire, I was hired to remove the wreckage and redesign a new building for the site. But I felt horrible about missing your birthday. I thought about you all day," he said as he hugged me. "Oh my, you feel like skin and bones," he gasped. "Are you feeling okay? You look exhausted and frail! Stella, what's wrong?"

"Oh, the poor girl came down with a touch of the flu right before her birthday, so it was probably best you weren't here for it. She slept for a week straight and hardly had any energy to eat. But she is feeling much better now, and I prepared a lovely supper for us," Mrs. Spangler said.

My father could tell we weren't our usual selves during his visit, especially since I didn't ask what was in the brown box. He looked at us quizzically, but we avoided looking at him. I sat on his lap and laid my head on his shoulder. I pushed him away when he tried to tickle me and buried my face in his neck. Bob sat quietly next to him while we listened to the radio. There was tension in the air, and our father noticed it. Nobody made eye contact with him while we ate supper.

"What's going on with the children?" he asked Mrs. Spangler after supper.

"Oh, I think they all came down with something when Stella was ill. They haven't been their normal selves for a week now. It was probably contagious."

"But Stella could hardly eat her food," he said, "I'm worried about how thin she is. They all may have been sick, but they look very sad."

Mrs. Spangler didn't respond as she cleaned the dishes in the sink. Once it was time for our father to leave, he asked me to open the gift he had brought me. It was a Raggedy Ann doll.

"Now, it's not as big as I wanted, but ..."

"No, Daddy, I love it! It's perfect!" I hugged the doll and then wrapped my arms around his neck. "Can you stay here a little longer? Please don't leave yet," I begged. My father hugged me tightly. The squeeze of his hug hurt my belly and ribs, but I didn't care.

"I can stay for a few more minutes. Maybe we can play a game of cards, would you like that, children?" Everyone nodded their heads except for me. I was too busy examining Raggedy Ann's blue floral dress and white pantaloons. She wore a white apron with pink stitching and a blue flower made with the same material as her dress.

The next day, Bob found me sitting on the front porch of the boarding house when he got home from school. I was cradling my Raggedy Ann doll with a blank stare on my face. "You don't look well. Do you want to come with me to the Jackson's store?" I nodded.

"Look who showed up!" Mr. Jackson said delightedly. But then concern washed over his face when he got a better look at me. His raised eyelids and the little wrinkles that appeared on his forehead made me feel uncomfortable. I wondered if he was upset that Bob brought me. "Bob, I'm glad you brought your sister with you. Stella, meet my wife, Mrs. Jackson."

I held my doll tightly to my chest and gave Mrs. Jackson a soft grin. She was a little plump lady with sweet eyes and a pretty smile. "It's nice to meet you, sweet Stella. I've heard so much about you. Can I give you a hug? Oh my, honey, you are a beautiful soul," she said when I didn't let go of her embrace. "I have a special surprise for you." She led me behind the counter.

I smiled as she handed me a plate of caramel. "A little birdy told me once that you liked caramel candy. Eat as much as you want, but not too much. I don't want you to have a sick stomach. You can take the rest home with you."

After Bob started his tasks, I could tell he was a good worker because of the way Mr. Jackson smiled at him. Bob didn't notice. He stayed focused on his jobs, but when he asked Bob questions about our family and where we lived, Bob's demeanor changed. He started glancing at me, and his stance stiffened. Bob found ways to politely avoid answering his questions by asking Mr. Jackson questions about his tasks. Mr. Jackson didn't press Bob with any more questions.

"Stella, we live next door, and I have a pot roast in the oven that I need to check on. Do you want to come with me?" I nodded, and we walked hand in hand out of the store.

When we returned, I had a broad smile on my face. Mrs. Jackson carried a covered pot.

"Something smells delicious," Mr. Jackson said approvingly to his wife.

"Yes, indeed. Stella helped me so much in the kitchen I would have felt guilty for not sharing our lovely meal."

Bob looked like his mouth was watering. Mrs. Jackson removed the lid to give him a peek inside. It was pot roast with cooked potatoes and carrots. "All I ask is that you return the empty dish when you come to work tomorrow."

"Yes, ma'am, I will."

I sat on Mrs. Jackson's lap while Bob finished his chores. I liked sitting on her lap. I liked the way it felt when she played with my hair. "We never had a little girl. Our boys are grown men now," she said.

That wasn't the only time Mrs. Jackson sent Bob home with leftovers. Bob snuck dishes into the boarding house a few times a month while we lived there. Mrs. Spangler never knew.

Chapter 24

BEFORE WE KNEW IT, fall was right around the corner. Our father had been living on Frebis Avenue without us for a year. I remember it was a warm fall that year, and we sat outside on the front porch longer in the evenings than usual because the air wasn't cold. Bob and I enjoyed playing hand-clapping games, and Eleanor and Charles read books or played cards with each other. One evening, a stray cat walked up the front steps and meowed at us. "Hey, little fellow, what are you doin' here?" Bob asked as he scratched the top of the cat's head and around his chin. The cat meowed while rubbing against him. The meows spoke to us in an urgent, high-pitched tone.

"Oh, no, little girl. Are you a hungry mama?" Eleanor asked.

"How do you know it's a girl?" I asked.

"Because if you look at her belly, you can tell she's had babies. Look at her nipples."

"Nipples," Bob giggled. "That word is funny, nipples." He chuckled and giggled some more. I didn't understand what was so funny, but I giggled too. Charles rolled his eyes at us.

"We should feed her," I said. "She looks very skinny and hungry. What should we feed her?"

"I'll sneak into the kitchen and get a little cup of milk," Bob said. When he returned, the cat slurped up the milk. After she drank it, she rubbed her body against my legs and purred loudly as I petted her.

"Be careful, she could have a disease," Charles warned. But I didn't care. I loved feeling her rubbing her soft fur against my legs and purring.

"She's got a loud motor," Bob said as he scratched under her chin. She had a large patch of white fur under her chin that led down to her chest. Her body was covered with orange and white stripes, and she had big green eyes. "Where have you been living? Do you still have your babies?"

My eyes grew large when I looked at Bob. "Should we look for them? We should look for her babies!" I squealed.

"No," Charles said. "It's getting late. We should probably go inside now before Mrs. Spangler looks for us." Eleanor and Charles opened the front door and said goodnight to the cat and told us to come inside too. But I couldn't. I wanted to pet the cat some more. I wanted to find her babies.

"I feel sorry for her, Bob. She seems sad," I said while rubbing my hand down the cat's back and running my fingers through her tail.

After that evening, the cat visited us around dusk every day. Bob brought home cat food Mrs. Jackson gave him. We poured some in a bowl and hid it under the front porch in the evenings so Mrs. Spangler wouldn't see it. We named her Tabby, and I fell in love with her. We never found her babies. Eleanor said that after some time, all kittens leave their mamas. I thought that sounded horrible. I would never leave my mama. I would want her to stay with me. But every evening, like clockwork, Tabby would appear on the front porch looking for attention.

While Bob and I were petting her one evening, Mrs. Spangler's son walked up the steps leading to the porch and snarled at us. "My mom ain't gonna let you keep that cat. You better stop feeding her so she doesn't come around anymore. Where you gettin' the food, anyway?"

We ignored him. My lips fluttered for a second, but I didn't answer. We didn't like Albert. He scared me and seemed mean. We stroked Tabby's back and rubbed her head while she purred between Bob and me. "What's wrong? Cat got your tongue?" Albert snickered. I didn't know what that meant. Bob and I continued petting Tabby and avoided making any eye contact with Albert. His heavy boots made the floorboards rattle when he opened the front door. When it slammed behind him, it scared Tabby, and she scurried under the front porch.

"There's food and water for her under there. Let's go to bed now, it's getting late." Bob said.

Not long after that evening, Tabby stopped visiting us. I sat on the front porch every evening waiting for her, but she never came. I called her name and shook her food bowl, but no Tabby. Bob sat with me and held my hand when I cried. Then he would walk up and down the street shaking her bowl and calling her name, but no response. We did that for weeks and were devastated when she didn't appear. With winter coming, it was getting dark and cold earlier in the evenings. But every morning, Bob and I would still look under the front porch to see if any food was missing. When Mrs. Spangler found out, she was angry. "I should give you both a slap on the ear! What were you thinking? We're not feeding every stray cat in this neighborhood." She emptied the food bowl in her garbage can. "You better get rid of the rest of the cat food, or you'll be sorry. There're enough strays living here, we don't need anymore."

"Yes, ma'am," we sniffled and ran to Bob's bedroom. Charles and Eleanor were sitting in between their beds playing cards. I plopped myself down on Eleanor's bed and cried.

"What do you think happened to Tabby?" Bob asked.

"I don't know, but you better get rid of that cat food like she asked," Charles said. Bob slid under his bed and grabbed the rest of the cat food he had from the Jacksons' store. I watched him walk outside and throw it in the garbage can with a frown on his face. When he looked up, he saw Albert. He smiled at Bob. His smile was as cold and prickly as the frost that had formed on the grass. The hairs on the back of my neck stood up, and a cold chill ran through my body. Albert didn't say a word to Bob. His expression turned flat, yet daunting. His black eyes fixed intently on Bob like he was trying to challenge him, but for what? Bob stared back at Albert, and then Bob must've known it had to do with Tabby. He glowered at Albert like he wanted to throttle him. He closed the lid on the garbage can and, with the corners of his mouth turned downward, he shoved his hands in his pockets and walked back inside.

It was our second December in the boarding house on Southwood Avenue. Mrs. Spangler was meaner and acting strangely again. She cried more and yelled obscenities at the kitchen wall like she was scolding it. It was odd watching her scream at the wall in German. I didn't know what she was saying, but I knew she was angry at someone. Her wrath gave me goosebumps when I spied on her from the kitchen doorway. She smoked more cigarettes and drank more whiskey in December while she sat at her kitchen table raging obscenities at a poor wall that did nothing wrong.

During that December, she bought new dresses to impress our father when he visited. She flaunted herself around him and flirted with him. She looked silly to me. It irritated our father, so sometimes he cut his visits short, which, in turn, irritated us. She only wore those dresses once. After he left, Mrs. Spangler's mood changed, and she cried in her bedroom as she cut up the dress she wore that Sunday. It only happened a few times, but it was the strangest thing to watch. Bob and I would press our ears against her bedroom door and listen to her rants. Then we cracked the door slightly open to peer inside. She looked delusional, like a creepy witch. It frightened me, so I would run away, but Bob never did. He stayed and spied on her until her ranting stopped.

Christmas was on a Sunday that year, so our father had the whole day to visit us. Mrs. Spangler managed to make a turkey dinner with all the trimmings. She wasn't the best cook, but we didn't complain because it was the most food we ate. We still had sour looks on our faces. Christmas wasn't what it once was.

Mrs. Spangler pretended to like us in front of our father when he visited. That made it worse because we were forced to pretend that was our normal. But it wasn't. Our normal wasn't normal. After our father left his visits, she turned back into the same mean witch she was during the week. She spoke cruelly to us. She would tell us our behavior was horrible when we did nothing wrong. One of her favorite punishments was making us stand with our noses against the wall. I'm not sure how long we had to stand, but I remember feeling wobbly and fatigued after time passed. The pain that ran down both sides of my neck into my shoulder blades was unbearable. If we looked at one another, she would put a book on our heads. She was determined to break us. And sadly, she was succeeding. We all lost a little piece of ourselves every day. Little by little, she was whittling away at our spirit like a carpenter with a piece of wood. We were all slowly changing into different children on Southwood Avenue. I most certainly changed the most.

Chapter **25**

WINTER HAD FINALLY ENDED, and my sixth birthday was rapidly approaching. One morning, Bob found me lying on the sofa in the front room, wrapped up in a blanket.

"What do you want for your birthday this year?" Bob asked me.

"A teddy bear," I sniffled as I wiped my nose with the sleeve of my dress. I had a horrible sickness that refused to go away. Every time I told Mrs. Spangler I wasn't feeling well, she told me to get a drink of water, and that I would be fine.

"Are you still sick?" Bob's brow wrinkled, and he put his hand on my clammy forehead.

"Yes," I sniffled some more. "My head hurts, and I'm really cold."

"You're running a fever," Bob sighed. "Has Mrs. Spangler given you any aspirin?

"No, she keeps telling me I'll be fine." I started crying. "My head hurts so bad."

Bob ran to the kitchen, and I heard him rummaging around. He came back with a cold, wet cloth and gently laid it on my forehead. "I'll be right back," he said. He ran upstairs and by the sound of his quickened footsteps,

I could tell he was in Mrs. Spangler's bedroom. He ran back downstairs with a white pill in his hand.

"Here, take this. And then let's lie head to toe. I'll stay with you until you feel better." I swallowed the white pill and forced a small smile. My lips were cracked and chapped, but I couldn't help but smile at Bob. We lay on the sofa head to toe, and then I fell asleep.

I woke up to heavy footsteps walking through the front door. I glanced at Bob, who was sleeping. I felt delirious, and chills ran down my spine to my feet. My vision was blurry, but it looked like Albert was standing over us with an orange tabby cat in his hands. My stomach tightened, and my jaw clenched. "Is that Tabby?" I whispered. Then I heard a monstrous laugh and the sound of heavy boots walking away. I nudged Bob's cheek with my foot to wake him. "Did you see that?" I asked.

Bob stirred in his sleep and yawned. "See what?"

"Albert and Tabby. I think I just saw him with her."

Bob sat straight up. "Are you sure?"

"I don't know." I started crying, and my stomach tightened again. "I think I did." Bob jumped off the sofa and briskly walked around the house, looking for Albert and Tabby.

"I don't see them anywhere, and his bedroom is locked, so I can't check in there," he breathlessly said when he returned to the sofa.

"I know I saw him!" I cried. "At least, I'm pretty sure I did."

"It's okay, Stella. Go back to sleep, and I'll look around for them some more." I rolled over and fell back to sleep.

I dreamed about Albert for the first time while I was sleeping on the couch. I dreamt he had Tabby locked in his bedroom and was teasing her. He had a bowl full of cat food, and every time he put it in front of her, he would take it away. She meowed miserably in my dream. It was a high, scary pitch meow like when we first met her. I later woke from my dream screaming Tabby's name. I lurched from the sofa and ran to find her. Albert's bedroom door was locked, so I kicked it. Bob suddenly grabbed my shoulder and swung me around. "Stella, go back and lie down. I looked. Tabby is not here," he said.

Something interesting happened during one of our father's visits one Sunday in the summer of 1922. Mrs. Spangler was good at telling lies when he visited. She didn't every week, but maybe once a month she would tell him about the fun things we did. Sometimes, they were small fibs, which always made her look good like she was "mother of the year." But they were all lies, pretending everyone was happy, and we sat there and didn't say otherwise. It wasn't worth it. But then, I think my father caught on when she said we went to Olentangy Park. That was her biggest lie yet. He looked surprised to hear she took us there, so he asked many questions. Mrs. Spangler ignored his questions and fabricated a story about our fun adventures there. Then my father said something interesting. "I heard The Loop the Loop is not working anymore, which is a shame because that was always one of our favorite rides." He looked at her closely.

"Yes, that was very disappointing for the children because they were looking forward to that ride." He caught her. He caught her in a lie. That was not true. The Loop the Loop was not out of commission and was not one of our favorite rides because I threw up the first time we rode it. My vomit on my siblings ruined the fun of that ride for us. Charles and Eleanor's jaws dropped open, and they shifted around in their seats when she said that. And then they gave our father a pointed look. Their eyes were pleading with him to challenge her more. We knew he knew she was lying. The room grew stiff and awkward. Bob let out a little gasp, and I fidgeted with the radio that was sitting next to us. Disappointment sunk into our father's eyes. He knew she was lying too, but he didn't say anything more. Why didn't he challenge her statement? Maybe because he was not the type of person to start arguments, unlike our mother. But I could tell by the look on her face that day, Eleanor felt betrayed. She looked at our father incredulously and walked out of the front room. She never looked at our father the same after that.

Father sat quietly on the couch for the rest of his visit. He scratched the stubble on his chin one too many times, and his jaw tensed. I could tell he was deep in thought. It made me nervous to look at him as I chewed on my lip. He wasn't his jovial self, and he didn't try to tickle Bob and me. He seemed hurt. He looked wistful. We hadn't been to Olentangy Park since our mother left. Bob, Eleanor, and Charles were outside playing stickball in the front yard with other children in the neighborhood, but I sat with my father in the front room of the boarding house. I traced the lines on the palm of his hands with my finger, and then I played with his curly arm hair. "How come your arms are so hairy?" I asked. He laughed and hugged me, but then his eyes squinted and glazed over. I studied his melancholy face while Mrs. Spangler prepared supper. He suddenly looked different to me. He looked smaller. He looked weak for the first time. I wrapped my arms around his neck and kissed the back of it. He smelled like fresh soap. "When can we come home, Daddy?" He let out a heavy sigh and wrapped his arms around me. He didn't let go. When I pulled out of his hug, I noticed his eyes were wet.

"It's not time yet, sweetheart. I hate to say it, but it's not the right time yet. It's too soon. But Daddy misses you and loves you very much."

Then, he pulled me up to his shoulders, and I straddled them. I placed my hands on his head while I rode around on his shoulders. He pretended he was a horse as he snorted and rubbed his foot on the ground. It was one of my favorite games to play with him. I laughed when he neighed and whinnied as he walked out the front door to watch the children play stickball. Bob was running toward us. "Where are you going?" Father asked.

"To find another ball. We lost the one we had." Bob was breathing heavily and sweating.

"I'll help you!" I slid off my father's shoulders and ran after Bob. I found him in his bedroom, lying on the floor on his belly. Half of his body was under his bed. It looked like the bed was eating him! "Did you find another one?"

My throat narrowed when I saw Bob pull a bag of cat food out from under his bed. We looked at each other incredulously. "What? How did that get there? Did you find Tabby?"

"No," Bob said. His eyebrows pulled together, and he stared at me. "I threw this away last winter when Charles told me to." Bob wiped a bead of sweat from his brow and stood up. "How did this get back under my bed?"

I shrugged, "I didn't do it."

"Well, someone did! And I bet I know who."

"Who?" My eyes widened.

"Albert," Bob said to me knowingly. "I bet it was Albert. He wants me to get in trouble. He wants his mom to find it and whip me for not throwing it out. I hate her rotten son!"

"Or do you think he has Tabby hidden in his bedroom?"

"No, we would have heard her. I think he's just trying to get me into trouble. He loves watching us get into trouble, especially me." Bob shoved the cat food into one of his dresser drawers. "I'll get rid of it tonight." He turned to leave. The heaviness of his steps made me jump. I had never seen Bob so angry.

Before I left his room, I opened his drawer, scooped some cat food out with my hand, and put it in the pockets of my dress. I wasn't sure what I was going to do with it at the time, but I knew I wanted some.

Later, I pushed some kibble under Albert's door. "Tabby," I whispered from under his door. "Tabby!" I waved my fingers under the door and called her name over and over, but she never came. I badly wanted to feel her soft fur rub against my fingers. I wanted her to come to the food. I wanted to know she was okay. Once I realized she wasn't in Albert's room, I sat against his door and cried.

Chapter **26**

ONE SUNDAY IN THE FALL OF 1922, our father looked exhausted when he visited us. He had finished the construction of the new football stadium at Ohio State University and was working other construction jobs simultaneously. When I sat on his lap to snuggle with him, Mrs. Spangler demanded I leave my father alone because he looked drained. "Stella, get off of him. You're getting too big to sit on your father's lap," she snorted. I was only six years old.

"I didn't know there was an age limit," my father snapped.

Mrs. Spangler huffed at that comment. She could tell it upset my father. She squinted her eyes at him. Their relationship was evolving into something different. My father wasn't trying as hard to appease her. He wasn't hiding his true emotions as well as he once did. Mrs. Spangler was catching on, so she tried to deflect the situation. She told me to go to her bedroom and nap in her bed. I had already stopped taking naps, but I wanted to see her bedroom, and she knew I would love that. My father kissed my forehead and said he would see me when I woke. He was too tired to argue with Mrs. Spangler, even though he wanted to visit with me longer.

Initially, I hesitated to walk into her room because children were not allowed in her bedroom. It was off-limits to us, but then I scurried inside.

Even though I wanted to see my father, being allowed to lie in her bed seemed like a big treat. I wanted to explore her room, open the drawers and look in her closet, but I knew better. However, I peered inside her glass jewelry box. I saw different jewels, pretty earrings, necklaces, and bracelets. I couldn't help myself, so I lifted the lid and grabbed a necklace with an emerald stone. I placed it around my neck and admired myself in the mirror. I thought I looked beautiful. Suddenly, I heard a noise in the hallway, so I immediately dropped the necklace back into the jewelry box before slipping into her bed. "Who's there?" I asked. No one answered.

I squirmed around in her bed and shifted some more, trying to find a comfortable spot. I changed pillows and moved around again. Her sheets felt cool against my skin, and her blankets made me feel like I was in a cocoon. Lying in a real bed felt like a present. I turned over and noticed a picture of Mrs. Spangler, a man, and her son on her nightstand. They weren't smiling in the photograph and looked unhappy. Albert was a child in the photo. He looked to be around my age. I wondered if the man was his father. We didn't know much about him, other than that he was no longer living, and Mrs. Spangler seemed mad at him. Especially when she cursed the walls in her kitchen. It made me feel sad. Nobody in the boarding house liked Albert, though. He was mean and rude. Suddenly, I felt someone slipping into bed with me. It startled me initially, but I thought it was my father since he was tired. Maybe Mrs. Spangler told him to nap too. But when I turned, I saw it was not my father. A heavy body sat on top of me. It was Albert.

He smelled funny and had a devilish look on his face. *What's happening?* I thought to myself. Before I could speak, he covered my mouth with his hand and whispered in my ear, "Don't yell, or I'll kill you." His hand was pressed hard against my mouth. It was sweaty, and I felt the calluses on his hand against my lips. He pinned me to the bed with his other hand on my shoulder when he was on me. He warned me that he had a knife and would use it if I made a noise. A sudden surge of fright went through my entire body. My eyes opened wide, and my face tensed. I couldn't scream even if I tried because the weight from his body paralyzed me with fear. Then he whispered if I were good, I would get a huge piece of sponge cake with extra fruit that his mom had made earlier that day. I knew something felt wrong. My throat closed up, and I couldn't breathe. Then, my innocence was taken from me by an eighteen-year-old monster that Sunday afternoon.

I was lying motionless on his mother's bed after he left. I heard faint voices escaping from the kitchen, but I didn't want to hear what they were saying. I didn't understand why I was in Mrs. Spangler's bed. I tried to call out for my father, but my mouth wouldn't open. I couldn't muster the word "Daddy." I felt weak and sore, and I felt tired. *What happened?* I wondered, but my mind felt suffocated. I wanted to get up and run but couldn't move. My heart started thumping loudly, and I felt like it was pounding in my throat all the way to my ears. I squeezed my eyes shut and tried remembering why I was in Mrs. Spangler's bedroom. Then, I rolled over and slept.

I am unsure how long I slept, but I knew I wanted out of Mrs. Spangler's bed when I woke up. I limped to the water closet and shut the door. I slid down the bathroom wall and sat on the cold tile while I hugged my legs. I realized I was bleeding a little and felt sore below my belly, but I didn't understand why. I started humming to myself with my head between my knees. "Baa Baa Black Sheep" did not satisfy my pain. I rocked back and forth, squeezing my knees against my ears. A breeze blew through the open window. It made me shiver, and I held my knees tighter. I could hear children playing stickball outside. I was confused about why I wasn't with them. I wanted someone to find me. I wanted my father, but nobody came. *Daddy, Daddy, where are you?* repeated through my mind. Then, I cried, but it was a silent cry; only wet tears streamed down my face. I pictured the sponge cake my mother made me on my fourth birthday. I thought about how pretty it looked, decorated with fresh fruit, and how good it tasted. I wanted sponge cake.

My body mechanically made it to the attic. I looked out the window that overlooked Mrs. Spangler's front yard. I saw my father's car parked on the side of the street. I pressed my forehead against the cold glass of the window. My breath made a circular ring on it. I put my finger on the circle and traced the ring. "Daddy, Daddy, Daddy!" I yelled inside my head as I pressed harder against the window with my forehead. Then I heard my father's voice. He was saying something to Mrs. Spangler. I heard him say my name. I heard him ask about me. I heard him say he wanted to kiss me goodbye. But then I heard Mrs. Spangler's rancid voice. I heard her say, "Stella is still sleeping. She's probably not feeling well. I'll tell her you said goodbye when I go upstairs to check on her." Then I heard the bang of the storm door slam shut, and I watched my father walk to his car. I wanted him to look up and see me in the window. I wanted him to know that I was not sleeping. I wanted him to know I was in pain. I wanted him to know I was scared. But I didn't have the energy to scream for him. I closed my eyes, banged my head against the window and whimpered as I fell to the ground.

When I woke up, I was lying on the hard, cold attic floor. My body ached. The full moon shining brightly through the window gave me enough light to see the other children sleeping. I slowly walked to my straw mattress. I tucked my knees up as close as I could to get them to my chest and sucked my thumb. My mother had rid me of that habit, but it comforted me now as I hugged my knees. I wasn't afraid of being scolded for having my thumb in my mouth. It made me feel good while I tried to remember my day. I remembered Mrs. Spangler making a sponge cake with half-spoiled fruit on it, but I couldn't remember eating it. I wondered why I couldn't remember anything other than being sent to Mrs. Spangler's bed right after my father arrived.

I wondered why the vision of Albert was in my mind. Why do I smell him and his hot breath? I wondered why I woke up on the attic floor with pain below my belly. I was confused and scared. I sucked my thumb raw that night as I laid on my stick mattress and stared at the full moon. I wanted to be home. I wanted my father.

Chapter 27

I HAD A HORRIBLE DREAM THAT NIGHT, and when I woke up the next morning, my mind couldn't help but replay it in my head. It felt so real that I needed to convince myself that it didn't happen. I dreamt that I needed a tooth pulled by a dentist, so my father gave me two dollars to pay for it. When I reached the office, I went into panic mode. I couldn't find the two dollars. I searched my entire body for the money. I kicked off my boots and pulled my coat pockets inside out, but I couldn't find it. Then I heard the sound of cracking. It sounded like ice splintering. Suddenly, my mouth felt strange and full. I felt petrified. I knew something was very wrong. I looked into a mirror and saw my teeth breaking and falling out of my mouth. I tried stopping it. I tried to hold them in place, but I couldn't. Every tooth shattered and fell to the floor. I cried uncontrollably while I tried picking up my teeth. I screamed for help, but no one was there. And then I woke. I immediately felt my mouth. I touched every tooth with my tongue. They felt secure, so I wiggled each tooth with my finger, just to make sure. My mind felt anxious. I didn't feel I could leave the fetal position I was lying in. I was scared because the dream felt real, even though I knew it was only a dream. I was the only one in the attic. I could hear the other children and my siblings moving around in the house. Then I remembered it was a Monday. We had school.

I was walking slower than everyone else while we staggered to school that day. Charles and Eleanor kept looking back at me, and I didn't like how they looked at me. I felt like their eyes were burning me. It was a chilly morning, but I felt hot, and every place on my head itched. When my scalp tingled, I scratched it, then I scratched my chin, then my neck, then my eyebrow, and the side of my nose. I couldn't get the hot feeling out of my body and my itching to stop. I came to a halt.

"You're acting strange. What's wrong?" Eleanor asked. I didn't answer her. I could hear her, but I couldn't make my mouth work. I stared blankly at her and continued walking.

Then I felt Bob next to me. He grabbed my arm and whispered, "Please, tell me. Why didn't you eat dinner with us last night? Were you sleeping the whole time?"

I stared at Bob. He looked different to me. He wasn't smiling, and his curls weren't happily bouncing on his head like usual. "I don't know, but I feel itchy," was all that came out, and I walked away. A random tear slid down my face.

"What's going on with you?" Charles demanded in a voice that startled me out of my trance. He angrily wiped the single tear away from my face. My heart started thumping in my ears, and I felt nauseous. My limbs grew weak as Albert's face and bad breath intruded into my mind again. I was suddenly overcome with fear.

"I won't tell, I won't tell, I won't tell!" I blurted. I put my fingers in my ears and hummed loudly. Charles raised his eyebrows at my behavior. He grabbed my shoulders and shook me. I swayed back and forth, escaping his hold, and continued humming loudly with my fingers in my ears. I closed my eyes tightly while I swayed and hummed.

"Stop your nonsense," Charles bellowed. He hissed, "You're embarrassing me. People are watching! And we're running late for school." He pressed his hands on my shoulders. I didn't like that feeling. The pressure made me feel worse. I pushed his hands off of me. I wanted to run.

I stopped humming and opened my eyes. I stared at Charles, but my fingers were still in my ears. He looked like a scared little kid for the first time. He didn't look like Charles, which frightened me. My face grew tingly again, and I felt like I couldn't breathe. I opened my mouth, but then I closed it. I wondered if he was going to shake me again. I thought if he shook me hard enough, then I could escape from the fog I was suffocating in. But I didn't want him to touch me and he didn't. Instead, Bob and Eleanor grabbed my hands, and we walked to school without saying another word.

I didn't focus on my studies that day. I felt blind going through the motions of our daily routines. My first grade teacher asked me if anything was wrong, but I shook my head no. I knew she didn't believe me because she pressed her lips together, which looked like a thin line on her quizzical face. "Stella, are you sure you're all right?" she said with her hands on her hips. I nodded my head yes as I stared at the ground. I tucked a lock of my hair behind my ear. The brown leather hand-me-down boots I received from Eleanor were too big for me, and I felt a blister forming. *I must get thicker socks*, I thought to myself as I slipped into my private shell, where I felt safe. I was protected in that shell. I knew nobody would hurt me while I was hiding there.

Not long after that day at school, my teacher and another woman visited Mrs. Spangler at her house. I heard whispering when they met, and it was about me. I remember feeling scared that I was in trouble for something as I sat on the top step and listened from the second level. But I had no idea what it could be about. The meeting didn't last long. I ran and hid in the water closet when I heard Mrs. Spangler say, "I will keep a watchful eye over her, but she seems fine when she's here." Then I heard the click-clacking sounds of footsteps moving toward the front door and Mrs. Spangler slamming it shut. I waited for her to find me, but she didn't. She never told me what the meeting was about.

Every day was a blur for me after that, but I remember peanut butter. We were given two crackers with peanut butter smeared on top for a school snack. I loved the taste of peanut butter. I had never had it until elementary school. It was the only food I could stomach. I wasn't eating much. I think even Mrs. Spangler became a bit concerned. I wasn't asking annoying questions. I was unemotional when I played with Bob. I felt numb and machine-like. I didn't like the stares I received from the other children. It made me feel insecure, like I did something wrong, that I was a bad girl. I was always somewhat timid with people I didn't know, but I also wasn't the happy and outgoing tomboy I once was. I had become the twins and Samuel.

I was sitting on the second-level steps near the washroom waiting for my father one Sunday when I heard him say, "Mrs. Spangler, we need to talk," as he walked through the front door. "I've been thinking a lot about the children. Especially Stella. They look miserable when I visit, and they don't look happy when they see me anymore. Stella is too skinny. She hardly eats supper when I'm here. She's not right. Is there something I should know about?"

I slipped downstairs to eavesdrop. He sternly looked into her eyes so she couldn't avoid the conversation.

"No, everything is fine during the week, Frank. Maybe when they see you, they are reminded of their mother. Have you thought of that? Maybe they just miss her," she said deliberately. "I mean, what kind of woman just gets up and leaves her family behind?"

My father's eyes narrowed. "I'd prefer you keep my wife out of this." He walked out of the kitchen and sat on the front porch.

Mrs. Spangler decided it was time to move me into my father's old bedroom. She was hoping to rent it, but she felt she had no choice with my father's constant questions. That move made me closer to Albert's bedroom. Two years ago, I would have been elated to be out of the dreary attic and away from the children who wouldn't speak to me, but now I missed it. At least I felt safe there.

Albert was my monster now. In my dreams, the monster said, "Bye, bye little Stella," as he wagged his little finger at me. That was what he said to me when he left his mother's bedroom the first time he violated me. Those four words haunted me afterward. I woke from my nightmares with those words burning in my ears. "Bye, bye, little Stella" made an imprint that I couldn't erase. Every day, I lived in fear that I would hear those words spew out of his hot, smelly mouth again. I avoided Albert as much as I could. I hated living on Southwood Avenue with a monster and a witch that I couldn't escape from, not even in my dreams.

After I moved out of the attic, Albert hovered over me whenever we were in the same room. He stared at me with a smirk on his face. He eyed me with warning eyes. Then, about six months later, he assaulted me for the second time. It was before my seventh birthday. He snuck into the little bedroom I was sleeping in next to his mother's room. I woke to his sweaty, callused hand over my mouth. The devilish look on his face returned when he was staring down at me. I tried to squirm out of his hold, but I couldn't. My tiny body lay under his.

But then something different happened. My body drifted above me, and I climbed into another world. I was wearing a beautiful white silk dress trimmed in lace. I was in a lush garden that was full of daisies. I ran barefoot through the different mazes in the garden. A tiny angel appeared on my shoulder. She whispered, "This is not real. You are not Stella right now. Run as fast as possible and gather all the daisies that you can hold. Run, run and smell their wonderful fragrance! Close your eyes, smell the flowers, and hide them so nobody will find them. And then, you'll be Stella again. You can do this. The garden will keep you safe." The tiny angel's whispers comforted me, and I smiled at the little angel. I smelled the herbaceous green scent of the cheerful yellow-and-white daisies I collected in the garden, then hid them so nobody would find them.

After my seventh birthday, Albert didn't come into my room anymore. He was afraid his mother would find out. He started forcing me into his bedroom, where he could lock the door. But one night, he forgot to lock his bedroom door. I heard a faint noise from the hallway that interrupted my tiny angel's whispers soothing my ears. I saw the door crack open. Charles was peering through it! I felt paralyzed, but I wanted to yell his name. *Charles!* my mind screamed. *Charles, help me! Charles! Charles!* My mind yelled louder. I called for Charles over and over. But as quickly as I saw him peering through the door, he quickly left my sight. I felt betrayed by Charles. I grew confused. *This isn't real!* rang through my mind, and I drifted above my body.

"You're right, this isn't real. You need to run. You'll be okay if you run," my tiny angel whispered. "Ignore him. Ignore Charles, he can't help you. Find your daisies and smell them. Their wonderful fragrance will make you feel better. And then, you'll be Stella again."

Charles avoided me the next day. He refused to look at me from across the table when we ate dinner that evening. His face appeared pale, and he ate faster than usual. Then I stopped looking at him. My pleading eyes made me tired, and I didn't want to see his face anymore.

"Stella, eat your meal," Mrs. Spangler squawked. She sounded like the scary geese that were in her basement. "You're losing too much weight, and I'm tired of your father hounding me with questions! Oh, and when he visits this Sunday, try to look happy. I'm sick of seeing that depressed look on your face. It's getting to be a little too much."

I sat at the table with a scowl on my face. I pushed my food around on my plate. I felt like I was going to get sick looking at the room-temperature gravy over the mushy biscuit. I couldn't eat, and I was mad at Charles. I felt like he let me down when I needed him the most, like he stranded me on a desert island. I felt betrayed and alone. But what I didn't understand was that Charles was scared, and he was shocked by what he saw. He worked all day, pushing the sight out of his mind. He didn't want to picture it anymore. So he tore the sight out of his mind and threw it in the garbage like crumpled paper. *That never happened,* he told himself, and he never thought about it again. But I remained quiet in my silent torture. I withdrew deeper and deeper into my protective shell.

Chapter 28

ONE SATURDAY IN THE SUMMER OF 1923, we were sitting in the front room listening to a story on the radio when Eleanor screamed. We saw a woman peering through the window at us. At first, we were startled, but then Eleanor cupped her hands over her mouth and shrieked, "Oh my God, it's Mother!" My siblings ran to the window to get a better look, but she was already walking away. They hurried outside, but she disappeared in a parked automobile on the side of the street. I heard Eleanor scream, "Mother, wait! Come back!" She wailed as she raced after the car that pulled out of the parking spot and drove away from Southwood Avenue.

I heard a loud thud. Charles punched one of the pillars that stood outside the house. "I can't believe her," he bellowed. His knuckles bled as he stormed into the kitchen to wash them. Bob cried as he returned inside and sat next to me. Eleanor stormed through the front door sweaty and distraught. She ran to her bedroom. I remained silent, sitting on the dusty rug in the front room. I remember feeling scared, but I didn't recognize the face peeping through the window. I had forgotten what she looked like. It felt like having a case of blindness. It stole my ability to remember my mother's face. So, I remained in my private shell. I didn't want to leave it.

No one talked about seeing our mother when our father visited the next day. Bob didn't want to be tickled, and Charles and Eleanor weren't in the mood to play cards. They retreated to different areas of the house. I rode one of the tricycles in the backyard. It felt uncomfortable because my legs were too long for the trike. I looked like the twins when I saw them riding the tricycles when their legs were too big. I slowly rode in circles with no place to go. I didn't hum or sing. I just pedaled around with a blank stare on my face, just like the twins did when I first met them.

"Something doesn't feel right. Please tell me. Is there something going on that I don't know about? The children are worse today."

Mrs. Spangler shrugged. "Frank, you know Charles and Eleanor are almost in their teens. You know that's an awkward stage. I'm not sure what's going on with Bob, but I know Stella isn't doing well in school. She's failing her studies. She's probably afraid you'll find out."

When our father left that day, Charles walked him to his car. We watched from the front porch, Mrs. Spangler looming over us. We leaned forward and strained to listen to their conversation.

"Dad, we saw our mother yesterday. We caught her looking at us through the front window, but she left so fast we didn't have a chance to talk to her. Why would she do that? What do you think she wanted?" His eyes grew wide. My father shook his head incredulously and sighed. He wiped his brow and shook his head again. I watched the expression on his face change from bewilderment to anger to sadness when he spoke.

"I'm sorry, Charles. That wasn't fair. It must have been difficult for you all. Aunt Lucille told me about her father's death, your grandfather. She asked me where you were staying. I didn't think before I told her. I didn't know your mother was coming to Columbus to settle his estate. I can't speak to why your mother does what she does. I think she's dealing with her own issues. She has been for a while. But I know she loves all four of you. It's hard to understand but try not to dwell on what your mother does or doesn't do. I gave up trying to figure her out years ago. I know that sounds harsh, but it's the truth." I watched Charles hug my father. I could tell Charles wasn't satisfied with what our father said. His face was drawn up. He was stewing over something again. He shoved his hands in his pockets and kicked the dirt around on the ground while our father drove away. I locked eyes with him for the first time since the night he was in the hallway. I recognized the look in his eyes. They looked dark and cloudy at the same time. They looked sad and desperate. They looked like the way I felt every day.

Chapter **29**

I NOTICED A BOOK ON ALBERT'S BOOKSHELF called *The Incredible Book About Everyday Knots* next to a box of Lincoln Logs when he was on top of me one night before I left my body. A burning feeling ran down my throat, and I swallowed bile that turned my stomach. I stared at the book and the Lincoln Logs before my body went numb and floated above. My tiny angel whispered, "Knots, knots, knots, Stella. You must defeat your monster now. Read about the knots. Study how to make different kinds of knots. Knots can be your friend. Forget about the Lincoln Logs. You have something more important to do." My tiny angel suddenly seemed different. Her encouraging whispers sounded like demands as I listened to her. "This *is* real now, Stella, but you can do it. You are a strong and courageous girl. You must prepare yourself to defeat your monster. You can do it. He's stealing more than just your Lincoln Logs from you. Take back what belongs to you!"

After leaving Albert's room that night, I thought about what my tiny angel had said. I lay in my bed and thought about the Lincoln Logs he stole from Bob and me. And I realized Albert was stealing something more from me. Something more sacred. Something he shouldn't have. Something that only belonged to me. I slept a little sounder that night because I understood what she meant, and I was certain that I would take back what belonged to me.

The next day, I crept into his bedroom and stole *The Incredible Book About Everyday Knots*. I felt nervous entering his room; I hated being there. My heart pounded heavily in my chest as I slipped the book off the shelf. Then I grabbed the box of Lincoln Logs. I took the risk and didn't care if Albert noticed that they were missing. My pulse was rapid, and my hands were clammy as I scurried up the attic steps. I knew of good hiding places there. I was excited to tell Bob but then realized he might ask too many questions, so I decided not to. I felt sad that we couldn't play with the Lincoln Logs together, but I felt great triumph that I had them back. I liked the fact that I stole from Albert. I read and studied the book daily when no one was watching. The book taught me how to make many different types of knots, and it gave me comfort because I was developing a plan in my mind.

It was a chilling and dangerous plan to escape with Bob from Southwood Avenue. I imagined my plan over and over. I recited it in my mind when I was at school, when I was sitting in Mrs. Spangler's front room, before I fell asleep at night, wherever I was. First, we needed rope, lots and lots of rope, a heavy pot, and two handkerchiefs. I imagined the scenario with great detail. First, a hard whack to Albert's head with the heavy pot. It had to be hard, extremely hard, to knock him out. That would be Bob's job, but I would happily do it if Bob didn't want to. Then the rope. We needed lots of rope for my plan to work. I imagined Mrs. Spangler as a witch engulfed in flames with the rope tied around her to a tree. Then I imagined tying Albert's hands and feet with the rope, like a pig on a stick, and throwing him into the Olentangy River. And the handkerchiefs were the easy part; Bob and I would shove them into their mouths to keep them quiet. It was a frightening plan, but it gave me a sense of comfort when I needed it.

I loved to read books. I taught myself how to read at a very young age. Out of boredom, I started reading the McGuffey Readers series when I was home with my mother while my siblings were at school. But once my mother saw how fast I caught on to reading, she introduced me to more challenging books. Charles and Eleanor loved to read too, and they had many books that I gobbled down while they were at school.

I found pleasure in reading *The Incredible Book About Everyday Knots*. It wasn't the type of book I would pick to read on my own as a seven-year-old girl. I would have preferred a fairy tale, a mystery, or an adventure story. But I felt joy learning about the different knots and imagining my plan. It sounded morbid, but it made me happy. It was the only thing that made me happy then. It gave me strength when I needed to feel strength. It gave me courage when I needed to feel courage. It gave me hope when I felt hopeless. My aspiration was that one day, Bob and I would run away from Southwood Avenue and leave the torture behind. Leave the monster and the witch that haunted me daily to their own demise. The desire that I would return back to my old self that I missed gave me motivation, and I would break out of Albert's invisible claim over me.

Chapter 30

NOT LONG AFTER WE SAW OUR MOTHER peering through the window, Charles left the boarding house and moved home with our father. My other siblings and I were jealous. We wanted to go with him. We sat on Eleanor's bed and watched Charles walk around the bedroom, packing different belongings in his bag and taking them out again. He had a weird look on his face.

"What's wrong, Charles?" Eleanor asked. "I thought you'd be more excited to leave this awful place. You look like you don't want to leave."

Charles sighed heavily and looked at us. "I don't know. I thought I would feel happier. But I feel horrible leaving you." Our mouths gaped open, and our brows raised. Charles put a shirt in his bag and took it out. "Bob, why don't I leave you some of my clothes? I'm outgrowing most of them." It felt good to me that Charles was feeling bad. It was the first time I saw him look remorseful. I sat on Eleanor's bed and stared at him. He looked different to me. Or maybe I just felt different when looking at him. I didn't feel I needed him anymore. I didn't feel like I needed his approval. Bob was fidgeting on the bed. It was annoying me, so I got up to leave. But that's when I heard Bob ask Charles for help.

Bob asked him to tell our father how we were treated. He thought if our father knew the truth, he would allow all of us to come home.

"I don't think telling him the truth is a good idea. Mrs. Spangler would just deny everything. And think about it, Bob. Why do you think Dad keeps us here? He doesn't want Stella to be alone. I think he changed after Mother left. I think he thinks he can't handle raising four kids alone. I think he's scared. And I know Mother hurt him. That's why he never talks about her. She hurt him, and he knows she hurt us. I don't think he's been in his right mind since the night Mother left with Stella."

"Why only Stella?" Bob asked.

"I don't know. But our family has never been right. You probably don't remember, but I do. Something has always been off, especially with Mother."

"So you're not going to tell him about Mrs. Spangler?"

"No, I think that would be a huge mistake. She'll lie like always, and then she'll take her anger out on you. Just give it some more time. Let me do some thinking."

We stood on the front porch and waved goodbye to Charles when he looked back at us. All of our eyes were swelling with tears, even Charles. He looked stiff as he walked down the street. He stopped and turned toward us before he was too far away and yelled, "I'll come visit. This won't be the last time you'll see me. You'll be home soon too."

After he moved out of the boarding house, I came up with a plan to keep Albert away from me. "Bob, why don't you take my bedroom now that Charles is gone? I want to be with Eleanor, and my bedroom has a new mattress. You'll like it." Bob moved into the bedroom next door to Mrs. Spangler, and I moved in with Eleanor. Mrs. Spangler was furious that we made the move without her permission.

"It will please our father," I told her. "I'll feel happier being with Eleanor. I'll smile more, just like you asked." She sneered at me, but she didn't contest. She went back to the kitchen to finish her half-smoked cigarette.

I loved sharing a room with Eleanor. We slept in the bigger bed together, just like when we were home. I knew I was safe from Albert by sleeping with her. She spent more time with me and Bob. She played games with us when we weren't at school or working for Mrs. Spangler. Now that Charles was gone, Mrs. Spangler expected us to do more chores. Cutting wood for the winter was our favorite because we envisioned Mrs. Spangler's face on every piece of wood we split in half. I saw Mrs. Spangler and Albert's face in the wood. I was too young to chop the wood, so my job was to put the pieces into a pile on the side of the house. I loved piling up the wood, imagining the witch and the monster's cruel faces whenever I threw a piece of wood onto the other.

"Albert is strange, isn't he?" Eleanor asked me one evening in our bedroom while brushing my hair. "Why do you think he's always staring at you? He doesn't talk to anyone in the house, but I often catch him staring at you." I thought about telling her the truth about Albert. I wanted reassurance that what he was doing to me was not normal. I wanted to tell her about Charles and how he let me down. I wanted to ask her if Charles was just scared like me. I wanted to tell her about my tiny angel. I wanted reassurance from Eleanor that my angel was right. But then fear and shame overtook me, and I decided not to say anything.

"I don't know why," I lied, but I wondered if she was suspecting something. Even if she did, Eleanor didn't press me for more information. It disappointed me that she didn't.

A year later, Eleanor moved home with our father and Charles. I was sad when I heard the news because Albert was not abusing me with Eleanor around. The day Eleanor left was an emotional day for Bob and me. Mrs. Spangler could tell we were upset and told us we could go with Eleanor too. We couldn't believe it! We ran upstairs to pack our belongings.

"Stella, this is great! I'm so happy we're leaving too!" My heart raced with excitement. I eagerly stuffed my best clothing into a bag.

"Come on, Bob, let's go!"

Then we heard Mrs. Spangler summon us as we walked down the steps with our bag of clothes. "Come say goodbye to my sweet Eleanor," Mrs. Spangler said sarcastically with wicked laughter.

As we ran down the steps, Bob asked, "What do you mean say goodbye? We are going with her. You said we could." We saw Eleanor standing by the front door with her small suitcase and a frown on her face. "Eleanor, wait, we're coming too."

Mrs. Spangler let out an evil laugh. "No, you aren't. You're staying here with me. Why would you think you could leave? It's not your time yet. Social services would find you. You're stupid kids. Unpack those bags and help me with dinner."

We were devastated. A tear crawled down both our faces as we embraced Eleanor and hugged her goodbye. But Eleanor stood tall and had a reassuring look on her face. When she hugged us, she whispered different messages to each of us, and they were important messages.

"Bob, keep watch over Stella. I'm worried about her. I don't like the way Albert looks at her." Bob hugged her and nodded his head.

"I will," he whispered back into her ear.

She then hugged me. "You're a smart and strong girl. Don't forget that." Then her last sentence surprised me. Eleanor cupped her hand around my ear, and her whisper grew quieter when she said, "There's rat poison in the basement on the top shelf where the cleaning supplies are kept."

Mrs. Spangler leaned in closer to try to hear. "What are you whispering about?"

"Nothing you'd care about," Eleanor sneered. Then, she placed her hand on the door handle and waited for a second before she turned to Mrs. Spangler, "You better keep a better eye on your son. He's stealing from you. He knows where you hide your money."

Bob cupped his hands over his mouth and chuckled. We were surprised that Eleanor tattled on Albert. Mrs. Spangler huffed and then half-ran into the kitchen. She was wearing the same shoes she had on the day we met her. They squeaked to the kitchen and then all over the kitchen floor. We heard her cursing while cabinets and drawers were opening and slamming shut.

"What are you looking at?" she spat at us as she rushed up the steps to her bedroom and slammed her door shut.

We stood on the front porch, and quiet tears rolled down our faces. We waved goodbye to Eleanor as she walked down the street. But I was also thinking about what she had said to me. My mouth watered, and my head spun with thoughts about rat poison. *The Incredible Book About Everyday Knots* didn't seem important anymore.

Chapter **31**

"DON'T MOVE, DON'T MOVE, DON'T MOVE," I repeated to myself every night as I watched the doorknob from my bed. If I saw the doorknob move, I knew what to expect, it would be Albert. I stared at my doorknob every night with nausea and prayed I didn't see it shift. Now that Eleanor was gone, Albert was my monster again. Mrs. Spangler moved me back into the small bedroom attached to her room because two young brothers moved in. They shared the other room with Bob. They were waiting to be placed with someone. We didn't know much about them other than their mother died.

I thought about rat poison every day. I thought about it every time I saw Albert's disgusting face. My tiny angel disappeared, and I no longer heard her whispers. I don't know why she left. I developed a new way that helped me escape when he was on me. My imagination helped me pretend Albert was my husband, but he was very mean. So, I decided to poison him slowly. I sprinkled a little rat poison on the food I prepared for him. I was careful not to put too much in, so he didn't taste it. I laughed to myself every time I watched him take a bite. "Honey, this is delicious! It tastes a little different, but it's good."

"Thank you. I made it special just for you. I hope you like the new spices." I winked at him with a sly smile.

And in my imagination, Albert was becoming weaker and weaker until he died. These scenarios I created in my mind helped me in many ways. They put me to sleep at night. They kept my mind busy at school. They kept me from feeling the abuse when it happened.

Once, I got the nerve to ask Albert, "Why do you do this to me? Why me?"

He answered, "Because I can." I didn't understand what he meant. He made me feel ashamed. I felt guilty and mad at myself for not trying to stop him when it first started. I wanted to tell someone badly, but I was embarrassed. I was afraid no one would believe me.

My life was a nightmare you can't wake from. I was too skinny, and my body felt weak and tired all the time. Every day, I felt a sense of loss, like a part of my soul was being chipped away. I continued to mourn for my old self. I missed my father but was also angry with him. I was angry that he moved us to Southwood Avenue. But I was angrier at my mother since she was the reason we moved. Her rebellion changed our family. Her mutiny from my father changed my life.

But it got to the point that I didn't want to cry anymore. Crying didn't help me, so I stopped. I remember once my teacher at school told someone, "Crying over it won't make it clean." I wondered what she meant by that, but I was too afraid to ask. I felt like the kids at school didn't like me, except for a girl named Nancy. We sat beside each other in class and played together. The twins and Samuel were finally adopted by a family in Upper Arlington, so they stopped attending my school.

Bob wasn't getting along with the two brothers he shared a bedroom with. He asked Mrs. Spangler to move them to the attic, but she said no because they weren't going to stay for much longer. "Why do you think she said the boys aren't staying for much longer? Do you know where they are going?" Bob asked me.

"I don't know, but something seems different with her. She's lost weight and is coughing a lot. I don't know what's going on with her, but she's not the same."

I often wondered if she knew what Albert was doing to me. Or, if I told her, would she believe me? She might have asked Albert to hurt me in the first place because she never liked me. Maybe that was what Albert meant when he said, "Because I can."

One afternoon, when Bob and I were walking home from school, we saw Albert with his friends across the street from Southwood Avenue. They were leaning against the side of a brick building, smoking cigarettes. When Albert noticed me, he stared straight through me. He wagged his little finger at me and then laughed. My face grew a deep shade of red. He turned and whispered something to his friends. *What did he tell them?* I wondered. He was snickering. I felt angry. I felt like I wanted to scream. I wanted to push him through the brick wall he was leaning against. My stomach turned, and I looked away. I pressed my lips together so hard I felt like my teeth would cut through them. Bob asked me what was wrong.

"Nothing," I said. "Let's walk faster, I don't want to be late." I grabbed his hand, and we silently walked to the boarding house.

Mrs. Spangler was waiting for us at the front door with her arms crossed. She glared at us as we walked through the door and yelled, "Where have you been, you little shits? You're supposed to be sweeping the floors." She grabbed the broom that was resting against the wall and started hitting us with it, but she was hitting us with the head of the broom. Bob started laughing at that, which flustered her. Then, she turned the broom over and continued hitting us with the wooden handle. "Why are you getting home from school so late?" she scolded. The whacks to my shoulders and back hurt, but not as bad as being spanked with the rod. Mrs. Spangler also wasn't hitting us as hard as she used to. She started wheezing and coughing. She covered her mouth with a handkerchief and coughed up phlegm. She couldn't stop coughing. It looked like she was choking on whatever she coughed up. She lost her energy and stopped.

"We aren't late!" Bob yelled as he pointed to the clock hanging on the wall. When she turned to look at the clock, Bob grabbed the broom from her. She glanced at the clock and then lazily walked to her armchair. She sat down on the edge of it. She was sweating. She looked pale. She then reclined in the chair with her face in her hands. She was wheezing and coughing again. Then, she started crying, but Bob and I didn't care. We wanted her to cry because we despised her. I would have felt sorry for her if she was nice. Then, her cries soon turned into uncontrollable wails.

She started screaming, but there was a rattle in her scream. It sounded different, and then it gurgled. Both hands were on her forehead when she wheezed, "I hate my life! I hate my life! I hate my life!" Bob and I stared at her while she slouched in her chair and cried. Her behavior was always unpredictable, so we weren't surprised, but I was somewhat scared. I didn't feel scared she would do anything to us, I was scared of what she was going to do to herself.

"Stop looking at me," she grunted when she finally stood up and walked to the kitchen. We waited for a second, and then we quietly peeked through the doorway. She was banging her head against the kitchen table; a glass of whiskey sat in front of her next to an ashtray full of her cigarette butts.

"Do you want us to go outside and leave you alone?" Bob asked. She didn't respond. She whimpered into her hand. "Can I help you to your chair? I'll turn the radio on." She nodded.

Bob and I helped her walk back into the front room. We knew she would go right to sleep because we smelled whiskey on her breath, and she shuffled uneasily, like she had too much to drink. I sat on the other chair and turned the radio to her favorite station. Bob went back into the kitchen to empty her ashtray and put the whiskey away. Then, Albert walked through the front door with the same disgusting, smug look he always wore. He tried to wake his mom, but she didn't budge. He sat across from me on the couch and stared at me.

"I saw you walking home from school today," he snickered. "I know you saw me. I saw you looking at me. You looked like a scared little lamb."

Bob walked into the front room at that moment. He heard what Albert said, and he noticed how he looked at me. Then Bob asked him a dangerous question he should not have asked. "Why do you always stare at my sister? You're always staring at her, and I want to know why."

"I don't, you little shit. Mind your own goddamn business." Before Bob could respond, Albert got up from the couch, grabbed Bob around his throat, and pushed him against the wall where the wallpaper was peeling off. He squeezed Bob's throat with both hands, and his face turned a deep crimson color. I started to panic, and my body froze. I wasn't sure if I could move or pull myself off the chair to rescue Bob.

"Stop!" I blurted. Bob put his arms behind him, ripped some of the dangling wallpaper off, and crumbled it into Albert's mouth. Spent adrenaline drained Albert's body and shock took over. He didn't expect Bob to fight back, so he released his hold on him when he spit the wallpaper out.

"Bob, let's get out of here before he tries to kill you!" I screamed.

Bob coughed and rubbed his throat. His blond curls dripped with sweat. "You're crazy, just like your crazy mother," he gasped.

Albert ignored Bob's comment. He spit on the floor again and glared at us. Then he looked at me with the same smug smile.

"Don't wait up for me." He wagged his little finger at me. "Bye, bye, little Stella," he said as he walked out the front door. Mrs. Spangler stirred a bit when the front door slammed shut. She mumbled something under her breath and moved her head from side to side. But she slept through the whole commotion.

Chapter **32**

SINCE OUR FATHER DISLIKED HOW SAD WE LOOKED when he visited us on Sundays, he started taking us to his friend Ed Chaplin's house after Charles and Eleanor moved home. He picked us up around eight in the morning, so we spent the entire day away from Southwood Avenue. We had great meals there, much better than anything Mrs. Spangler made. They had children around our age in their neighborhood, so we played with them. Mr. Chaplin was a handy guy. He made bikes for Bob and me from parts of other used bikes he collected. Mr. Chaplin's house was on a paved street, making riding bikes smoother and more fun. We raced each other up and down the street, hooting and hollering all the way. I loved feeling the fresh air flow through my hair when we rode fast. We kept the bikes in his garage so we could use them when we visited. His wife also bought us a new pair of roller skates. I never received a present like that—a present I got just because someone wanted to be nice.

Ed and Nora Chaplin had three children. Bob and I played with the younger two because they were around our age. Their oldest son was Charles's age. He didn't play with us, but he was nice. His name was Curtis. He read a lot of books. I liked talking to him about the different books he read. Then he offered something extraordinary. He gave me the ones that he had read. I was thrilled to have my own books because I had none. He had so many that I could not take all of them at once. I picked out a new stack to take to the boarding house every Sunday. When we returned there, I hid them so Albert and Mrs. Spangler wouldn't find them. After I read a stack of books, I gave them to Eleanor and Charles. They visited us at the boarding house on Saturdays, but it felt more like they were checking in on us. They never stayed long, but I always looked forward to their visits.

On one Saturday, only Charles showed up. He brought us candy my father had given him. We sat on Mrs. Spangler's front porch so she wouldn't see us eating it.

"What's going on with her?" Charles asked. "She looks different and coughs a lot."

"We're not sure," Bob answered. "But we think she's sick with something serious. She sleeps more and doesn't have the energy to discipline us like she used to. Father hasn't noticed the change in her since we've been going to Mr. Chaplin's house on Sundays. I thought about telling him what was going on, but I didn't. I don't want him to be concerned about her because you know how he is. Oh, Charles, I have something to show you. I'll be right back."

After Bob went into the house, I asked, "Why do you think Bob said that? That he didn't want Father to be concerned about her."

"Probably because if he knew she was sick, he would stop taking you to the Chaplins. He would want to see her. Even though Dad doesn't like her, he still cares for people. He would want to help her somehow."

I suddenly felt the blood in my body growing hot, and my lips tightened. A pit had already formed in my stomach. I squeezed my eyebrows together when I asked, "Then why didn't you help me that night? You know, the time I was trapped in Albert's room, and he was on top of me." I couldn't believe I said that. My stomach turned, and I felt my face tense, and my throat closed.

Charles's face went white. He shifted his position in his chair and looked down. His breathing grew heavy, and he stopped making eye contact with me. "I don't know what you're talking about. I never saw you in his room."

"Yes, you did, and he was hurting me, and you saw. Why didn't you help me?"

"Stella, I don't know what you're talking about," he stammered. "Maybe you're confused. I've never seen you in Albert's bedroom."

Unknowingly, Bob halted my conversation with Charles. "Mr. Jackson gave me a new comic. Look!" he said.

I was a little upset Bob came back so quickly because I wanted to say more to Charles. But I also felt like he had already silenced me. I was angry with him, just like that night at the supper table. He made me feel insignificant. He made me feel embarrassed for even asking him, as if I were lying about it. Why would he do that to me? Charles and I never spoke about it again. I wanted to leave and hide in my protective shell at that moment, but I didn't. I just glared at him. I stared right through Charles while he and Bob talked about the stupid comic book. Charles knew I was glaring at him. I could tell by how many times he shifted in his seat. My face was tense, but not as tense as his.

Chapter 33

"DON'T MOVE, DON'T MOVE, DON'T MOVE," I repeated while watching the doorknob. I thought for sure I would see it move that night. Then I heard the creaking sound of the doorknob turning. I held my breath and pretended to be asleep, even though that never worked. But to my surprise, it wasn't Albert, it was Bob. He was sweaty and breathing heavily. His face was flushed when he asked me if I was okay.

"Yes, what's wrong?" I asked him.

"I don't know. I just woke up from a terrible dream, and I felt the sudden urge to check on you," he replied. "Are you sure you're okay? You seem startled."

"I'm okay, but don't leave. Come lie on the opposite end of my bed, you know, head to toe, like we do on the sofa." Bob crawled into bed with me and slept in my bedroom for the rest of the night.

The following day, he told me his horrible dream involved me. He said something was wrong with me but he didn't know what it was.

"The night Eleanor left, she told me to watch over you. She told me she didn't like how Albert looks at you, and I don't either. I know I can move home soon, but I'm not leaving you here. I think we should run away. Not run away, I mean go to Dad's house. We're not little kids anymore. You can take care of yourself, and I know I can. Who cares if social services get involved? We'll just hide from them if they visit the house."

"What do you think Dad will say when we come home? What if he sends us back here?"

"I don't think he will once he finds out how sick she is. She's not even babysitting or renting rooms anymore now that those two horrible brothers are gone. It's just us. We don't need to stay here. I already have a plan put in place. We just need to pick the right time." I wanted to tell Bob about the plan I had envisioned with the ropes, the fire, and the river, or just using the rat poison in the basement, but I realized I couldn't. It sounded crazy, and Bob would ask me why my plan was so morbid. Then I would have to tell him about Albert and why I hated him so much. And then that would make it feel real, and I wasn't ready to make it real yet. I wondered if Bob would look at me differently if I told him, and I didn't want that.

Our father focused on making extra money by working multiple construction jobs to buy land on Buckeye Lake. It was his dream to build a house next to the lake someday. In 1924, he helped renovate the local YMCA, and he helped build North High School, which became Everett Junior High School. The school was constructed on Arcadia Avenue, east of High Street. Then, he helped build another high school because Columbus was booming with people moving into the city. It was called South High School and constructed on Ann Street the same year. Ann Street was close to Southwood Avenue. Occasionally, my father took Bob and me to his work sites on Saturdays because we loved walking through the constructed buildings. It was great fun imagining how the building would look once completed. We also loved leaving Southwood Avenue whenever we could escape the dreadful house. Mrs. Spangler's coughing all the time irritated my ears. She stopped wearing her usual outfits and walked around the house in her nightgown with a bottle of whiskey in one hand and a cigarette in the other. She looked like a walking corpse.

"Your father is here!" she hacked while looking out of the front window one Sunday morning. "Don't be too long at that Ed's house today. I have chores for you to do when you return."

"Why doesn't Albert have any chores? He's your son. Dad is paying you money to take care of us, not to treat us like servants," Bob said.

"What he does or doesn't do is none of your goddamn business, you little shit!" she said as she tugged hard on Bob's earlobe. "You're lucky I didn't smack that smirk off your face."

"You're lucky we don't tell our father how you treat us," he said with a squinted eye. The older Bob got, the more he wasn't afraid of Mrs. Spangler. He reminded me of Eleanor.

"Tell him, for all I care! He won't believe you after I have a word with him." Then she bent down and grabbed me around my chin so I would have to look in her dark and scary eyes. "Tell him, Bob, and then see what will happen to Stella if you do."

"I'm not gonna tell him. I'm just saying you should be nicer to us because we aren't telling him," Bob said.

"Go on. Get out of here, you little shits. Get back at a decent hour. I'll need help with supper," she said as she coughed into her handkerchief. Bob and I ran through the front door to our father's car. Bob waved at Mrs. Spangler as we watched her standing in the window watching us.

"Bye bye, you little shit," Bob whispered only loud enough for me to hear. Then we started giggling.

"What's all that laughing about?" Father asked.

"Nothing," Bob said. "We're just glad to be with you. But we have to be back earlier today to help Mrs. Spangler cook supper."

"She looked different when I saw her in the window. Why does she need you back early and to help with dinner? We usually eat with the Chaplins."

"I don't know, Dad. It's probably because her stupid, lazy son is not helping her with dinner anymore," Bob lied. Albert never helped with dinner.

"How many people are renting rooms from her now?"

"I don't know. It comes and goes," Bob lied for the second time. He gave me a pointed stare to keep quiet, and I did. I figured he had his reasons why he wasn't telling our father the truth.

In April 1925, on my ninth birthday, my father, Charles, and Eleanor surprised me with a wonderful gift. He bought me a new bike. It was the first expensive gift I had ever received. It was a Colson Fairy bicycle, and I loved it. "Daddy, thank you so much!" I said as I hugged him. My father held on to my embrace longer than usual. I was over the moon with excitement! We celebrated my birthday at our father's house that year. I told him it would be more special for me to be at his house. Bob and I took turns riding on Frebis Avenue and Ann Street all day. When it was time to leave, I rode the bike back to Southwood Avenue, and Bob ran next to me. We parked it in the backyard.

The next day, before it was time for us to leave for school, we found the Colson Fairy on the side of her house. The front fork and handlebars were bent, the chain was disconnected, and the tires were slashed. Rage took over me. I screamed for Mrs. Spangler.

"Look what your son did to my new bike!" I was sure it was him. He was capable of anything, and torturing me was his favorite hobby.

"Albert didn't do that," Mrs. Spangler snorted. I knew there was no point in arguing with her, but I was mad.

"Yes, he did! I know it was him! It's always him! He's a monster!" I screamed as I stormed past her and ran to my bedroom, slamming the front door behind me. She was quick on her heels and followed right behind me. Her walk quickened, and she didn't seem as frail as usual. She threw open my dresser drawers, yanked my clothes out, and threw them like she was a mad teenage girl with nothing to wear. With every piece she tossed out, she yelled obscenities at me.

"Then leave, you little shit! Leave!" she spat as she threw my clothes at me. "Take your trash and leave!" I covered my head with my hands, wondering if she was going to hit me. "You're not my problem anymore. I have enough of my own problems," she yelled as she hurled the last piece of clothing I owned at me. I was speechless. I didn't know what to do. I stood and stared at the heap of clothing that sat at my feet. Mrs. Spangler stormed out of my bedroom, and then we heard her slam her bedroom door shut. Bob grabbed my hand and motioned for us to leave. As we walked to school, he assured me that Mr. Chaplin could fix the bike. A sick feeling was forming inside my stomach, and my mouth watered like I was going to throw up. I could hardly concentrate on what Bob was saying to me. I didn't want to go to school. I wanted to run. I wanted to run home to our father's house.

"Bob, I hate her. I hate her son, and I hate her stupid house. I want to be home with Father. I can't stay here anymore."

"I know," Bob said. "We won't. It's time now. We'll leave tonight."

After school that day, I found Bob trying to fix my bike on his own. His blond hair was wet from sweat, and he looked frustrated. He didn't know I was watching him. I stared at him for a while because he reminded me of my father. When he noticed me watching him, he smiled at me. "Hi, Stella. I fixed some of the parts that he damaged and the bike's frame the best I could, but the tires are still deflated. We'll have to buy new ones. I'm sure Dad will help with that."

"Thank you! It looks so much better. We're leaving tonight, right? I can't bear to be here for another day. I don't care if Father is cross with us for leaving."

"Yes, we are. And I was just going to say that too," Bob said.

Chapter 34

BOB TOLD ME NOT TO PACK A BAG the night we left Southwood Avenue. He said we didn't want to look suspicious while walking home if someone saw us. "Why would we want anything from this place anyway? Just a few clothes will do," he said. "Let's wait until everyone is asleep, and then we'll leave." The blood running through my veins felt hot with anticipation when he said that. I had never run away before. I was scared of getting caught, even though I wanted out of the boarding house. Then it occurred to me what the date was. It was the day after my birthday. The same date when my mother ran away from our family.

While we ate dinner, we listened to the radio with Mrs. Spangler. *The Eveready Hour* was playing in the background. She could barely eat and looked even more frail. We suspected she was sick from smoking so much. She carried the same handkerchief with her to cough into. Most times, she coughed up blood. She tried hiding it from us but wasn't very good at it, especially since I did the wash. I would have felt sorry for her if she hadn't been so cruel to us. She didn't look at us or speak to us during dinner, but we didn't look at her either. I felt nervous about our plan. Every time I looked at Bob, he nodded at me and gave me a reassuring smile.

Albert walked into the kitchen while we were finishing eating. He grabbed a piece of biscuit off my plate and plopped it in his mouth. Then he spit it on the floor with disgust and wiped his mouth. "It's cold," he complained.

"Mine's hot, Albert," his mother said to him as she pushed her plate toward him and coughed. Albert slid a chair around and straddled it as he ate the rest of his mother's dinner. He stared at me with every bite, so I focused on my cold plate of food. I could hear Bob stirring in his chair.

"Hey, little Stella," Albert said with a wag of his finger when he drank from his mother's teacup. He made a face. I suspect it had whiskey in it. He shoveled her food in his mouth as he stared at me. I got up from the table and cleaned my plate. Bob did too, and then we walked to the front room.

"Don't take my chair by the radio," Mrs. Spangler hacked as she sat at the kitchen table, resting her head in her hand.

Bob and I sat in the front room, patiently waiting for Albert to leave. We could hear him rummaging through his mother's drawers in her bedroom. We knew he was looking for money. Then Mrs. Spangler lumbered into the living room and plopped into her chair. She fell right to sleep. I squirmed when I heard Albert's loud footsteps stomp down the stairs. He sat next to me on the couch. He put his arm on the back of it behind my head. He smirked at Bob and asked, "How long has my mom been asleep?" Bob ignored his question. Albert walked over to his mom and tried to wake her, but she slept soundly in her chair and didn't wake. "That bratty sister of yours told my mom I knew where she hid her money. Now I can't find any," Albert said as he walked into the kitchen, opening and slamming cabinets shut. "Bitch," he hissed and then walked back into the living room. Albert grinned, wagged his little finger at me, and said, "Don't wait up for me, little Stella." He walked toward the door.

That's when Bob sprang off the floor and jumped on Albert's back. "Don't you look at my sister! Don't you talk to my sister! Don't go near my sister!" Bob yelled as he hung onto his shoulders. It didn't take long for Albert to turn around and put Bob in a headlock. Bob's feet shuffled below him as he looked up at Albert. His face was flushed and sweaty. They were each wrestling to gain control. Albert's mom stirred.

"What's going on?" she asked.

"Nothing," Albert said as he released Bob. She coughed into her handkerchief and fell back to sleep after saying something in German.

Albert stared at me like he wanted to kill me. I nervously said, "Bob, Albert doesn't bother me, so don't worry about him. Everything's fine." Bob knew I was lying, but he didn't challenge me. Albert's expression changed, and then he opened the front door, turned around, wagged his little finger at me, and left with the door slamming shut behind him. I thought to myself, *I will never see that stupid little finger again.*

Bob and I immediately looked at each other and knew this was the opportunity to leave. We quietly walked upstairs to our bedrooms. As discussed earlier, we did not pack a bag, but we put on a few layers of our best clothes. I shoved my Raggedy Ann doll and my teddy bear inside my coat before I buttoned it. We crept down the steps together, holding our breath. My face tensed up, and I gave Bob a scared look. He gave me a reassuring nod. "It's okay," he mouthed.

We had to walk through the front room where Mrs. Spangler was sleeping in her chair. I was terrified she would wake up and catch us. We crept to avoid making any noise. I was afraid we would run into Albert after we left. He often hung out with friends close to his mom's house. Bob slowly opened the front door and then the screen door, motioning for me to go first. We slipped out and looked around to see if anyone was watching us. By then, the Hendersons had moved out of their house, so we knew they weren't watching. We crept off the front porch and retrieved my bike. Bob pushed it as it wobbled down Southwood Avenue toward Ann Street. A loud crack of thunder roared in the background, and we jumped. We looked up at the dark sky and saw a streak of lightning splinter through the ominous clouds that were moving quickly. I shuttered as rain began to fall. It came down slow at first, and then it poured.

"Bob, I'm scared!" I yelled over the loud booms of thunder. "It feels like it's raining sideways. It's hitting my face so hard, I can barely see." Our layers of clothing became soaked. I felt heavier and heavier as each layer absorbed the rainwater.

"I know. Just keep walking," Bob screamed breathlessly as he turned around to check on me. I could tell he was struggling with pushing the bike up Ann Street. Puddles of rain were everywhere, and we couldn't avoid stepping in them. My feet felt like prunes inside my boots. It reminded me that I had forgotten to put on layers of socks.

Once we reached the corner of Ann Street and Frebis Avenue, we looked at each other incredulously. We were soaking wet and looked like drowned rats as we turned right on Frebis Avenue. "We've made it this far," Bob gasped from exhaustion from pushing my bike. "But we still have a little way to go. I wish we could run, but I can't with the bike."

"I don't think I could run if I wanted to. I'm soaked to the bone, and my clothes are heavy on me. And I'm getting scared again. I'm happy but scared at the same time. What if Father sends us back?"

"He won't. Everything will be okay, trust me. Nothing bad will happen to us ever again." I tried to take turns pushing my bike with Bob, but he wouldn't let me. The rain let up and sprinkled down on us as we walked on Frebis Avenue. We were close to our father's house. My walk felt lighter. We breathed in the air a little differently that night. We felt like caged birds that were finally free.

Chapter 35

WHEN WE ARRIVED AT OUR FATHER'S HOUSE, we were dripping wet and out of breath. Charles was sitting on the front porch as if he were waiting for us to come home. When he saw us, he ran inside and yelled for our father. Bob carried my bike up the porch steps and parked it in the corner of the front porch. Our father and Eleanor greeted us at the front door.

"Bob, Stella, what's going on? Why are you here?" Father asked.

Bob looked down and saw the pool of water that was forming around our feet. "We're sopping wet, Dad, I don't want to track this into the house." He wiped his brow and gave a shivering smile. "But we're home!" he said with excitement and a bit of uncertainty in his voice. "We can't live there anymore. Mrs. Spangler is sick, really sick, so we left. We want to be home with you. Why do you look funny? Are you angry with us?"

"No, of course not. I'm just surprised. We will need to discuss this more later. Why are you wearing layers of clothing? Does Mrs. Spangler know you left?"

"Yes," Bob said and gave me a warning look not to tell the truth. "She can't take care of us anymore because she's so sick. We didn't have a bag to pack our belongings, so we just picked our nicest clothes to bring home."

"Eleanor, grab them a towel and something to put their wet clothes in." Our father scratched his forehead. He looked concerned, and you could tell he was deep in thought. "Maybe I should stop by her house tomorrow. Are you sure she knows you left? I'm not sure if this is the best idea."

"Dad, it's fine. She practically told us to leave. She said she was unable to care for us and to go home. She's not renting out rooms anymore. We're old enough now to care for ourselves. Everything will be fine. You don't need to check on her tomorrow."

Bob and I were thrilled to be home! It didn't take long for us to feel like our old selves again. We quickly made friends with the children who lived on our father's street. We played outside with them every day and roller-skated on the brick road. Soon after we moved home, we were incredibly excited when the road got paved. We could skate smoother and faster, and our bikes rode better. We played outside until 10:00 p.m. most nights, but then Charles told us that things were getting out of hand. He scolded us frequently about staying out too late in the evenings, especially on school nights. It felt like he was trying to take the role of our father. But Bob and I didn't care what Charles said, and if our father was okay with us staying out late on a school night, we did. I was trying to break free of the protective shell I hid inside.

When I went to bed at night, I finally felt safe. I no longer stared at the doorknob and prayed. However, I continued to have insomnia. I couldn't sleep because nightmares of Southwood Avenue plagued my dreams. So, I figured the later I stayed up, the fewer dreams I would have, but that was not the case. When I did fall asleep, my dreams were about the horrors I went through on Southwood Avenue. My dreams were always the same. I was in Mrs. Spangler's basement, hiding from Albert. He called my name while trying to open the basement door. I couldn't get the door to stay closed. No matter how hard I tried, the basement door refused to stay put, so I pulled hard on the doorknob to keep it shut, listening to Albert on the other side. His evil, monster voice was whispering my name outside the door.

"Stella, oh little Stella ... I'm not gonna hurt you ... Stella, come on, little Stella ... let me in, little Stella." Then, my dream shifted to being in Mrs. Spangler's bedroom, and I couldn't get her door to stay locked. He pushed his body against the door, and the harder I tried to keep it shut, the harder he would push on it. "Stella, oh little Stella ... I'm not gonna hurt you ... Stella, come on, little Stella ... LET ME IN!" the monster roared. I always woke up at that exact same moment in my dream. It was right when he pushed through the door and grabbed me around my throat. I woke up with a pounding heart and shivering with anxiety from those dreams. My nightgown would be soaked with sweat, so I always had to change into a new one. My heart thumped so loudly it felt like it was in my throat. I placed my hand over my throat and felt the sensation of it pulsing. The pounding kept me from falling back to sleep. It felt strange. I didn't know your heart could pound in your throat. Sometimes, it also pounded in my ears. I tried taking deep breaths to make it disappear, but that didn't work. I switched positions a dozen times, trying to find solace but never could. I would finally get out of bed and find a book to read. Charles and Eleanor still had the books from Curtis. Even though I read them all, I picked one of my favorites and reread the book until my eyes grew tired and burned. Then I lay in bed and closed my eyes, but sometimes they wouldn't stay shut. I would study the different shadows that danced across the floors and walls of my room. Sometimes, I whispered Eleanor's name, hoping she would wake, but she didn't.

Chapter **36**

OUR FRIENDS CAME OVER AND ASKED US TO PLAY hide-and-seek one evening. Bob didn't want to play for some reason, and Charles told us we should go to bed because we had school the next day. But it was our last week of school, and it was a warm evening in early June. I wanted to play outside because I was so happy to be home. "Come on, Bob, please, play a few games." I talked Bob into it despite Charles's advice. I loved the rush of hiding from people. I had my secret places where I hid, and no one would ever find me. It was my turn to be the looker first. "One, two, three, four, five," I counted with my eyes closed. I counted slowly but loudly to thirty. My head rested against the maple tree in my father's front yard. "Ready or not, here I come!" I yelled with excitement.

During our second round of hide-and-seek, one of Bob's friends, Paul, dragged him to a sewer hole. "No one will ever find us down there," he said as he pointed. "Help me lift the lid, and you can climb down first."

Bob climbed down the steps. "I'm smothering! I can't breathe!" he yelled to his friend above. "Don't come down, I'm coming up." He was gasping and wheezing for air. "Get help!" was the last thing Bob said. His legs grew weak, and they could no longer help him up the steps. Bob slid to the bottom of the hole.

I remember hearing piercing screams. It came from one of the boys we were playing with. He was yelling for his parents to come outside. They were bloodcurdling screams. Then a jolt of commotion sprang into my ears while I hid under my neighbor's front porch. I knew something was happening. Something terrible was wrong. I dragged myself from underneath the porch and ran to the scene in disbelief. I watched my father and Charles go down a sewer hole. "What's happening?" I yelled. Kids were crying. I heard Bob's name. I felt confused. I didn't understand why my father and Charles were in the sewer. Where was Bob?

What we didn't know was that the water at the bottom of the sewer had chemicals in it. Sewer gas had accumulated down there. It overcame Bob. He died inside the hole before anyone could help him. My father and Charles were also overwhelmed by the fumes and could not reach him. All three of them were trapped in the sewer hole. I frantically watched one of my neighbors with a towrope in his hands lower himself into the hole. He had his shirt covering his mouth and nose. I watched that same man pull himself out of the hole, coughing and gasping. I felt like I was holding my breath underwater as I watched. He came up with Charles and dropped his body to the ground before he went back into the sewer hole. Charles's limp body didn't move. He was unconscious. Paul's mom laid her head on Charles's chest. She was shaking and crying when she screamed, "He's breathing, but barely!"

Another man ran over to help, with his handkerchief tied around his nose and mouth. The two men went down together to retrieve my father. They had trouble pulling him up as he weighed two hundred pounds, and the rope had slid around his neck; they feared he would choke to death. But then another brave soul ran to his rescue and helped them get my father out. He was unconscious too. Bob was still at the bottom of the fifteen-foot hole. I looked at my father and Charles lying on the ground. "Go back down there and get Bob! Go down and get him!" I screamed at my neighbors. "Someone help him!" I yelled. I sprung from person to person, grabbing their hands and begging for someone to help. An ominous hush circled the crowd. Nobody knew what to do.

My father and Charles were lying motionless on the road. I looked up at the full moon in the dark sky. I was shaking with fear. The wailing sound of sirens was deafening in my ears. When help approached, it made everything real.

My father and Charles were driven to Mercy Hospital, but Eleanor and I stayed behind. After Bob's body was recovered and I saw him lying on the ground, I threw up everything that was in my stomach. I ran to Bob and shook his lifeless body. I dry-heaved, and my vision blurred. "Wake up, Bob, wake up!" I demanded. I started sobbing when someone pulled me off his chest. "NO!" I yelled, NO!" Everyone was crying around me. A neighbor grabbed me and tried to calm me, but his words only worsened things. I didn't want to be touched; I didn't want a hug. I roared, "NOOOO!" and I pushed him away from me. Then our next-door neighbors led me inside my house. I kicked and screamed when they laid me on the davenport. The kids we played with were in my house. I didn't want to hear their voices or their whispers. I remember feeling like my body had left itself again, like with Albert. I was floating overhead, watching the neighbors whisper to each other below. But I wasn't in a beautiful garden. I was in a pool of dark, cloudy water.

Later that night, Eleanor received word that our father and Charles survived and would be okay but were staying in the hospital for a little more time. I was relieved but stayed in bed for three days without eating. Waves of intense and difficult emotions settled into my body. I felt shocked and numb. I even questioned if it really happened. My body felt empty and cold. I could not get myself warm. I shook with anxiety. Bob's death hurt me more than anything I had experienced on Southwood Avenue. I thought about Bob's body lying in a casket at Sherman D. Brown Chapel, waiting to be buried. I thought about him being all alone there. I felt guilty and angry, as if I wanted retribution. I couldn't stop thinking about Bob's friend Paul, who told him to hide there.

Eleanor contacted our mother and Aunt Lucille to tell them the devastating news. Aunt Lucille and our mother were living together now. I was angry that Eleanor corresponded with them. Actually, I'm unsure if I felt anger or jealousy, but the night I watched as Eleanor cut clippings out of newspapers sent me into a rage. Articles about the horrible events surrounding Bob's death were in *The Columbus Dispatch* and other local newspapers. "What are you doing?" I asked.

"I'm sending these clippings to Mother and Aunt Lucille."

"Why? They don't deserve them. If they cared, they would be here with us right now. Bob is dead! Charles and Father almost died while trying to save him, but they can't get on a train and come to Bob's funeral. Aunt Lucille should know how hard this is on us. She lost a child too. Has she even called the hospital to check on them?" I kicked the stack of newspapers sitting in front of Eleanor over as I stormed out of the room.

Our father delayed Bob's funeral service, hoping my mother and aunt would attend, but they didn't. Mother's relationship with Richard wasn't going well. Then, when she heard about Bob's death, she went into a horrible state and couldn't get out of bed. Aunt Lucille said she developed "issues" and had to be hospitalized. She stayed in Florida to help care for my mother. She feared our mother wouldn't eat if she left her alone. I think Aunt Lucille didn't have it in her to attend another child's funeral, but Uncle John showed. I was angry with my mother and my aunt, but I couldn't blame them because I didn't want to go to his funeral either. I didn't want to see Bob's lifeless body in his casket. I just wanted to hide under my neighbor's porch again and never come out.

Before we were to leave for Bob's funeral, my father came into my bedroom and sat on my bed. I was hiding under the covers. He was quiet at first and didn't say anything to me. Then he pulled the covers off my head and said, "Stella, Bob would want you to be there and to be strong. You were his best friend. He is in heaven now and at peace. He would want you to be at peace too." I flung myself off my bed and cried the hardest I have ever cried. I sobbed messy, hot tears that wouldn't stop. I kneeled on the side of my bed with my face hidden in my blankets. I was drowning in my grief and guilt under my blankets. It was my idea to play hide-and-seek that night. I didn't feel at peace, and I was mad at my father for saying that.

"Why? Why Bob? Why couldn't it have been that other boy he was with? Why Bob? Why did Bob have to be the one who died? How do you know he's in heaven?"

A look of distress covered my father's face. He breathed heavily and said, "I don't know, Stella. All I know is that if you only focus on the 'whys' in life, then you will never understand the 'why nots' in life. Focusing only on the 'whys' won't help you now. 'Why Bob?' won't help you. It won't help you understand or feel peace. And I do believe he's in heaven."

But I didn't understand what my father meant. I felt more irritated with him and with everything around me. I wanted to get back into my bed and hide under my blankets. I didn't want Bob in heaven, I wanted him with me.

A crowd of people attended Bob's funeral. I knew I wouldn't see my mother, but I still looked for her. I sat in the first pew with Eleanor, Charles, Father, and the Chaplins. Eleanor held my hand the entire time, but that did not give me the comfort I needed. I remember seeing black. Everyone was wearing black. I remember seeing all of Bob's friends and his schoolteachers. I remember hearing Mr. and Mrs. Jackson crying in the pew behind me. I remember children singing songs, but I can't remember the names of the songs. I remember seeing Bob in his casket. I remember he looked stiff but peaceful. I remember the funeral, but I don't remember anything about it at the same time. My father spoke at his funeral, but I don't remember what he said. I only thought about begging Bob to play hide-and-seek that night. *Why did I have to insist on playing? Why didn't I listen to Charles?* Why, why, why consumed my thoughts.

I remember how I felt at the funeral. I felt cold. I felt hot. I felt angry. I felt sad. I felt mad ... mad at everybody. Especially with the boy who showed Bob the sewer hole. I was still angry with Paul, even though Charles said it was not his fault. But why didn't he die? It was his idea. Why did Bob have to go down first? Why Bob? Then I remembered what my dad had said to me earlier that day. "You will never understand the 'why nots' in life if you only focus on the 'whys.'"

Chapter **37**

I DIDN'T RETURN TO SCHOOL AFTER BOB DIED. We only had a week left anyway. At that time, I went to Southwood Elementary School. I disliked it there. During the next school year, I was absent a lot. I continued writing my own excuse notes, and nobody, not even my father, caught on. He never saw my report cards or checked in with me about how I was doing in school. I was miserable. I was timid and hardly talked to anyone. My teacher was mean. She made me sit in the corner and wear a dunce hat once because I was late for school one morning. I felt humiliated and embarrassed and didn't want to be there anymore.

A new school called Lincoln Park Elementary was built, so I decided to leave Southwood Elementary and attend it for the rest of my time. My father never knew I had transferred schools because I never told him. I couldn't handle being at Southwood after Bob died because we went there together. The stares I received from the children were the worst. I needed a fresh start, and I thought Lincoln Park would help, and it did.

"I'm moving to Springfield and staying with Aunt Elizabeth," Eleanor stated one afternoon. Her news surprised us, especially our father. He wasn't close with his sister or her husband even though they only lived less than sixty miles away. He was shocked when he found out Eleanor had been conversing with her through letters since she left the boarding house, explaining to her how unhappy and depressed she was. It was Aunt Elizabeth's idea for Eleanor to stay with them. She only had one child, and he wasn't living with them anymore.

"I'd rather move to Florida to be with Mom, but I don't think she wants me. She seems to be wrapped up with that Richard." Father ignored that comment.

"Why are you so unhappy living here?"

"Because, Dad, I just am. I need a change. I hate being here. I'm reminded of Bob all the time, and I hate Columbus. It's hard for me to explain. But there's plenty of room for me at Aunt Elizabeth's house. I'll stay in her son's old bedroom. She said William never visits, and she'll love having my company."

My father was upset, but he allowed it after speaking with his sister. When Eleanor was seventeen, she married a man named Nile Brantley in Springfield. We found out about their marriage after they were married because she knew we didn't care for him. My father was furious about her decision because he didn't think Nile was a good person. He didn't like where they lived after they married. They were poor and had little to eat because Nile was lazy and disliked working. He would shoot the deer that walked in their front yard for food, and that disgusted my father. He couldn't believe Eleanor would marry a man like Nile. He told her she would regret marrying him one day, and that caused a rift between them. But our father wasn't going to allow their difference of opinions to ruin their relationship. He maintained a connection with Eleanor and was polite to Nile. They had twin boys named Edward and Neil. But Eleanor wasn't the same Eleanor we once knew, especially after she had her children. She didn't seem as powerful to me anymore. She wasn't the courageous girl she once was.

Eleanor loved to read, but she was never a writer. After she moved to Springfield, I found a poem she wrote. She placed it in one of my dresser drawers for me to find. My body tingled, and my throat closed while I read the poem:

Bob Miller's Fate

It was a warm night,
On the seventh of June.
The children were playing,
But the play stopped too soon.
They were playing hide-and-seek,
The game they all like.
The base was a telephone pole,
Close to the pike.
Bob went to hide the second time,
This time not on the grass.
But instead he hid,
In a sewer filled with gas.
Bob had a larger brother,
The kind that's brave and true.
He went down after Bob,
Before the circumstances, he knew.
When Charles went into the hole,
His brother to rescue.
The gas that filled the sewer,
Made him unconscious too.
These boys had a father,
Who loved and cared for them all.
He was the next to hear,
Of these two boys fall.
He went into the sewer,
The sewer filled with gas.

And when he too was overcome,
They both lay in a mass.
Oh, that was the worst night,
That ever met our eyes.
A man took a rope to the bottom,
And Bob began to rise.
We can't express in words,
The gratefulness for the men.
Who rescued the Miller three,
Out of that gas-filled den.
Bob never will have a chance,
In this old world to roam.
For God on that warm night in June
Called his loved one home.

I cradled the poem against my chest like a mother would cradle a newborn baby. I never shared the poem with anyone, including my father or Charles. I'm not sure why I didn't want to show it to anyone. Maybe I didn't want someone to take the poem from me. I wanted it to remain only mine. I thought it belonged to me and no one else. I think that's why Eleanor hid it in my drawer, so only I could find it. I think if Eleanor wanted other people to read it, she would have left it on our kitchen table. Maybe she needed to get her words out and then pretend it never happened. Maybe if she shared it with others, it would make Bob's death real to her. I remembered how she coped during stressful times at the boarding house. "This never happened. Go to bed and wake up the next morning thinking everything was just a bad dream. This never happened," she would say. Her words comforted me as a child, and I did what she said, but now, looking back, I'm not sure that was the best advice.

After Eleanor left, I took over the cooking. My father left me a list and money daily and expected me to cook dinner for our family and often for some people he worked with on his construction sites. Some didn't have much money to spend on food. He didn't want them to go hungry. I felt a lot of pressure to do all the cooking. I had no idea how to cook, but I quickly learned at ten years old. My favorite meals to cook were baked pork chops and meatloaf. My father loved anything that went well with roasted potatoes and carrots. Luckily, those two dishes tasted well with potatoes and carrots. "Perfect," I said out loud as I pulled the roasting pan out of the oven one evening. I placed it on the counter and admired how good it looked, and it smelled delicious.

"Mrs. Jackson would be proud of you," I heard Bob say from behind me. A jolt of energy shocked my body, and I quickly turned around, but Bob wasn't there.

"Bob!" I screamed as I ran from the kitchen. I was panting heavily while I looked for him. "Bob! Where are you?" But then my body went limp, and my jaw tensed. I knew I wasn't going to find him. I knew where he was, and it wasn't with me in our house. I slid to the ground and hugged my legs as I cried. My lips quivered as I sobbed, "Bob," one last time. I wanted to hear his voice again, but I didn't.

"Stella, Charles, look what I bought you!" our father excitedly said one afternoon. "I think you will love this!" Our father tried to get our minds off Bob. He managed to buy us a used piano. He had an uncle named Will, who was a concert pianist. He was very extravagant, and I enjoyed being around him, but he also scared me at the same time. Probably because he told the strangest stories when he ate dinner with us. At least, I thought they were strange because I didn't always understand them. They seemed too adult for me, but Charles always laughed and asked questions.

He wore fancy clothes and rings. I wasn't used to seeing a man wearing so many rings. He gave Charles and me piano lessons. Charles excelled with the piano and got exceptionally good, but not me. I would hide during the lessons, but my great-uncle Will was very kind and understanding. He didn't put pressure on me, which made me happy. I loved listening to him and Charles play the piano together. He rode his bike to our house weekly to give us lessons. He lived on High Street near the University District. One day, while riding his bike to our home, he was hit by a car on Neil Avenue. He was in the hospital for a long time. He never recovered from his injuries, and before he died, he gave my father a beautiful diamond ring. The diamond had been in their family, and my uncle wore it in a man's ring. It was an old European cut diamond, over a carat in size. When my father showed me the ring, it fell out of his hand, and we could not find it. We frantically looked everywhere. My father wasn't the type of person to panic easily, but he was hysterical. "Stella! Please crawl around and help me. We can't lose this ring. Why did I have to be so clumsy?" Finally, he realized it fell into the cuff of his pants. We laughed nervously about that.

My relationship with Charles significantly changed after Bob died. We formed a bond, the kind I always yearned for. We spoke about Bob often. We laughed about the funny things he did and cried together through our grief. Our father often said Bob was watching us from heaven and smiling down on us, and that he was happy that Charles and I were so close. It annoyed Charles when my father spoke like that.

"Saying that may give you comfort, but it doesn't give me comfort, Dad. How do you know there's a heaven? How do you know people can see us from heaven? I'd rather have Bob here, living with us, not smiling down on us from heaven. And I can't stand it when people say he's in a better place now. He was in a pretty good place here with our family, with his friends, with Stella." Charles wiped his eyes and walked out of the room. My father and I looked at each other dubiously, not knowing what to say to each other, so we didn't say anything. But after some time, my father went to Charles. He was sitting on the front porch.

"I'm sorry I upset you, Charles. Everyone grieves differently, and I will be more careful with my words ... with how I grieve. I won't push my beliefs on you. That was never my intention. I wish Bob were here with us too. We are all struggling with why Bob died that night. Why did he die and we didn't? But then I am thankful that it was only one son I lost and not both of you." He put his arm around Charles's shoulders and leaned into him. I was listening from the storm door. My eyes burned from the tears that welled inside them. I didn't want them to see me eavesdropping, so I tiptoed to my bedroom and cried into my pillow.

Charles was an excellent student in high school and won academic awards. Later, he was accepted to Ohio State University, and he majored in business. He met a girl named Ruth at Ohio State. One day, I found his marriage license to Ruth hidden in a drawer in Charles's bedroom. He did not want our father to know he was married. He wanted more time before he told our father that Ruth was pregnant. I held that secret over his head for months. When I was twelve years old, Ruth moved in with us before the baby was born. My father was supportive because he liked Ruth. I liked Ruth too. She was good for Charles. She had a spunk about her that helped Charles not be so uptight. I helped Ruth with their baby, Marilyn. She was a beautiful baby. She had Charles's blue eyes and his good looks. I asked my father if he had any baby pictures of my mother so I could compare them, but my father said no. I loved cradling her in my arms and singing her songs. Her smile warmed my heart. Charles and Ruth left my father's house before Charles graduated from OSU. They rented a place near us. I could walk to their home, so I continued babysitting for them. But then, they moved about one hundred miles away to Middletown, Ohio, after Charles graduated from OSU and secured a job with a paper supply company.

Chapter **38**

WHEN I WAS IN JUNIOR HIGH, I first went to Barrett Junior High School, but the school was overly crowded. My class was in the furnace room. It was too warm and uncomfortable there, and I didn't like how crowded it was. Large crowds and feeling claustrophobic gave me anxiety, so I transferred to Roosevelt Junior High School. My father never knew I did that either. I remember walking into my new school and smelling vegetable soup cooking. It made me feel good. I learned how to sew at Roosevelt. I made a dress for Charles and Ruth's daughter, but she never got to wear it. I was proud of the dress and how unique it looked. It was a short-sleeved, dark-pink silk dress detailed with light-pink chiffon flowers at the top. A white silk ribbon lined the dress below the flowers and was made into a bow. It also had matching bloomers with white silk trim around the legs. My teacher loved it so much that she submitted it for a competition displayed in an art gallery. "I'm so proud of you, sweetheart," soothed my father while we admired it in the gallery. We went there several times to look at the dress. The last time we visited the gallery, I froze when we turned the corner to where the dress was displayed. I saw a glimpse of Bob staring at the dress with his hands and forehead pressed against the glass window in front of it. My heart fluttered.

"Did you see him?" I asked my father.

"See who?" he asked.

"Never mind," I quietly said.

Sometimes, I would wake up in the middle of the night swearing Bob had just woken me. I felt the touch of his fingers touching mine. "Stella," he whispered in my ear. Then I heard his giggles and the pitter-patter sound of his feet running away as I woke.

In 1929, when I was thirteen years old, my father had to go out of town on a business trip. He did not want to leave me home alone, but he did. He had to go to New York City. Instead of riding by train, he took an aircraft from Port Columbus Airport that carried fourteen passengers. My father was excited to ride in his first aircraft. I was excited to be left home alone because I wanted to take my father's car for a ride. Our neighbor next door, George, was good friends with my father. George was to keep an eye on me while my father was in New York. After my father left, George knew I was planning something because I spent the better half of a day in my father's car, figuring things out.

"Stella, I know what you're planning. You best not take that machine out for a ride. Your father will not be happy," he warned me. But I quickly figured out how to drive it, and I took it out despite George's advice. Driving around Broad and High Streets was not scary for me, and I had no trouble. Although I had a little problem with the choke, I quickly figured it out. My father left me some money, so I used that money to fill the tank and replenish the gas I used. It cost around twenty or twenty-one cents per gallon. George was waiting on my front porch when I returned home. He looked displeased with me, but he also had a little smile on his face. His lips were tight but curved upward.

"Please, don't tell my father," I begged. "I did well, and the car is in perfect condition. I even filled it with gas."

"Stella, you're quite a girl," he murmured as he walked away, shaking his head. I'm unsure if he ever told my father because he never said anything to me about his car after he returned home.

I flourished in English and Language Arts in junior high and all throughout high school. I finally started to love school and felt safe coming out of my protective shell. I answered all the teachers' questions about the books we had to read. I gobbled up as many books as I could afford. Most books cost me ten cents. I started writing the title of every book I read in a journal. The list became so immense that it filled the entire notebook, and I had to buy a new one. Reading books put me into another world that wasn't mine. I loved getting lost in a good book. It took the mental chatter from inside my brain away. I immersed myself in other people's lives and felt what they felt. Books kept my mind off of thinking about Southwood Avenue and Bob.

I also loved to dance. I was still somewhat introverted but, like books, dancing also helped me escape into another world where I felt safe. I loved feeling like I could be free with myself. I took dance lessons for five years at Beaux Arts Dance Studio above Ben's Tavern. The lady who ran the studio liked me. Her name was Judith, and I loved the attention she gave me. She was from New York City. She had the best accent, and listening to her talk tickled me to death. Her voice was high yet sounded a bit nasal, and she pronounced her short vowels differently when she spoke. I had never heard anyone sound like her before. She had long, thin, muscular legs, and I was mesmerized by her.

"Stella, we are Leg Twins! Look, we have identical legs," she once told me.

"Oh, your legs are much nicer than mine," I replied with embarrassment because it was the nicest compliment I had ever received.

"Let's look at our legs in the mirror together! Don't be bashful, come now!" she said.

She spent extra time with me at the studio, which I adored. I loved the praise she gave me. "Lovely, Stella, you look quite lovely. Your lines are beautiful." Sometimes, we sat and talked after our lesson. She was the one who mainly talked, and that was great because I enjoyed listening to her. She loved horses almost more than dancing. She taught me about the different types of horses. I never knew there were so many different breeds.

I begged my father for a horse, but we could not afford one or the upkeep. Later, he paid for me to have private lessons. After one lesson, I rode so long that I couldn't sit down when I got home. I had horrible blisters on my rear end and couldn't remove my riding pants without my father's help. "Daddy!" I called. "Help me! I can't remove my pants! My bottom and legs hurt miserably." My father teased me for days about it.

Judith was a precious influence in my life. She mentored me and gave me joy. When she moved back to New York after her stay in Columbus, I missed her greatly. We kept in contact and wrote letters to each other. I saved every letter she wrote me. When I missed her, I reread old letters.

One of the letters I enjoyed the most read:

My Dearest Identical Leg Twin,

I am keeping busy in New York, but I miss you. I hope you are keeping up with your dance lessons. You are a beautiful dancer with a gifted talent, especially since you have my legs!

Are you still taking horseback riding lessons? I hope so. Ladies need to have hobbies of their own. It will help make you into a strong and independent woman. I suspect you are already turning into that on your own.

How are your studies going? Are you still doing well in literature? I am jealous of your love for reading. I wish I had the attention to sit and read an entire book. You go through a book in a day!

Stella, smile at yourself in front of your mirror more often. And when you do, look at what a strong and beautiful woman you are growing into. You should feel proud of yourself because I'm proud of you.

Much love,

Judith

Chapter **39**

I WAS THE FIRST STUDENT IN MY HIGH SCHOOL to wear black-and-white saddle shoes. My dad enjoyed shopping and wanted to make sure I had nice things to wear. That started a new trend with the girls at my school. Almost everyone started wearing black-and-white saddle shoes once they saw mine. I never would have described myself as a trendsetter, but I guess I was. It made me feel good even though I was embarrassed by the attention I received. I never told anyone, but the feeling of making an influence on others made an impression on me. I knew someday I wanted to work in a field where I could help others. But the absolute highlight of my high school years was when my father bought me a brand-new Model A car. It cost eight hundred dollars. I was flabbergasted! Because he was saving money to build a cottage on Buckeye Lake, I knew it was a financial stretch for him, but he always found ways to give me nice gifts.

I met my best friend, Dolores, at the beginning of high school. Dolores and I remained best friends for our entire lives. She and I were into shopping and looking good. We went to Lazarus weekly. It had an area with mark-downs where we bought most of our clothes. Dolores and I dressed up to go shopping. We wore high heels, white gloves, and fancy dresses. Dolores was the one who influenced me to dress up all the time. Her mother always wanted her to look perfect because they lived in a not-so-nice area of town.

When I was sixteen, my father finally had enough money to buy land at Buckeye Lake. He built the cottage he always dreamed of on a large plot of land, and we used it for family vacations. We loved to fish and celebrate the holidays there. Watching the fireworks over the water on the Fourth of July and New Year's Eve was breathtaking; you almost felt you were seeing them twice with their reflection in the water. The way the fireworks boomed and then spread their sparkling, colorful lights that soared through the sky like falling diamonds was beautiful.

We had a boat that I would row my family across the lake in to an ice-cream shop after supper. It surprised me no one helped me row the boat. I did it alone. Sometimes, I would see Bob sitting at the bow of the boat, trying to rock it back and forth while laughing. And sometimes, I would see Bob rowing the boat while I sat at its bow, watching his blond curls bounce back and forth on his head. He would smile and wink at me. I smiled back and gazed at him until he disappeared.

My favorite flavor to order at the ice-cream shop was strawberry. My father used to take his spoon, steal a bite of mine, and then smear a little on my nose. I don't know why he thought that was so funny. Charles, Ruth, and Marilyn joined us at the lake often. The funniest memory I will never forget was when Charles ate an ant sandwich—at least, that's what we ended up calling it. He had left the jelly out overnight and forgot to put the lid on it. We woke up early to fish the following day, and Charles decided he wanted a peanut butter-and-jelly sandwich. He didn't realize ants had gotten into the jelly. Once he realized what he was eating, he got sick everywhere. We laughed for days about that incident; even Charles laughed about it.

Even though my life was the best it had ever been, I mourned for Bob daily. I felt like a piece of my heart was missing, not just my heart but a piece of me; a piece of my soul. When Bob died, a part of me died with him. My nightmares never went away. If I wasn't dreaming about my monster, I was dreaming about Bob. I often woke up screaming for air. I felt like I was suffocating in that hole with him. My father tried to comfort me, but I felt embarrassed that he came into my bedroom and treated me like a child.

"You're okay, Stella. Everything is okay, sweetheart. It was just a bad dream." I wondered if he could hear my heart pounding. I wondered if he knew what my dream was about. I shook him away when he placed his hands on my shoulders.

"I'm okay. You can go now, I'm fine." I didn't want to be rude to him, but I didn't like to be touched, and my father didn't understand that. I knew he was trying to help, but I still didn't like the feeling of someone's hands on me. Especially when anxiety puts a chill through my body that I can't get rid of. I hated the feeling of someone's hands pressing on my shoulders. I would push them away. It made me feel controlled, and the last thing I wanted to feel was that someone was trying to control me. Especially when my anxiety was already taking control of my body, and I didn't know how to stop it. It made me shiver and shake. I would wrap myself up with blankets and pace my bedroom. Then, I would open my window and sit on the windowsill. I stared into the darkness, breathing in the air and allowing it to fill my chest. I studied the trees and how they swayed in the breeze. Their branches reminded me of a ballerina's arms, outstretched and waving gracefully through the air. The trees swaying softly in the night helped me feel calm and at peace.

One evening, when I returned home from horseback riding lessons, I found Albert sitting on my front porch. He was drinking a beer and smoking a cigarette. I felt terrified seeing him again. Cold goosebumps broke out on the back of my neck. I wondered why he was at my house. I put my hands behind my back so he could not see them tremble. I hadn't seen him since the night Bob and I had escaped from the boarding house. He looked smug sitting on my porch, and my heart pounded in my chest.

"Why are you here? You need to leave!" I forced the words out of my mouth. I felt weak in the knees, but I also felt strong at the same time. It was the oddest feeling. I couldn't believe how easy it was for me to tell him to leave. He glowered at me.

"My mother died of lung cancer. I thought you and your family would want to know. It was a while ago," he sighed. "But I wanted to see you, Stella. I miss you. How are you?"

"I'm sorry about your mother, but you need to leave now." I looked him straight in the eye. He had that same stupid smirk across his face. He stood taller but so did I. I wasn't the same little girl he was used to.

He replied, "You're not sorry," and then wagged his little finger at me like he used to. He took a knife from his pants pocket and started cleaning under his nails with it. It felt like he was trying to intimidate me. A cold shiver went through my spine, and my knees slightly wobbled. I felt my armpits sweating, but I wasn't going to waver. I wanted him gone.

"You need to leave now! I don't want to talk to you. I never want to see you again!"

"Stella, you were such a good little girl, don't be rude. You've grown into a beautiful woman. What are you, seventeen or eighteen years old now? I've missed you terribly. Are you home alone?"

At that moment, my father pulled his car into the driveway. I was so relieved! He didn't even pull his car into his usual spot. He stopped in the middle of the driveway. He got out of the car with a curious look on his face. His eyes darted between Albert and me. He knew something was not right.

"What's going on? Why are you here?" my father asked Albert.

"I just stopped by to tell you my mother passed away. Stella and I were just reminiscing about old times in the boarding house. But I should leave now. Have a good night, sir." Before Albert walked down the porch steps, he turned to me and said, "I'm living in my mother's house. She left it to me when she died. I'm running it as a boarding house too. You should come by and see it. There's a sweet little girl there who reminds me of you."

Albert sneered at me with the same disgusting smirk and wagged his little finger at me. "Bye, bye, little Stella."

I can't believe what I did. I strutted over to him, stared him in his dark eyes, and spit in his face.

"Get lost!" I crossed my arms over my chest and sneered back at him. I knew my face was flushed and turning red, but I didn't care. Albert wiped my spit off his face with the cuff of his sleeve. He let out a little chuckle and eyed me up and down.

"You should leave now, Albert," my father said as he stepped in front of me.

I turned and walked away. I scooted through my front door, put my hand over my mouth, and breathed a heavy sigh of disbelief. My hands trembled as I pushed the curtains back and watched Albert stroll down the street. A tear crept down my cheek as I thought of that little girl he spoke about. *Maybe he's lying? Maybe he was trying to get a rise out of me?* I thought. Memories of Albert and the boarding house invaded my mind. I didn't want Albert to control my feelings anymore, so I pushed the memories away. I wanted to change out of my riding clothes and wrap myself in a blanket.

"What was that about?" my father asked.

"Nothing. He's always been trouble." I sprinted upstairs.

"Stella!" He stopped me midflight. "Don't run away from me." I turned and looked at my father. He looked disturbed, and his eyes were full of concern. We just stared at each other, but he didn't ask me why I spit in Albert's face. I was relieved when he didn't ask me more questions. "I love you, sweetheart. Let me know if you need anything."

"I love you too. I'm going upstairs to change and rest before I make dinner." I would rather die than tell him the truth about Albert. I had never told my father about the abuse, and I wasn't about to then.

During my last few months of high school, I met a boy who moved across the street from my father and me on Frebis Avenue. His name was Thomas

Bennett. He lived on one side of a double with his mother and stepfather. He would sit on his front porch and watch me read books on my front porch. I was not interested in boys, and I was not interested in dating. I was eighteen years old, and I never had a boyfriend. I had never kissed a boy. I guess Tom was not a boy but a handsome young man. He was twenty-four years old, the same age as Charles. He asked me to go out with him often, but I always had an excuse not to. I thought he was too old for me. I also didn't trust people easily, especially men. Tom seemed nice, but I was scared to go out with him. Dolores never understood why I never dated, but she also didn't press the issue. I think she knew something I didn't want to talk about happened to me. Or maybe she didn't press me for more information because she didn't want to know the truth. Dolores and I were close, but she wasn't a deep talker. She liked to keep things fun and light.

<hr>

I graduated from South High School in 1934 with honors. My father was immensely proud of me.

I focused on getting a business degree after high school. I attended Bliss Business College for two and a half years. It was in the Market District south of Broad Street. Thomas drove a trolley that ended up replacing streetcars in Columbus in 1933. Converting to trolley buses meant that people could be picked up at the curb instead of the middle of the street. Thomas only worked with the trolley buses for a short time. Then, my father got him a job working with him. My father had to work extremely early in the mornings at Buckeye Stamping. He was the superintendent there, and the vice president was his friend Ed Chaplin. The workers stamped Bayer Aspirin boxes and other supplies. My father still dabbled in construction as a second job because times were hard due to the Depression.

My father loved Tom and encouraged me to give him a chance. I liked Tom, but I wouldn't say I liked how he dressed. I liked well-dressed men. I'm not sure why that was important to me because I never considered myself superficial. When I asked my father if I was, he said no. He told me my mother liked well-dressed men too. That was the first time my father mentioned her to me. I wanted to ask him more questions, like if I looked like her. I remember my aunt Lucille and Eleanor told me I did, but I didn't ask him. My father always seemed uncomfortable talking about my mother when Eleanor pressed him for information, and I wanted to respect his privacy because he was everything to me. I loved my father more than anything. I told Tom I would go out with him if he got new heels on his shoes and dressed up. He agreed, and we finally went out. He was friendly, made me laugh, and was a complete gentleman. He had a kind voice and reminded me of my father. I started to like and trust him.

As a graduation gift, he took me on a surprise outing. There was something in town called the Buckeye Donkey Ball Company. They entertained you by playing baseball on donkeys! What a weird event to watch, but we had great fun. I squealed, "Thomas! You know I love sports, but I never thought I would be watching this!" He smiled at me and put his hand on the small of my back. I didn't try to brush his touch off. It made me feel good. I smiled back at him, and he kissed my cheek.

Then, one day, he said, "Marry me, Stella. Let's get married before I have to move."

My heart sank. "What? What do you mean you have to move?"

Tom nodded his head. "I have to move to Middletown. I got a new job working at Armco Steel. I love you, Stella, and I will give you a good life," he gushed. "I promise I will make you happy. I want to have a family with you. Please give me the honor of being your husband! Marry me, Stella, and move to Middletown with me!"

I considered the proposal briefly but said, "I don't think that's a good idea, Tom. I care about you too, but I am focusing on myself and furthering my education right now. We don't need to rush into marriage just because you're moving. We can still be together, but I'm not ready for marriage. We must try to make it work long-distance for now."

Chapter **40**

TOM WAS PERSISTENT BUT ALSO PATIENT and didn't give up on me. He visited me in Columbus most weekends. He told my father how he wanted to marry me but couldn't afford an engagement ring that I deserved. My father gave him the old European cut diamond ring from his uncle Will. "Use this diamond and the gold. Have a jeweler make it into an exquisite engagement ring for Stella. She deserves this. I won't take no for an answer." He slipped the ring off his finger and handed it to Tom.

One evening, while Tom was visiting me, he got down on one knee. "Please do me the honor of marrying me! I want you to be my wife, Stella. I love you, and I can't live without you." I was shocked when Tom opened a small ring box. The solitaire diamond shined brightly inside the box. The sparkle mesmerized me. I couldn't stop staring at it.

I covered my mouth with my hand. My stomach fluttered like butterflies were swirling around. I never imagined having a ring so beautiful. "This is too much, Tom, you can't afford this."

"Your father helped me. The diamond has been in your family for years."

"Is this Uncle Will's diamond? I remember this," I smiled as I thought about the time it fell into the cuff of my father's pants. But I refused to put it on. "I care deeply for you, Tom. But I'm not ready yet. I told you before that I want to continue furthering my education and find happiness with myself before I'm able to make you happy."

"But you do make me happy, Stella! I love your independence, and I love the fact that you want to further your education. I'm happy that I met such a strong woman like you. Your education shouldn't stop us from getting married." He caressed my cheek and smiled at me. When he kissed my forehead, he asked, "Why did you say you needed to find happiness with yourself?"

I was tempted to avoid his question and just say yes to the marriage, but I held my ground. I was not ready to make a huge change in my life yet. Even though Tom did make me happy, I wanted to feel happiness on my own for a while longer. "It's complicated to explain, Tom. It has to do with my childhood ... after my mother left my family. I used to struggle with feeling happy when I was younger due to my living conditions. But I think I have moved past it, and I want to make sure I have completely moved past it before I make any big decisions. But rest assured, I love you too." Tears welled up in my eyes. "Give me a little more time, just a little more," I trailed off as I hugged him.

"Okay." Tom cleared his throat and asked, "Will you tell me about your childhood? You never talk about anything before your brother died. All I know is you lived in a boarding house for a period of time after your mother left. Was it five years? At least, that's what Charles told me."

"Did he tell you anything else?"

"No, he just said it was difficult on everybody, especially you."

"It was, but I learned a lot about myself while living there. Don't get me wrong, it wasn't a positive learning experience for me, but I managed, and I learned. I'm learning from it every day, and I will continue to learn about myself every day." I hugged Tom, and I pressed my face onto his shoulder and wrapped my arms around his neck. "I don't want to relive my past. Let's focus on the future. *Our* future. Please just be patient."

"I will," he said.

I wore the ring when I was alone in my house. How could I not? It was stunning! My father caught me wearing it one day.

"Stella, are you finally going to marry Tom?" he asked.

On Christmas Eve 1936, my father and I planned to visit Charles and his family in Middletown for the day. Since Thomas also lived in Middletown, my father insisted I wear the engagement ring while we visited Tom while we were there. As I looked into the mirror while I was getting ready to leave for Middletown, I thought of my mother. I grabbed a hand mirror and looked at my profile. I thought about the time my aunt Lucille told me I had my mother's profile. I wondered what my mother would do if she were me now. But she wasn't me, and I wasn't her. I only knew her from stories Eleanor shared. I took the engagement ring Tom had given me out of my drawer and wore it to Middletown. My father smiled during the entire car ride. I said yes to Tom on Christmas Eve. We went to a minister's home in New Port, Kentucky, and married on Christmas Day. It was nothing special, but the clothes we wore were glorious. After getting married, we walked around downtown. We felt like movie stars. I moved to Middletown the next week. We had a beautiful apartment downtown. I worked at a clothing store and oversaw three departments. I did all the buying for those departments. I felt so much happiness in my life. I stopped thinking about my past and continued focusing on my future; mine and Tom's future.

Tom and I had two children together. We had our first child, Jim, in 1938. He was a beautiful baby. He had blond curly hair and looked like Bob. In 1943, we had our second child, Anna. She looked just like me. After I gave birth to Anna, Tom moved to Lima, Ohio, to work in a lab. He moved by himself and mailed us money weekly. I moved in with my father on Frebis Avenue with Jim and Anna because we couldn't afford to keep our current house. At six years old, Jim rode the city bus to mail cookies and clean clothes to Tom in Lima. I can't believe I put that much responsibility on a child, but Jim did it. I struggled with Jim, even though he was extremely smart and independent. He was an ornery child who got into trouble often. He reminded me so much of Charles, even though he looked like Bob.

Poverty was everywhere in Columbus. It was a horrible time. I always felt sorry for the people who we called "tramps" riding the trains near my house. I often fed them and gave them water on my back porch. It scared Anna when they appeared, but she was just a little girl. She would hide behind the couch so they wouldn't see her. "Why are you so scared? You don't need to hide from them. They won't hurt you. They are people just like us but with less than us." Anna appeared from behind the couch and sat on my lap. She rested her head on my shoulder.

"I'm scared because they look dirty and tired and get food from strangers. We don't do that."

"Well, it's because we aren't homeless and searching for jobs. It doesn't mean they are bad people. They are trying to survive."

Jim was not afraid of them. He seemed intrigued by them. He helped me feed them and pour water for them. He tried to engage in conversations with them, but many were too preoccupied with eating to talk to a boy.

My father helped me with my children while Thomas was in Lima, but he was still working in construction. I helped him build a house down the road from us. Jim was in school, but I brought Anna with me because she was only three. After it was built, I painted the entire house by myself. Every day after work, I collapsed on the couch. My arms and legs felt like noodles. After I finished painting the house, I had extreme shoulder pain and stiffness. I didn't know it was a frozen shoulder at the time, but when I couldn't move my arm, my nervous system took a hit. Everything became too overwhelming for me. I was hospitalized for about a week. I was scared, and I couldn't stop crying, but I was determined to get better. My doctor, Dr. Reed, was a wonderful doctor during a very terrifying time for me. I confided to him about my past. "Stella, you experienced so much trauma and anxiety as a child, you just came to a breaking point in your life; it was bound to happen."

After my recovery, I obtained a job running a ladies' apparel department at Morehouse-Martens. It was known for its high-end merchandise. Lazarus Department Store was still popular at that time, but so was Morehouse-Martens. I rode the bus to work and home each day. My father was in semi-retirement and took care of Jim and Anna so I could work. My stomach churned, and I cried on the city bus every day because I missed Tom, and I felt bad that my father had to watch my children. I begged Tom to move home from Lima and find work in Columbus.

Chapter **41**

I ENJOYED WORKING AT MOREHOUSE-MARTENS, but I needed something more; I needed to feel more fulfilled and keep my mind busy. I joined the American Red Cross. The women who volunteered for the Red Cross wore gray dresses with gray caps, and we were called the Gray Ladies. We worked on West Broad Street and helped girls who were considered unruly, but most were homeless and had mental health issues. It felt a little like being a nurse and a counselor simultaneously. We worked with the girls to help them become independent and functional community members. One of the girls we worked with killed herself. It was a great sense of loss for us all. But I wasn't going to let that detour our goals as Gray Ladies. It gave me more drive to encourage everyone that there is hope in life and that learning the will to fight through adversity will make you stronger.

The Gray Ladies and I often drove together. Once, the black Dodge we were driving broke down on Broad Street. At that time, cars had carburetors, and I knew it had something to do with that. "I'll get out and fix it," I said. Many cars blew horns at me because we were stopped in the middle of the street. The hood was up, and I was leaning into the car with my dress on. My bottom and legs were the only thing showing. "Try starting the car again," I yelled. I heard men clapping, whistling, and yelling in the background once the sound of the engine roared. It embarrassed me as I slammed the hood shut and quickly got inside the car. I was too scared to look at them, but Dolores slipped out of the back seat of the car and stood next to it.

"Thank you! Thank you all!" she yelled and took a curtsy.

"Dolores, get in the car. You're so funny!" one of the Gray Ladies said. We laughed as we drove down the street.

My father knew living together in his house was too crowded since Tom had moved back to Columbus. One evening, he was reading a popular magazine called *Better Homes and Gardens* and found a plan for a house he loved. He decided to build it for my family, even though he was technically retired. He bought a spacious lot on the north end of Columbus on a street called Garden Road. When he told me the name of the street, it bothered me at first. I remember lying in bed at night wondering why the name Garden Road gave me a wave of anxiety. I spent sleepless nights wondering. Then, one night, I dreamed I was walking through a garden of daisies. I was wearing a beautiful white dress and running barefoot through the different mazes in the garden. Someone was speaking in my ear, telling me to gather all the daisies I could find. And then she told me to hide them. After I had a handful of daisies, I hid them in an attic next to a box of Lincoln Logs. I woke from my dream in a cold sweat. My nightgown was damp and sticking to my body. I quickly got out of bed to change. Thomas stirred in bed and asked me if I was okay. I told him yes and to go back to sleep. As I changed into a new nightgown, I felt like a little girl again. I stepped into the hallway to make sure my father was still sleeping. I didn't want him to wake up and check on me like he used to. Then, I opened the window to the bedroom I was sharing with Tom. I sat on the sill and breathed in the night air. The sky was dark, but the stars were bright. I watched the trees sway and dance in the cool breeze. I saw my first falling star that night, and when I did, I thought I heard the wind whisper, "You're strong," in my ear.

Materials and money were scarce when my father started building my home on Garden Road. He could only buy seven pieces of lumber at a time. My father had to ride the bus from the south end of Columbus to the north end and then walk a mile each time he worked on the house. It took about five years to finish it, costing around ten thousand dollars. It was a two-story, white stucco home with light blue shutters. It had a huge, beautiful picture window facing the front yard. The house had three bedrooms and one and a half baths with a one-car attached garage. It had hardwood floors and a stone chimney. My father was incredibly proud of the stone chimney he built because it was a skill many people didn't have then. He was delighted with the house when it was finished, and my family loved the home once we moved in. My father felt a great sense of pride, and I felt a great sense of gratitude. He provided my family with a wonderful gift, but it was the last selfless gift he gave to me.

In early 1950 my father said, "Stella, I've kept this to myself long enough. I'm not well. I feel fatigued every day. So I went to the doctor, and I was told I have sugar diabetes, and my organs are strained." I visited his house on the south end of Columbus almost daily for six years to bring him food and take care of his needs. He didn't want to go to a nursing home, and I couldn't blame him. I didn't want him in one either. Dolores offered to help me with his care. She always felt like he was a father to her. His kidneys were failing toward the end, and I felt like mine were shriveling up and failing too. I felt a horrible pain in my stomach daily. I was on autopilot and every day blurred together. I didn't have time to cry. I was too busy.

"How long has he been like this?" I asked Dolores who was caring for him when I arrived one day. He was sleeping soundly in his bed, but he was not coherent. His cheeks and nose were red, and he was running a fever. He was sweaty and clammy. His eyebrows were pulled down, and his mouth hung open. He looked sad and reminded me of a sick child. He had a heart attack and died while we were at his house that day. It was 1956. Dolores and I sat at his bedside and heard him suck in his last breath as we each held one of his hands. The last breath he inhaled startled us. It was loud. It almost sounded like he was choking on air. Our eyes widened and chins lowered; we looked at each other in disbelief.

"No, Daddy!" I whimpered as I laid my head on his chest. Memories of him lying next to Charles and the sewer hole Bob died in flooded my mind. I didn't want to believe it was true, just like when Bob died. I wasn't even crying when I looked at Dolores with incredulity. "Is he gone? He's gone, isn't he?" I asked her, even though I knew the answer. She shook her head yes. Neither one of us cried. We were in shock, even though we knew it was going to happen. Does the shock you feel make you not cry, or is it because it isn't real to you yet? "Bob, please get Daddy," I begged as I laid my head on his chest again.

"Dolores, you know he's a religious man. Will you pray for him? Please say a prayer for him. He would want someone to pray over his body. I don't think I can." I chewed on my lower lip. I remember she recited a beautiful prayer, but I can't remember what she said. My autopilot was kicking in. I was already thinking what I would say to Charles and Eleanor while I sat and caressed his clammy, pale face and stroked his curly gray-blond hair. I laid my head on his chest for the last time, and I told him I loved him. I whispered into his ear, "You were the best father anyone could have ever asked for."

Losing my father was a horrible loss for Tom and me, even though I avoided talking about how I was feeling to Tom. I wasn't ready, and he knew I wasn't ready. He didn't press me. He learned early in our relationship not to press me. "I don't feel I can function without him," I broke down and said to him one day. "He was the most important man in my life." That may have stung Thomas a little, but I think he understood what I meant when I said that. He knew I was always daddy's little girl.

"Stella, you were a wonderful daughter to him, and he knew it. You took great care of him for six years until the day he died. You went above and beyond for him, especially when he needed you the most. You were his best friend. Remember when you helped him build that house, and then you painted that entire house by yourself?"

"Yes," I cried.

"Well, it was your father who made sure you were getting the proper care when you were in the hospital. He watched over you every day while taking care of Jim and Anna. I felt so helpless because I was working so much. And to be honest, I was scared, but your father wasn't. He knew you would get better. He cared for you in a way I'm not sure I could have. He advocated for you. He did things I couldn't have handled without him."

I clutched Thomas's hands and pulled him close to me. "You could have," I gasped as I wrapped my arms around him. "I miss him so much," I cried against his chest. Warm tears streamed down my face and bled into Thomas's white shirt. I felt like I could hardly catch my breath. "My heart hurts so much. I feel like I can't swallow. I feel like I can't breathe. I feel like I did when my brother died. Nothing feels real. My father was everything to me. He was my best friend too." Thomas stroked my hair and rubbed my back. He was the only person that made me feel at peace when he did that. I leaned in closer to Thomas, and a heavy cry poured out of me. My entire body lost control, and I heaved up and down. Tom continued holding me against his chest, but he was careful not to put his hands on my shoulders. He knew I didn't like that feeling. He gently rubbed my back instead and allowed me to bleed his shirt wet with tears. He didn't try to shush me or soothe encouraging words in my ear. He just stood still, caressing the small of my back, and allowed me to have my moment.

Tom and I were best friends with Dolores and her husband, William, who went by Bill. They always made our outings fun and kept us laughing. Dolores was a tall woman, and Bill was short. They called themselves Big D and Tiny Wee. We loved going to Ohio State and attending college football games with them. Anna and Jim both graduated from Ohio State. It was also Charles and our father's alma mater, and Bill went there too. Tom and I also took many trips to Lake Erie with Dolores and her husband when we could get away from work. We bought an auto parts store before my father died. It flourished, and I loved the responsibility of being a business owner. My father was extremely proud of us.

My life drastically changed when Tom had his first stroke when he was in his early sixties. He was never the same after his stroke. He then experienced mini-strokes for years. It got to the point where he had to stop working, and we sold our business. Our son, Jim, felt helpless and wanted to help his father, so he bought him a pontoon boat for Buckeye Lake. Sadly, Tom never got to use it. A week later, in 1974, he had a major heart attack. We were at Sears shopping for a new dryer. Once Tom came home from the hospital, I cared for him. His body and mind were affected to the point that I had to order a hospital bed for him. I put it in our living room so I could tend to him more easily. Tom's needs were highly demanding, but I didn't want to put him in a nursing home.

I cared for Tom by myself for seven years. I had some help from different services that came to our house for free so I could run errands and shop for groceries. Anna did not live in Columbus anymore but frequently visited our house on weekends. Dolores helped me with Tom the best she could, but her husband had cancer and needed her care too. Charles gave me a wonderful gift. He supplemented my meager income since I could not work while caring for Tom. He gave me six hundred dollars a month. I didn't feel guilty for taking his handout. I felt a bit selfish, but I also felt like I deserved it. Charles and Ruth were wealthy. They owned a paper supply company they once worked at and were doing extremely well for themselves.

I promised Tom I would never allow him to die in a nursing home, so the last few years of his life were the worst for me. I hate to say it, but it became like caring for an infant. I had to feed him and change his diapers. I never bought the new dryer we were shopping for. I hung the laundry outside to dry. When Jim figured out I was hanging laundry, he bought me a new dryer. I washed a lot during the last few years due to Thomas's frequent accidents because I always wanted him in a clean bed and fresh clothes on him. When Jim and Anna visited, he didn't remember who they were in his final years. He was confused and called them by the wrong names. He didn't recognize them. Tom only recognized Anna's husband, Gene. Anna and Gene were both schoolteachers. He smiled at Gene when they visited. "Gene, how's teaching treating you?" he would manage to murmur from his bed.

When I was changing Tom's clothes one day, I noticed his feet and legs were gray and stiff. His body was sweaty, and his nose and cheeks were flushed a bright red color, just like how my father looked before he died. There was a gurgle to his breathing I had never heard before. I felt my heart pound, and my throat closed up. I knew it was bad, and he wasn't going to wake up. I got into bed with him and rested my head on his chest. I listened for a heartbeat. I could only hear my heart beating loudly; I couldn't differentiate between our two. I smoothed his hair away from his face and put a cold washcloth on his forehead. I gripped his hand tightly as I told him how much I loved him. I leaned into him and whispered into his ear, "Thomas, you have given me a great life, and I'm proud of what we've accomplished. You are also one of the most important men in my life, not just my father. I don't want you to be in pain anymore. You've gone through enough. If there's a light and you see it, go to it. If you see my father, go to him. Don't be afraid. Don't be afraid to leave me. I will miss you, but I am strong. I will be okay."

Tom died twenty minutes later. He was only seventy-one years old. After his funeral, I was tired and exhausted but had no regrets about caring for him. I told Anna I wouldn't have done it any differently. I was only sixty-five years old when I lost Tom in 1981. Now that I could work, I swore to focus on myself again. I knew my father and Tom would want me to.

Chapter **42**

AFTER TOM DIED, I STARTED VOLUNTEERING at Riverside Hospital. I worked in the emergency room, checking patients in. I loved working there because I wanted to keep my mind active and help others. It also gave me a sense of belonging because I made good friends at the hospital. I lived alone and missed Thomas greatly. I also had my share of stories to tell Dolores. I loved the fast-paced style of the ER and the odd things I would see. People came in due to stomach pain when it was constipation, scissors sticking out of someone's rear end, and ladybugs stuck in ears. I saw many unusual things, but it never bothered me. Dolores and I laughed hysterically with each other about some of my adventures at Riverside.

I could handle anything I experienced in the ER, but my worst experience was when I was seventy years old. A severely burned man was brought in. The ER buzzed with patients that day, but the burn victim took precedence. His wallet fell from his pocket when they rushed him through the doors on a gurney. I noticed it and picked it up. When I bent down to retrieve it, I winced when I saw how badly he was burned. I walked back to the check-in desk with his wallet. I sunk into my chair and looked at my coworker. My stomach turned. I wasn't sure why I was feeling so odd.

Somewhere in the pit of my gut, something didn't feel right. "Linda, the burned victim's wallet fell out of his pocket." I laid it on the desk. "Should we open it to get his information since he was never checked in?"

"Yes," Linda said. "Go ahead and open it. Maybe his insurance card is in there too."

When I opened the wallet, I found his driver's license. I suddenly went numb when I studied it. I could feel my face turn white, and my body was shaking.

"Are you okay?" Linda asked.

I shook my head. "No. Do you think you can check him in? I feel I am going to get sick all of a sudden." I could barely catch my breath as I slid the wallet to her and rushed to the restroom.

"Albert Spangler on Southwood Avenue," I heard Linda say while her fingers clicked on different keys on the keyboard.

I made it to the bathroom, slammed one of the stall doors closed, and grabbed the rim of the toilet. My stomach turned while I heaved into it. I couldn't believe it was Albert. I sat on my knees and heaved some more as I hung over the toilet. My mouth was watering, but nothing was coming up, only saliva. My stomach turned again. I hadn't seen Albert since he showed up on my front porch when I was seventeen years old. I thought about lying in Mrs. Spangler's bed at the boarding house. All of a sudden, I could smell Albert's disgusting breath and could feel his body on mine. His devilish smile imploded my vision of his burned face. I thought I could stomach anything in the ER, but I wasn't expecting to see Albert's charred body. I blew my nose with toilet paper, flushed it down the toilet, and closed the lid. I sat on the toilet lid and breathed in and out heavily, trying to regain my composure. I exited the stall and walked to the sink to wash my hands. I pressed my hands against the side of the sink, leaned into it, and looked at myself in the mirror. *You can do this, Stella,* I thought. *You can do this.*

I returned to my station, where Linda was still typing. She slid her glasses off and looked at me. "Are you okay? You look like you just saw a ghost."

"I did," I muttered under my breath as I sat down next to her.

"What?" Linda stopped typing.

"I'm not feeling well, and I may need to leave early today if I don't feel better."

"Oh, honey, I hope you're not coming down with the flu." Linda lowered her voice several notches. "Don't take this the wrong way, but you look awful. You're pale white. Yes, please go home and take care of yourself."

"I will in a little while. I need to finish up a few things first. I'll be back." My jaw clenched, but I forced a small smile as I left Linda sitting at our desk. My stomach quivered with anticipation as I walked down the hall, looking for Albert. I knew he would be in one of the critical care rooms.

I heard a man moaning in the last room on the left, and I knew it was Albert. I slid into his room as the doctors were removing what clothing he had left on him. The smell of burnt flesh waffled up my nose. His burns were worse than I thought. He looked grotesque. There was no way I would have recognized him if it wasn't for his wallet. The nurses and doctors were frantically working on him. My brow creased. I stared at them, opened-mouthed. *Don't help him!* I thought. *Leave my monster alone!* One of the doctors noticed me in the room and shot me a perturbed look.

"Ma'am, you need to leave," a nurse said as she closed the curtain in front of me. I quickly turned and walked back to the check-in desk where Linda was typing.

"Did you get done what you needed to do?" she asked.

"Yes and no," my throat tightened. "But I'm not feeling any better, so I will leave now since my shift is about over. I'll be back tomorrow."

"Are you okay to drive?"

"Yes, I live close by. I'll be okay, but thank you," I told her as I put my arms inside my coat sleeves and zipped my jacket all the way up. I felt bad for lying to Linda for the second time.

"Call me if you need anything. I hope you feel better soon and drive safely."

All I thought about when I returned home from Riverside was Albert and the different things I experienced on Southwood Avenue. My stomach was churning, and I felt cold, so I didn't remove my coat. I paced around my house so much I probably wore out the soles of my shoes. I turned the heat up. I knew it was my anxiety making me so cold. I picked at my hair and twirled it around and around through my fingers.

I remembered my father took pictures of us when we lived on Southwood Avenue. I found them in a cigar box after he died, and I kept them. For some reason, I wanted to see those pictures again. There weren't many, just a few of my siblings and me sitting with our father in the backyard. Some were of Eleanor, Bob, and me playing stickball; one of me wearing my hat sideways and my black button shoes that I loved wearing; and then I came to the picture that turned my stomach. I sunk into my couch with my jaw hung open. My mouth was dry, so I quickly retrieved a glass of water from the kitchen. But no matter how much water I drank, I couldn't make my mouth feel quenched. I returned to the couch, picked up the final picture, and studied it. There were eleven total in the picture. We were in the grass in front of the front porch of the boarding house. I was sitting on a wooden bench with one of the twins, Bob, and Samuel. Albert was standing behind me, next to his mom, with his hands resting on the back of the bench. It almost looked like they were resting on my shoulders. That gave me an eerie feeling. Eleanor and the other twin were standing next to Mrs. Spangler, who was holding a baby. There were two other boys in the picture. Mrs. Spangler used to babysit kids sometimes. The baby and the other boys were kids who lived down the street, and she used to watch them on occasion. Bob and I looked young in the photo, so it must have been taken after we first moved in; I looked to be around four. I actually laughed out loud when I studied Bob in the photo because of how his hair looked. I remember the time we played "Barber Shop," and he allowed me to cut his hair. Eleanor was furious with me when she caught us because I cut his bangs way too short and crooked; most of his hair was cut off. You couldn't tell he had curls. It surprised me that Charles was not in the picture, but he could have been the one who had taken it. I couldn't help but stare at Albert in the photo. I wanted to rip it up, but I didn't. I placed all the pictures back into my father's cigar box and put the box in a drawer.

The next morning, Albert still consumed my thoughts, and I wondered about his condition while I was getting ready for work. I got the nerve to call the front desk at the ER.

"Linda, what's the burn victim's condition?" I breathlessly asked.

"He died," Linda replied. "He inhaled too much smoke and ..." I hung up the phone before she finished her sentence.

When I returned to work, Linda asked me why I wanted to know about the man's status and then hung up on her. I didn't know what to say. I certainly wasn't going to tell Linda the truth. I apologized for the phone conversation and told her we had a bad connection. I felt horrible for lying to Linda again. But Linda believed me.

"Oh, the burned victim who died. Apparently, his house caught fire because he was smoking in bed. I think he lived alone. At least he was the only one home sleeping when it happened. He suffered from extreme smoke inhalation. He was in his early eighties. Nobody was able to reach his next of kin. The poor guy died alone with no family by his side."

The poor guy died alone with no family by his side! I thought. Her words burned my ears. She felt sorry for him, but I didn't. I almost told Linda not to feel sorry for him. I almost told her how I knew him and what kind of person he really was. It was on the tip of my tongue, but I forced it down. Instead, I sat next to Linda in my chair, and thought about his charred body. My mouth started watering, and I excused myself and went to the bathroom. While I was washing my hands, I stared blankly into the mirror. I splashed some water on my face and just stared at myself. I'm not sure how long I was in the bathroom, but it must have been a while because Linda peeked in to check on me. "Are you okay?"

"Yes," I said, taking one last look at myself in the mirror. "I'm fine. Actually, I'm good." I dried my hands and tugged at the hem of my volunteer hospital dress. Then, I rearranged a couple of my hairpins that had pulled back my curls. We worked for the rest of the day in silence.

My monster is dead, I thought while I automatically finished my daily routines. *My monster is dead*. I couldn't stop repeating those words in my mind while I worked that day.

As I drove home from Riverside Hospital, I thought about what my father told me before Bob's funeral. He said that instead of only focusing on the "why me?" in life, I should concentrate on the "why not me?" I suddenly realized what he meant. "Why me," attaches blame. It's negative feelings of feeling alone or painting a picture of being the only unlucky one in life; how victims may feel about their hardships. "Why not me?" is what a survivor may think. No one is more important than another. Bad things happen to good and bad people all the time. No one is in complete control. No one can avoid bad things; you can only learn from them. I missed my father. I missed Bob. I missed Thomas. I wished I could ask my father if my revelation was correct. I glanced at myself in my rearview mirror as I drove home, and when I did, I saw a survivor, a woman who never gave up on life's obstacles. I didn't see the scared little girl I used to see.

I called Dolores when I got home. When she answered the phone, I started crying. It was the first time I cried since Tom died. I couldn't get my words out, but she knew it was me. I heaved heavily into the phone. I felt childlike for doing so, but we had an unspoken bond.

"Stella, do you need me to come over? I'm right down the street. I'm here if you need anything."

"No, I just wanted to hear your voice. I'm okay. I just feel out of sorts today, but I'll be fine." I never told Dolores about Albert and the abuse I went through when I was young. I never told anybody other than Dr. Reed, and then my daughter, years later. Like Eleanor once said to me after we were sprayed with the garden hose by Mrs. Spangler in the backyard,

I pretended it never happened. And at times, it worked. But in reality, I couldn't pretend it never happened. I tried to convince myself that I could, but deep down within me, I couldn't remove myself from my experiences. They attached themselves to me and became a part of me. Pretending it never happened was just a Band-Aid, but I had ripped that Band-Aid off. My experiences influenced the person I became. My journey helped me feel happiness again. It helped me understand the saying, "Crying over it won't make it clean."

Chapter 43

I SOON BOUGHT A MEMBERSHIP AT A HEALTH SPA. I needed to release my thoughts and negative memories by focusing on something physical. I walked the track, used the free weights, and sat in the sauna daily. I loved going there. It improved my mental health and gave me something positive to do. After the day Albert came into the emergency room, all the horrible memories of Southwood Avenue flooded my mind, and I needed to flush them out of my system. The health spa became a sanctuary for me.

An uncomfortable incident happened once in the sauna. A man sat beside me while I was enjoying the hot steam soaking into my body. He said hello, and I pretended not to hear him. Then, after a few minutes, I felt his hand touch my thigh. I slapped it away and told him to get lost. But I wouldn't let that incident ruin the health spa for me. I continued going there, even though I saw him during my visits.

I told Dolores about it. "Yes, I slapped his hand away! It caught me off guard. I was disgusted he felt he had the right to do that!"

"Try to consider it a compliment that you are still an attractive woman, even as an old lady," Dolores chuckled.

I also met a few friends at the health spa who introduced me to a senior club called Dating for Mature Seniors. I was nervous when I attended the first function. I had no intention of dating anyone, so I wondered why I allowed my hospital friends to talk me into attending one of the senior functions.

I tried to get Dolores to go with me, but she said her husband wouldn't like it and declined. Bill died around the same time as Tom, and then she started dating a man who lived down the street from her. They weren't really married, but she called him her husband. She encouraged me to go anyway. "Maybe you'll meet the man of your dreams! You're not in a wheelchair yet; you should go!" Dolores laughed.

"Ha ha. Very funny." I smirked.

I sat away from the attendees and avoided talking to anyone. A man walked over to me and said hello. I noticed he had toilet paper hanging from the back of his pants. I politely let him know and then said I needed to leave. I told my friends I wasn't feeling well and left. That was the last time I participated in Dating for Mature Seniors.

Chapter **44**

IN 1998, AT EIGHTY-TWO YEARS OLD, I wasn't ready to leave Columbus, but I knew it was the right thing to do. I knew it was time to leave the only city I loved and be near my daughter and her family in a small suburb called Milford, Ohio. It broke my heart to put my home up for sale. I stood on my driveway and stared at the For Sale sign that was pounded into my front yard. I had a lump in my throat I couldn't manage to swallow. Memories flooded my mind. I fought the bad memories away. I didn't want to think about the seven years I cared for Tom in that house. I didn't want to reflect on the last moment I watched Dolores wave goodbye and walk down my driveway for the last time. I told myself to remember the good memories. I sat on the front stoop of my porch and ruminated about my father and the pride he felt after he built Tom and me the house. I thought about his pleased smile when he showed me the stone fireplace. I remembered my son teaching our black poodle, Bom-Bom, how to play hide-and-seek in the house. I remembered watching my daughter walk down the steps in a beautiful aqua-velvet gown before she attended her first high school dance. I remembered my husband reading the newspaper in his favorite chair. I thought about the giggles my three granddaughters made every time they visited me because I showered them with desserts and candy they weren't used to having. I loved my house on Garden Road. I knew I was going to miss it dearly. But I also knew living in Milford, less than a mile away from Anna and her family, was what I needed. I was happy there for twelve years. I was a great-grandma to eight children who visited me often. The highlight of their visits was my bird, Buster. He was a yellow-and-white cockatiel with a bright-yellow mohawk and orange cheeks. He flew around my family room, visiting from person to person while perching on their shoulders. My great-grandchildren were the most impressed, especially when he asked them, "What are you doing?" They fed him crackers and held him. He would sing "Happy Birthday," which made everyone laugh.

Charles continued supplementing my social security income with a monthly allowance. He raised it to eight hundred dollars a month after his wife died and put it into a trust for me so I would continue receiving money with the assumption he would die before me. He swore me to secrecy not to tell Eleanor or his daughter. I kept his secret, but I would give Eleanor money from time to time when she needed it. Then, in March 2001, Charles died. Eleanor and I were at a loss for words when we met at the funeral home in Middletown. We sat next to each other during his service, holding hands, and it felt like holding hands with an old friend you once knew. We both breathed heavily and shed tears at the same time. We both were at a loss; *we are the only two left*, I thought. After his funeral, when we said our goodbyes, it felt like two trains passing each other in the night.

Six months later, I received word from Eleanor's sons that she died suddenly. She was living alone in Tampa after our mother passed away. When the police found her, she was in her bed with a picture of our mother in her hands. It was our mother's high school graduation photo when she was eighteen. It was a picture of her profile. Eleanor's sons later gave me the picture, and I shuddered when I saw how much I looked like her. A surge of adrenaline filled my body, and my heart raced. I had always thought she was bold. I thought she was brave. But I suddenly realized our tenacity and loyalties did not mirror each other at all. I did not flee. I chose to fight.

AUTHOR'S REFLECTION

IN MARCH 2014, I GOT THE CALL that no one ever wants to hear, "Melissa, you need to come home now." It was a Wednesday, and I had just said good-bye to my students and was walking back to my classroom when my mother called me. She said my grandma didn't have long and that I should come home to say goodbye. I sat at my desk and cried for the first time. I knew my grandma entered hospice earlier that week, but it didn't become real to me until my mother's phone call asking me to come home. Teary-eyed, I organized my lesson plans for the substitute teacher who would cover for me. I flew to my mother's home in Ohio the next day, leaving my husband and children behind. My boys were young, and selfishly, I wanted to grieve without taking care of them. I wanted to know they were home safe with my husband so I could focus only on my grandma.

I remember how my grandma looked when I saw her at the nursing home the evening I flew in. She was lying in bed wearing clean, pink silk pajamas with the covers pulled up to her waist. Her eyes were shut, and she was sleeping peacefully. She didn't look like a person lying on her deathbed. She looked perfect. I sat at her side and grabbed her hand. It was warm and soft. I guess I thought it would be cold and stiff, but she felt like the same grandma when I rubbed her hand against my cheek and whispered her name. I thought maybe she would wake up, but she didn't. My mom, sisters, and I talked for a while, and then I told them to go home and rest. I said that I would stay with her for the night since they had spent all week by her side. At first, they were hesitant to leave, but the hospice nurse reassured them that Grandma wasn't ready to leave us yet. I sat next to my grandma for the rest of the night, caressing her hand and speaking about my grandma to the hospice nurse. I told the nurse all about her. We talked all night long. The nurse was impressed with the amazing person my grandma was. It made me proud to speak of her.

The next morning, my dad, mom, and sisters were by my side, admiring how peaceful she still looked. There wasn't anything we could do but wait. What an odd experience; waiting for someone to die, especially someone who looked as quiet and serene as my grandma did. By then, we had a new hospice nurse in the room with us. She examined my grandmother for the second time and announced, "She doesn't seem to want to leave." That made all of us cry, especially my mom.

Throughout the morning, my mom kept looking at the door to my grandmother's room, waiting for her brother to walk in, but he didn't. She finally called him and asked him if he was going to come and say good-bye. He lived in Columbus, which was only a two-hour drive. I'm unsure what they talked about, but I remember my mom putting the phone to my grandmother's ear, and he talked to her. My mom hung up the phone when he finished and said to my grandma, "Well, Mother, everyone has said goodbye now." Then, she played some of my grandma's favorite Frank Sinatra songs on her phone, and we all sat and waited with lumps in our throats and tears in our eyes.

The hospice nurse examined my grandma again around noon. "She still doesn't look ready to leave, even though her breathing is very shallow and her heart rate has weakened," she said. Nurses and other facility members who were there that afternoon came in and said their goodbyes to my grandma. She was well-liked and well-taken care of in that nursing home.

Then, my grandma suddenly slipped out of this world after a minister prayed over her body. She left at 1:00 p.m. on Friday, March 21, 2014. She was almost ninety-eight years old. What an incredible life.

My grandma was the matriarch of our family, even though if you asked her, she would blush and shake her head no and say, "Your mother is." But she truly was, if you ask me. She was the only grandparent I knew. My other grandparents didn't live long enough for me to remember them, but I had forty wonderful years with my grandma. She filled the void of missing three other grandparents. No one asked her to, but she filled that void all on her own, not only for me but for my sisters too. My mother was, and is, a strong influence in our family, but she learned from my grandmother. Grandma's tenacity and independence influenced me. She had a healthy body and mind. Growing up, I saw her mowing her own grass, cleaning her own house, toying with her own car, and making her own choices. She took care of herself and did not rely on anyone else to do so. Reading and self-care were important to my grandma. There was rarely a day that went by when she didn't visit the health spa and then walk around her neighborhood. She exercised into her nineties and only stopped when her balance became so bad that she had to for her own safety. She was also an avid reader and read many, many books. We often shared the books we read with each other. She was not only a good role model but also a friend, especially to my mother. My mom often said that Grandma was her best friend, even when she was a young adult.

If I had to choose one word to describe my grandma, I would pick brave. I don't mean that she was courageous without showing fear. She showed and felt fear in her life at times; don't we all? What I mean by brave is that she faced and endured dangers or horrible conditions in her life and then grew from them. She didn't let the obstacles she faced define her life. She used those obstacles to make herself stronger, smarter, and wiser. When she was eighty years old, two women tried to rob her at gunpoint in a mall parking lot. My grandma was determined not to give them her purse, and she fought back. She survived the robbery with a few cuts and bruises, but they did not get away with my grandma's purse. She fought until help arrived.

Her courage also gave her a humorous and loving personality. She loved to laugh, and she loved intensely. It wasn't hard to make my grandma laugh, and it wasn't hard to feel love from her. She gave more than she took. She laughed more than she cried. She listened more than she talked. And she sang when no one else was singing.

Writing this book was emotional for me in many ways. I thought about things I didn't want to think about. I wrote about things that made me proud. I wrote about things that made me sad. I walked in someone else's footsteps. I asked questions about things that didn't always have answers. I wondered about things I had never experienced. I dreamt about scenarios that may or may not have been true. I questioned myself, and I questioned others, but the only person I was not able to question was my grandma. I miss her deeply.

ACKNOWLEDGMENTS

MY INCREDIBLE JOURNEY in writing this book began with my mom. I could not have written it without her blessing. I would also like to thank everyone who supported me, worked with me, and helped me navigate this exciting adventure as a first-time author. I would especially like to thank my husband, Aaron, and our sons, Griffin and Jake, for their patience while I took time away from them to accomplish something that was important to me.

ABOUT THE AUTHOR

MELISSA (MCENDREE) SIMONYE is a wife, mother, small business owner, and retired elementary school teacher of twenty-five years. She explored her love for writing in high school by expressing herself through poetry. She grew up in Ohio and graduated from college with a master's degree in education. As an educator, her passion was inspiring her students  to love reading by exposing them to authentic literature that spoke to her students' individuality. Reading about courageous people also fascinated Melissa, especially strong women who made a mark in history. Melissa has lived in Colorado since 2003. She now works with her husband running their small business. Whenever she can escape her busy life, she exercises, travels, reads books, and writes at her kitchen table, surrounded by her two cats and two dogs. This is Melissa's first novel, inspired by her extraordinary grandmother's life experiences.

For more information, visit www.melissasimonye.com.

INVITE MELISSA TO
YOUR BOOK CLUB!

Melissa would love to visit your book club via videoconferencing or in person. Please contact Melissa directly through her website at www.melissasimonye.com to schedule her appearance at your next book club meeting.

Made in the USA
Columbia, SC
11 December 2024

49000399R00167